THE TOMB OF ETERNITY

(Joe Hawke #3)

Rob Jones

THE TOMB OF ETERNITY is a work of fiction. All names, characters, places and occurrences are entirely fictional products of the author's imagination or are used fictitiously. Any resemblance to current events or locales, or to persons living or dead, is entirely coincidental.

Other Books by Rob Jones

The Joe Hawke Series

The Vault of Poseidon (Joe Hawke #1)
Thunder God (Joe Hawke #2)
The Tomb of Eternity (Joe Hawke #3)
The Curse of Medusa (Joe Hawke #4)
Valhalla Gold (Joe Hawke #5)
The Aztec Prophecy (Joe Hawke #6)
The Secret of Atlantis (Joe Hawke #7)
The Lost City (Joe Hawke #8)

This novel is an action-adventure thriller and includes archaeological, military and mystery themes. I welcome constructive comments and I'm always happy to get your feedback.

Website: www.robjonesnovels.com

Facebook: https://www.facebook.com/RobJonesNovels/

Email: robjonesnovels@gmail.com

Twitter: @AuthorRobJones

DEDICATION

For T

THE TOMB OF ETERNITY

CHAPTER ONE

New York

The view of Manhattan was obscured by heavy cloud as the Boeing banked to starboard and began its final descent into the city. An exhausted Joe Hawke snatched a glimpse of the Chrysler Building before it was blocked by more of the same cloud. Next to him, Lea Donovan, the Irishwoman he trusted more than anyone else in the world slept fitfully, and across the aisle Ryan Bale stared into nothing without blinking or moving.

Hawke looked away and closed his eyes. It was less than a day since Nightingale had sent him the text saying she was being kidnapped. He had stared at those words dozens of times during the flight, each time hoping he had made some kind of a mistake, that maybe it was a joke after all.

As for the picture of the man she had sent before he snatched her – the hideous, blurred image of her tormentor looming over her with what looked like a kitchen knife in his hand – he felt an uncontrollable rage rise in him every time he looked at it.

Lea had done as promised and taken the situation straight to Sir Richard Eden, but as he was listening patiently to her words, Hawke was already booking the flight to New York. He appreciated the open offer of help, but he was reluctant to take it.

The last time he had led a crew of people into a mission, two of them hadn't come back, and he wouldn't forget how Olivia Hart and Sophie Durand had died – on his watch, under his command. He saw Sophie's death in Ryan's face every time he looked at him. He clenched his jaw and looked down to see he'd squeezed all the blood from his knuckles. This time he wanted to face the enemy alone and be responsible for only himself, but Lea would have none of it.

"Where you go, I go, Joe Hawke," she had said.

Ryan agreed with a non-committal shrug of his shoulders.

So now the three of them flew into New York.

He looked ahead with hatred in his heart, and knew there was a lot of hard, dangerous work to do if he was going to rescue Nightingale. The big question on his mind was why had she been taken? Was it simply to strike at him somehow – some kind of personal vendetta – or did it have something to do with the cursed Map of Immortality?

He didn't know for sure, but he had a bad feeling the damned map was behind everything, and if all of this weren't bad enough, his mind was also being tortured by the thought of Dragonfly's treachery, a woman he now cursed himself for trusting with such an important mission. It was another terrible lapse of judgement that made him question all over again his ability to be leading people into such danger.

When they boarded the aircraft in Hong Kong, Eden had contacted Lea and told her he was already on

Dragonfly's trail. He had sent Scarlet Sloane and Bradley Karlsson to Germany to start the hunt for the Chinese assassin and the map which she had taken from the burning tomb back in Xian. Hawke knew he had to save his old CIA friend first, but the thought of hunting down Lexi Zhang and settling his account with her was almost enough to quell the rage rising in his heart.

At least, he considered bitterly, all of this had pushed thoughts of his wife, Liz, to the back of his mind. Even now after he'd had time to think about what Hart had told him on their way to Xian, he could hardly bring himself to believe a word of it, and yet… He knew in his heart what she had told him was true. His wife had not been who he thought she was. He had to accept the terrible truth that throughout their relationship she had been someone else – someone with a secret past, who had lied to him every day they had been together. That tore him up almost as much as the savage murder which he had witnessed on their honeymoon.

The aircraft turned once again and lined up for its final approach. Lea stirred from her sleep and stretched her arms. She looked tired, Hawke thought. He watched her buckle her seatbelt and prepare for the landing, but then he saw Ryan and his mind drifted to the terrible loss the young lad had sustained when the Lotus's underlings had murdered his girlfriend while she was trying to save his life. He knew what he was going through, but it was pointless to say it. Absent-mindedly he buckled up as Lea checked her phone.

"Anything?" he asked.

She nodded and swept her hair up behind her ears. "A message from Richard – just reiterating that we should focus on finding Nightingale because he's going to put Scarlet on the search for Lexi. As for Nightingale, I asked him to run some traces on her calls to try and get an address."

Hawke considered the plan for a moment and decided that if anyone could track Lexi Zhang down then that person was Cairo Sloane. "Let's hope she can find her then," he said, thinking once again about her betrayal of him and his friends back in Xian.

"What's the matter?" Lea asked.

"Nothing…it's just that I was the one who dragged Lexi into all of this – it's my fault that we got shafted over the map. I knew I couldn't trust her… I just can't believe I introduced her to everyone and seriously put your lives into her hands."

Lea sighed. "Don't be so bloody melodramatic, Joe Hawke!"

"Eh?"

"You heard me well enough."

"Well, sure, but…"

"But you were expecting some sympathy? Well forget it, boyo. We're all big grown-ups around here you know, with the exception of Ryan, at least."

"I heard that," Ryan mumbled with his eyes closed.

"The point is that we made our own judgement about Lexi Zhang and whether or not to trust her. It's not all down to you, so pull your head out of your arse and focus on finding Nightingale, got it?"

Hawke smiled. "Got it."

"That's what I like to hear. Now, is it too late to order some beer and peanuts?" As she spoke she craned her neck above the headrest of the chair in front and tried to find a flight assistant. Hawke shook his head and turned to the window.

Below them now he saw the squat buildings of an industrial zone adjacent to the airport, and thousands of cars snaking their way in and out of the sprawling city.

The flaps were now fully deployed and the odd silence of final approach filled the cabin. He hadn't been to America since Eddie Kosinski had released him from CIA custody, and as the plane touched down on US soil and the cascade reversers were deployed, he half wondered if they would let him back in again.

"I'll find out soon enough," he said to himself.

They taxied slowly to the gate and a gentle drizzle began to fall.

*

A short car ride through the city brought them to their destination – what looked from the outside like a pretty expensive condo building in the Tribeca district. Yellow cabs honked horns and fought for supremacy somewhere in the distance, and a few dozen people hurried along the sidewalks wrapped in scarves and gloves. The cold sky promised snow, but for now it was still just drizzle. In the distance a giant billboard flashed an image of the latest iPhone, but everyone was too cold to notice.

"Joe?"

It was Lea. Her voice was quiet, and she gently brushed his arm when she spoke.

"Yeah?"

"We're here, babe."

He looked at her distractedly, not even seeing her, and then stared up at the building while a solemn Ryan Bale paid the cab driver.

"This is it?" he said.

Lea shrugged. "Sure. This is the location Richard traced her last call to."

Thank God for Richard, was all Hawke could think. He had never met anyone with more influence and reach than Sir Richard Eden, and, he suspected, more money.

Right now, Hawke was so angry he just wanted to punch his way through the problem, but having Eden use his MI5 contacts to trace Nightingale's call was a stroke of genius from Lea. He knew it almost certainly meant the difference between life and death for his old CIA friend, wherever the hell she was right now.

"Let's start this, then," he said, steeling himself for another fight. He turned to Lea, lowered his voice and quietly gestured to Ryan over at the cab. "You really think he's up to it?"

She nodded. "I think so. I think he got a lot of it out of his heart last night – I've never seen Ryan drink an entire bottle of Scotch like that before. I know he must be totally crushed inside, but he seems to be projecting his anger outwards."

"Is that a good thing?"

"I don't know…"

"Sounds unpredictable to me, but…"

"But we both know we're going to need him."

Hawke nodded. "Exactly."

"And…"

Hawke flicked his eyes to Lea. "What?"

"He says he won't stop until he's killed everyone in Sheng's team."

"They're already all dead – apart from Luk, of course, and a few lackeys."

Lea shuddered when Hawke mentioned Luk. The last time she had seen him he was fleeing for his worthless life from the burning tomb of the Emperor Qin, and the time before that she was chained down to a boatshed bench while Luk sharpened a cut-throat razor. Now, he was out there somewhere, anywhere. She couldn't bear to think about it.

"Don't remind me about that weirdo, please. I'm just saying I think he's alright but we can't rule out him doing something crazy – dropping off the grid and going it alone, or something like that. He wouldn't last five minutes, Joe."

"We're not going to let that happen, all right? But now we have to focus."

Hawke pulled up his collar and walked toward the apartment building. It was time to stop asking questions and start finding answers.

CHAPTER TWO

Berlin

Dragonfly lit the cigarette and held the smoke deep down inside. She sighed, and with the gentle exhalation the hot smoke flowed smoothly out of her body and into the cold Berlin sky. All was fair in love and war, or so they said, and yet… She shook the thought from her mind and watched the traffic below her hotel room.

Yes, she had betrayed Joe Hawke. She knew that. It was part of the game. She had taken the map from Sheng Fang, prising it from his dead hands – but she had no choice. Sorokin had contacted her just hours before. He had sent her a simple message explaining that he knew her darkest secret, and would reveal it to Hawke and everyone else she knew if she didn't comply. The information was safe, he had said. He'd been very reassuring. Kill me and it will be released to the world. Get me the map or they find out, he had told her. One false move and they find out, he had said. It didn't look like he was kidding around.

She knew she would get her revenge on Sorokin – no one threatened her and got away with it, but she also knew she had to play along – play for time – do as the Russian told her until the moment for revenge presented itself. As it turned out that happened sooner than she thought when an unknown hit-man took Sorokin out of the game on the taxi rank outside the airport in Berlin. As far as the old Chinese proverb went, the hen had flown, but the egg was not necessarily broken.

But it would be if Joe Hawke ever got his hands on that information about her.

As for who else knew what Sorokin had discovered about her past, she could never know. That was the life she led, but at least it was one less fire to put out. She knew she would have to find out if Sorokin was telling the truth about the information being hidden away somewhere, but there was no time for that now.

She also knew there was much more damage to undo – Hawke and the others would take some persuading that she had not deliberately betrayed them, especially considering that she could never tell them the truth about why she had done so – she would have to get creative on that score and cook something up for them. More lies… and then there was this damned map… She had to do something with it before Sorokin's killers came calling a second time.

She gazed down into the city. An absent-minded flick of the cigarette knocked a cloud of ash over the balcony. She watched it drift through the air, its aimless trajectory reminding her sadly of her own bitter past. Even here, so far away from her life in China, that dark, repressed history had a way of rising up and almost choking her. If only she could go back in time, she thought…

Now, just because she didn't want them to, her mind filled with memories of the past. The day she left home to join the Ministry, her training, how the State took her under its wing and showed her everything. Her first kill – it was a shooting in Pyongyang and she still had nightmares about it… The first time she met Joe Hawke in Zambia – she was there to investigate corruption. Someone was diverting Chinese state development funds into a private account in the Caribbean when he should have been increasing productivity in the Chambishi copper mine. She had persuaded him to return the money before placing him on early retirement. Or that's what the government told his family, anyway. The reality was somewhat different.

Hawke was there as part of a joint SBS-SAS team protecting a British trade envoy and his team in the country who were there to talk about investment opportunities. There had been a terror threat made against the envoy and Hawke and his squadron travelled alongside the officials in civvies, posing as administrators.

They had met in a restaurant in Lusaka, each pretending to be someone they were not, but each had the skills and experience to know the other was lying. It wasn't long before they had each other's true story and a few bottles of Mosi lager on the side. They had spent three nights with each other, totally against the rules, but neither seemed to care. The mission had ended badly for the British, but a success for the Chinese, and she was given a special commendation when she got home.

Now, if Hawke refused to believe her she would have to add yet another betrayal to the ash-heap of her memories. But maybe she could fix it. Just maybe.

She stood motionless and considered her position. She was alone in a German hotel room with the Map of Immortality – the object of the most insane desire in history. Sorokin had taken them there to meet with a man who promised to translate the map. Probably just a charlatan, she thought, and rolled it out on the bed. She took a long look at the thing that had caused so much trouble and death. She felt like using it as an ashtray.

It was, sadly, unintelligible. She was angry with herself for being so naïve – she had pretty much expected it to be a map of some kind of territory with something approximating a big red cross on it to show where the hidden treasure was. Instead she was confronted with an illegible, messy scrawl – some kind of code – that reminded her of Egyptian hieroglyphics. Whatever it was, it meant nothing to her, and it wasn't the sort of thing you could Google, either. She had no chance of finding the elixir without the others' help, and she knew it.

The problem was she had no idea how Hawke and the others were going to react when she got back in touch with them, and whether they'd believe her story about Sorokin and the blackmail. She decided on a story about her parents being held hostage by the Russian, and she could show them the images of her 'parents' at gunpoint – such things could be faked easily enough. She knew it and they knew it, too. They would just have to take her word for it.

Another problem was just who the hell had tried to kill her at Tegel Airport, and taken Sorokin out of the game at the same time. Was she the primary target, or Sorokin? She had no idea, but she knew that no one got away with trying to kill the Dragonfly, not even for possession of the oldest treasure map on earth. Whoever it was had better start thinking about updating their last will and testament.

She picked up the hotel telephone and made a quick call to the front desk. As she waited, she looked once again at the map, and noticed for the first time that one of the edges was slightly frayed. She raised an eyebrow as she took a closer took, but then someone answered the phone.

"Reception."

"This is Room 76 calling," she said quietly. "I wonder if you could please give me the address of a reliable bank. I need to put something in a safety deposit box."

"You are quite welcome to use the safe in your room. They are perfectly substantial for most valuables."

"This isn't *most valuables*," she said sharply. She had read about a steep rise in the number of professional and opportunist burglaries in Berlin apartments and hotel rooms. This wasn't the time to test the accuracy of that particular journalism.

"I see, please wait."

She looked at the ceiling and took a deep breath. Why was she doing this? Maybe it was time to leave it all behind. Just walk away and settle down, maybe with a guy like Joe Hawke – or then again…

"Madam?"

"Yes, go ahead."

"Forgive the delay, but not all banks in Berlin allow access to a safety deposit box unless you are an account holder. The nearest bank is a Deutsche Bank which is on the same street as this hotel, or you could try the Berliner Bank a little further along. I believe they might be able to assist you."

"Thank you." She hung up, and looked at her cell phone, sitting innocuously on the hotel desk beside the window. She could just *call* him, she thought.

Hi Joe, it's Lexi – back from the dead.

No, not right now. She had business to attend to.

She pursed her lips and pulled another cigarette out of the packet. She hated German cigarettes but they were all the local store had left. She stared at the little warning on the packet as she struck the match and held the tiny flame under the tip of the cigarette, igniting the tobacco shreds – *Rauchen kann tödlich sein* – smoking can be deadly. So can a lot of things, she thought, as she blew out the match and stepped back out to the balcony.

So can a lot of things.

Including me.

When she'd finished smoking, she put the map in her bag and slid her gun inside her jacket. Cigarettes in the pocket, and the door clicked shut behind her as she moved along the silent corridor toward the elevators.

CHAPTER THREE

Moscow

Nightingale opened her eyes, but saw only darkness. *Where am I?* She breathed faster as she struggled to make sense of her new world. The man who had dragged her from the wardrobe had put a black sack over her head, and gagged her with what felt like a long piece of rough cloth.

The mere thought of him made her feel sick with fear.

She remembered him now. The feel of his heavy hands as he grabbed her head and shoulder and wrenched her from her hiding place. The smell of him as he hauled her into the light – cheap vodka and coffee. The sound of his foreign curses as he stumbled over her wheelchair and kicked it across the room in a fit of incandescent, animal rage.

The CIA was a long time ago, but she'd focused and recalled her training. Stay calm, assess the situation, don't aggravate the hostage taker. More than that, she tried to stay positive and thought about her rescue… but no one knew where she was apart from the one person she trusted more than anyone else, and his name was Joe Hawke. Had he got her message?

Her terrified mind went over that night yet again. The second her CCTV cameras were shut off she had known something was wrong, and immediately grabbed her cell phone. A second later she heard her door being kicked down. Without thinking about what to do, she tipped herself up in her wheel chair and crashed to the ground.

Then, she had heard the man in the hall, searching for her.

She dragged herself across the floor, dragging the weight of her dead legs behind her with all her might, knowing she could have only seconds to live. She crawled into the wardrobe in her bedroom and texted Hawke. “Someone’s in my apartment. I’m hiding in my wardrobe. They’re trying to kill me. Help.”

And then she saw the man boot his way into her bedroom, kicking the door away like it was balsa wood. She watched him through the slits in the Venetian door of her wardrobe as he stalked into the small room. His tight, lean chest heaved up and down as he breathed in fast. He was alert and pumped with adrenalin.

Then he saw the hiding place.

She knew what she had to do. She flicked her phone to camera mode and began taking pictures through the slits. The man drew a long kitchen knife – one of hers – and she thought it was all over. She attached the image to the text and sent it to Hawke.

The man wrenched the door open and slapped the camera from her hand before dragging her out into the room by her hair. She screamed and tried to fight back but it was useless. Then she saw him pull back his right arm and make a fist. It reminded her of a coiled spring.

He punched her, and her world ended.

Now she winced at the pain from the punch, but at least she was alive. How long she had been unconscious for was a mystery, but it was possible she had been drugged. She thought she could hear someone moving around in the room and then she heard a second man enter. They spoke in rapid Russian for a few seconds and then someone spoke to her in heavily accented English.

“Tell me about Joe Hawke,” the voice said.

She recognized the accent as southern Russian. “I…where am I?”

A hard slap across her face came from out of nowhere and nearly knocked her out of the chair. She gasped for air and tried to stop the dizziness which was now making her head spin. There followed a few seconds of ominous silence and her mind buzzed with thoughts of why this was happening to her, and what she could do to protect herself.

The man sighed. “I ask the questions. I want to know about Joe Hawke, the British Special Forces man. Tell me about him, or you get another slap.”

In her new world of darkness, the panic began to rise like waves on an icy black sea. She tried to calm herself, but she had been out of the field for so long that dealing with situations like this wasn’t easy – and she knew she could never run from this nightmare. In the background, she heard more men speaking in rapid Russian, but her lack of training in the language reduced it to incomprehensible noise. How many were now in the room with her – watching her, listening to her panicked breathing?

“I don’t really know Joe Hawke, he was…”

Another slap, this time from the other direction, and much harder. This one knocked her from the chair and she crashed onto the ground. It felt like cold concrete. For a few short moments she thought she was going to throw up in the sack, but she fought hard to control the nausea and bring her hyperventilation once again under some kind of control.

“We’re not going to start with lies,” the voice said. It was harder this time, but lower – almost a hoarse whisper. “We know you have a long history with the Englishman. Tell us about that history.”

Without any warning, she felt two huge hands grab her by the shoulders and haul her back onto the chair. There was a lot of power in that grip, she considered. It was easy to imagine them squeezing her tighter and shattering her shoulder bones. Then she heard some kind of duct tape being pulled from a roll. Seconds later someone was taping her wrists and ankles to the chair. "This way, I don't have to pick you up when I hit you next time. Now, tell me about Joe Hawke."

Nightingale's mind raced with so many emotions – fear, panic, rage – concern for Hawke – terror for herself. She had no idea where she was in the world, no idea who the men in the room were, or what they wanted with Hawke. She knew she had to play for time at the very least, so she had to tell them what they wanted to hear. She also knew she had to tell them the truth because she had no idea what they already knew. All of this, she considered, could be a test to gauge her reliability.

And she didn't want any more of those slaps.

"Joe Hawke," she began, "is a former sergeant in the Special Boat Service, or the SBS. It's the Royal Navy equivalent of the British Army's SAS, and a seriously tough outfit of Special Forces operatives. They're dangerous men and they usually work without a formal commander."

"We know this. We have men like this. Tell me things I don't know."

She flinched when she heard some rustling, but then came the unmistakable sound of a Zippo lighter. A second later the smell of strong cigarette smoke drifted over to her, followed by a deep, satisfied sigh.

She continued. "He was a commissioned officer in the Royal Marines Commandos, rising to the rank of major, but demoted to sergeant a few years after being recruited by the SBS."

"Why?"

"He was reduced in rank after going absent without leave."

"Why?"

"I don't know…" she heard the man's clothes rustle as he raised his hand to strike her. "I swear I don't know! It's the truth. He went AWOL a few years ago when he was about to be deployed abroad during an important mission. He never told me why, just that he had something more important to do. I always presumed that meant family, but all he told me was that he was lucky not to have been thrown out of the armed forces altogether. I guess that didn't happen because he's so highly skilled and experienced."

The rustling stopped. "Interesting. When did you first cross paths with Mr Hawke?"

"During a joint US-UK mission in the Balkans. He was on a covert mission to infiltrate a terror group and I helped him escape from them. He always said I'd saved his life and he owed me forever." Despite the terror she was feeling, she almost smiled at the memory.

"And why are you so interested in Ancient Egypt?"

"I'm sorry?" The question had come out of nowhere – she recognized it as a classic technique to disorient people during interrogations. She thought for the first time that maybe these people did this for a living – or had done once in the past, at least.

"We have been watching you for a long time – in fact since the first time you started working for Hawke and Eden. After that we started, how shall we say – listening into your life."

"You hacked me?"

"Don't be so surprised. Your reputation as a computer genius is well-founded, but a former KGB man like me is not without certain contacts. It was not hard for me to find someone to hack you, and what we found was very interesting, as you know."

"I don't know what you're talking about."

The man sighed again, and with no warning tore the sack off her head. She blinked in the bright light and saw opposite her a broad-faced man with dark hair and thin lips. Three thick scars ran down the side of his face.

"Don't play stupid games with me. You know what we're talking about. You have been researching the Map of Immortality in great detail, and your research is excellent, but of more interest to me is the person you speak with on email – codename Mercurio."

She flicked a glance at the man and immediately gave herself away. Now she knew why they had taken her – they wanted her to get to someone else. Someone who was critical to the search for the map.

He laughed. "Thank you for confirming you know Mercurio. This makes me happy, but the only problem I have now is that I do not know what Mercurio's real name is, or where he sleeps through the night. You will furnish me with this information."

"And what if I don't know it?" It was a gamble, but worth a try.

"I know you do. It is obvious from your email exchanges that you know each other's real names and addresses."

She was cornered, and she felt an indignant rage rise in her at being treated this way. "I just can't tell you what you want to know, whoever the hell you are!"

The man stroked her face with his cigarette hand, his expression almost approaching something like admiration. "I think you could be persuaded," was all he said as he left the room.

*

"It's time he knew – is he in or out?"

Sir Richard Eden MP spun slowly in his chair and watched the mist roll over the River Thames. London was cold tonight. He considered her words carefully. She was right, of course, but there was more to the problem than she knew.

"Richard?"

He turned back to face her. To say she was good-looking was an understatement, although there was a sad coldness to her face that made most men wary. Her hair was black, and she wore it up, no-nonsense. Black fingernail polish, lean, slim arms. She drummed the arm of her chair.

"What?" he asked, finally.

She sighed and rolled her eyes. "Hawke. Is he *in* or *out*?"

A long silence. "As you know, Scarlet, I'll need to talk to Lea about that, and she's in New York, as we both know." He paused a beat as he watched her reaction, then he spoke again. "But what do you think?"

"He's an arrogant bastard but the best there is. I say he's in."

Eden nodded vehemently. "He would bring valuable skills and experience to us, but…" his voice drifted. "It's a long way to Elysium."

Even though he had uttered it, the word caught Eden off-guard. Could a man like Joe Hawke be brought to a place like Elysium? Perhaps, he considered, but then again, perhaps not. It wasn't the kind of place to which you invited just anyone, that was for sure.

He glanced once again at Scarlet Sloane, and it seemed like she was in agreement. "It *is* a long way, yes, but much quicker since you bought your new jet."

"Talking of which," Eden said, changing the subject. "You might need to use it soon. We have information about the Chinese double agent Zhang Xiaoli, otherwise known as Dragonfly."

Scarlet raised an eyebrow. "Is she dead, or it is *bad* news?"

Eden gave her a sarcastic glance. "As we both know, she was last seen flying to Berlin with a Russian whom Sheng had paid to take the Tesla device to Tokyo. The Russian's name was Yevgeny Sorokin, a medium-level player in the Moscow underworld who double-crossed Sheng because he decided he wanted to live forever."

"A modest goal."

"Quite, but he was a very dangerous individual."

"*Was*?"

"He was shot and killed in an ambush when he was with Zhang outside Tegel Airport in Berlin moments after leaving customs. He'd barely been on German soil fifteen minutes. We believe the assassin was Kamchatka."

Scarlet leaned forward, her interest finally roused. "You mean Kodiak?"

Eden nodded. The Russians called the hired killer *Kamchatka*, named after the brown bear. For their own reasons the CIA and MI6 had renamed him Kodiak. Either way, he was one of the most ruthless professional killers on the market, and renowned for his total lack of ethics and extremely ruthless methods. "The very same – Ekel Kvashnin."

Scarlet considered the new information for a few moments. "But I thought he'd retired."

"Apparently not. He's in the field and active and I hardly need to tell you how bloody dangerous he is. We think he was trying to kill Zhang as well as Sorokin and get his hands on the map."

"Lexi's being hunted by the Kodiak?"

Eden nodded grimly.

"Good," Scarlet said sharply. "She bloody well deserves it."

"That's as may be, but either way we have to get to her before he does or she's dead and the map's gone forever."

Scarlet played with her lighter. "And where did we get this information from?"

Eden waited a moment before answering, the hint of a twinkle in his eye. "That's the interesting part – from Lexi Zhang herself."

Scarlet's eyes narrowed with suspicion. "Now this *has* to be a joke."

"I'm afraid not, no. She called me recently to explain that Sorokin had blackmailed her into taking the map and she had no choice. Now that Sorokin is dead she wants to return it to us."

"Now I really have heard *everything*, Richard! Please tell me you don't believe this bullshit."

"We'll have to see."

Scarlet shook her head and frowned. "Blackmailing her – how?"

"She claims he'd taken her parents hostage and was threatening to kill them if she didn't get the map for him."

She laughed. "No. Total bullshit – sorry."

"That's for you to find out, so sorry about that."

Scarlet offered a bitter laugh. "I thought it might be… but I don't trust her – I think she's up to something."

"Perhaps, but it's your mission like it or not. I want the map back and we can worry about whether Lexi Zhang is lying to us or not later. Just be cautious, that's all."

"Of course I will be. I'm not in the least bit concerned about Blowfly, or whatever she's called. If she crosses me I'll finish her." She crossed her legs and sighed, silent for a while. Then she spoke again. "What you said about Kodiak..."

"Kvashnin?"

"Right - an ape like that wouldn't be working solo. Who's his organ grinder?"

"We don't know. He's worked for every scumbag in Russia and a good many in the Middle East over the years too, so it could be anyone. Clearly if he's trying to take out Lexi Zhang then this has to be about the map and nothing else, so I'm guessing Sorokin was just collateral damage. We can safely presume someone else has heard chatter about the search for immortality and wants some for himself."

"And we can get an idea of how serious he is by the fact he hired Kodiak."

"Indeed, which is why you're going to Berlin. We know Dragonfly is there with the map, and I want you to retrieve it."

"When?"

"As soon as possible. We'll coordinate with Lexi but I want you to get there in advance and check the place for any trouble first."

"Of course."

"And you're going with Karlsson."

"Oh, *please*. Can't I take a potato instead? It'd be of more use."

Eden sighed, unamused. "The Americans are forcefully insisting on being part of this and he's the man they want in it. I get the feeling someone pretty high up the food chain in DC has started pulling strings on this one. Is that going to be a problem?"

Scarlet leaned back in her chair and swung her boots up onto Eden's desk, causing him to raise an eyebrow. "Bradley Karlsson? I've known tougher Teddy Bears. I can bring him to heel."

CHAPTER FOUR

Hawke didn't have to break the door down. That had already happened when the knifeman snatched Nightingale. Now it was closed in the frame but unlocked, and the lock mechanism was smashed out leaving a rugged hole where it had once protected her, or so she had probably thought.

He and Lea split up and searched the apartment for any trouble while Ryan stayed outside and watched the corridor.

It was a spacious loft apartment with polished hardwood floors and neat white walls, one of which was an enormous bookcase from floor to ceiling. A large semi-circle window looked out over a chilly Manhattan and let in the sound of the traffic far below.

Built-in spotlights shone down from the ceiling, and several well-kept house plants added a splash of color throughout the long, tidy room. In the center of the space was a circular desk with a serious array of laptops and computers on it. No sign of any struggle in here.

Lea looked at the tidy apartment. "She was pretty organized. My flat looks like a cross between a food fight competition and Tornado Alley."

"I remember only too well," Hawke said as he moved through to the bedroom where the trouble had begun. In here, a pot plant had been knocked over and the soil was all over a plush, cream rug. In the obvious struggle, books and ornaments had been smashed off the shelves and were now strewn over the floor.

Worse than that was the sight of a wheelchair on its side in the center of the bedroom. It looked like someone had given it a good kicking and one of the main wheels was slightly bent off its axle. Hawke felt like he was intruding into the very heart of Nightingale's secret world, but he knew he had no choice if he was to stand the slightest chance of getting her back – of bringing this nightmare to an end once and for all.

Lea joined him. "All clear back there, but… wait – is that a *wheelchair*?"

Hawke nodded grimly. "I had no idea. She never told me anything about it." He opened the wardrobe door and looked inside. "This is where she took the pictures of the guy who snatched her. I recognize the view from inside. Bastards."

Lea put her gun in the holster and looked at Hawke. "What's our next play?"

Hawke sighed and took a second to think. Whoever had taken Nightingale must have had a damned good reason to do so, and whoever it was had nearly a full day's head-start on them.

He turned to Lea. "Ryan needs to get those computers fired up, don't you think?"

Lea nodded gently and went to get Ryan.

Hawke picked up the wheelchair and set it back on its wheels, drumming his fingers on the handles at the rear as his mind wandered. Just who the hell would smash into Nightingale's apartment and kidnap her, but leave all of her computer gear? Clearly no one from her CIA past, he thought. This was starting to look personal, and his feeling that her disappearance might be connected to the hunt for the map was getting stronger – it would be just too much of a coincidence for it to be anything else.

He glanced quickly over her bedroom one more time, but the feeling of guilt returned. He had spoken to this woman so many times before, and she had saved his life, but she had never really invited him into her personal life. Now she was gone, and he was standing in the center of her universe, it all felt wrong.

On the side of her bed was a framed photo of a woman he presumed was her, with another man. He picked it up and looked at Nightingale for the first time. She was slim, with pale brown curly hair and sparkling green eyes. An innocent, honest smile made her look young and kind, but he knew this was a woman with a past. The man in the picture had seriously perfect hair with a dash of silver at the temples. At first glance he thought it must be a boyfriend, but then he thought he saw a resemblance and decided the man could easily be her brother. Whoever he was, Hawke thought he reminded him strongly of someone else, but couldn't put his finger on it.

"Joe!" It was Lea, calling him from the main room. He set the picture carefully down on the side table and stepped back into the other room to see Ryan walking around the table activating all the computers, his face a study of solemn determination.

"Any luck?" he asked.

"Just firing these babies up," Ryan said. Since the murder of Sophie Durand back in Tokyo, Hawke had noticed that Ryan was avoiding eye contact with him whenever he could, and keeping his quips to a minimum. Not surprising, Hawke thought, but he hoped that inside, Ryan had everything under control. He had gone through the same when Liz was killed in Hanoi – shot right in front of him – and it had been hard enough for a man with his training to deal with. How a loose-cannon like Ryan Bale might react was impossible to guess, but Hawke feared the worst. Most concerning was Ryan's refusal to talk about it, but he knew he shouldn't be pushed.

Ryan pulled a swivel chair over from another desk and began to work with the various screens in front of him around the table. "Looks like she didn't get out much," he said, and then stopped himself before going any further. "Sorry, Joe… I didn't mean anything by that."

"Forget about it," said the former SBS man. "I only found out about the wheelchair a few moments ago myself."

Ryan made no reply, but carried on looking through the computers. Hawke made a search through the bookshelves and anywhere else he could think of – inside kitchen cupboards, under the furniture, even inside the air-conditioning ducts, but he found nothing.

"Looks like she was pretty lonely," Lea said, glancing around the apartment.

Hawke nodded in response but said nothing.

Lea looked at him for a moment. "What is it, Joe?"

"Nothing… just that it's suddenly hit me just how little I really know about her – there's nothing here even with her name on it – nothing. She's gone out of her way to remove herself from the world, even inside her own apartment."

"Spooky, if you ask me," Lea said.

"What about on there?" Hawke asked Ryan. "Any names or anything that can help identify her?"

Ryan shook his head. "Not really. First, the only name I can find anywhere is Nightingale, and second, whoever she is, as far as computer skills go she's way above my pay grade…"

Lea sighed. "I don't know what to make of it."

"Exactly," Hawke replied. "We really are coming to a dead end."

"No, I mean that Ryan just admitted someone else was better than him at something and I really can't believe I heard that right."

Ryan sighed. "The only way you could get any funnier, Lea, is if you put on a clown outfit, you know that, right?"

"Zip it, Ry."

"With a big, red nose."

Hawke looked at them both. "Guys, I need some focus in here right now, yeah?"

"Sorry…"

"What about the desktop?" Hawke asked.

"I'll fire it up."

"Woah!" Ryan said.

"What is it?" Hawke leaned in to look.

"Looks like your little Nightingale has more than a passing interest in the Map of Immortality – check this out!"

Hawke looked at the screen and saw a long list of files. "What are they?"

"These ones here are all named after Egyptian gods."

Ryan clicked on a file and opened it.

Lea whistled. "Oh my…"

"My sentiments exactly," Ryan said.

They were now looking at a PDF full of text and symbols.

"Isn't that one called a wank or something?" Lea said, winking at Hawke behind Ryan's back.

"It's called an *Ankh*," Ryan said, sighing and shaking his head. "It's the ancient Egyptian symbol of eternal life, called the *crux ansata* in Latin, which means the cross with a handle."

"And they called it that because it looks like a cross with a handle on it, right?"

Ryan craned his neck to look at Lea. “You *are* kidding me, yes?”

Lea laughed. “Of course I’m kidding, Ry! You are so easy…”

Ryan was unamused. “The ancients called this symbol the breath of life or the key of the Nile and it’s one of the oldest symbols in the world. It’s found on carvings thousands of years old but no two Egyptologists can agree on its true origins.”

Hawke frowned. “Which is a mystery almost as interesting as why Nightingale has hundreds of files relating to ancient Egypt and immortality on her computer.”

“Hey! A girl can be interested in ancient Egypt, can’t she?” Lea said.

Ryan stared at the laptop. “Sure she can, but I think this goes way above *interested* – there are countless files on here, and the research just goes on and on. There’s also an email trail here to a mystery man called Mercurio who seems to know more about this stuff than anyone.”

Hawke stood up and scratched the stubble on his chin. “When did she start researching all this and talking to this…*Mercurio*?”

Ryan took a few moments to flick through the files. “Er… looks like around the time we were trying to stop Zaugg finding the vault of Poseidon.”

Lea sighed. “Great, so we’re to blame…”

“It gets better,” Ryan said,

“What is it?”

“A lot of these files look like they originated in the US Defense Department – the Pentagon.”

Hawke looked shocked. “Really?”

Ryan nodded. “And they’re pretty highly classified as well, unfortunately someone’s spoiled all the fun and all the good bits have been redacted.”

"Eh?" Hawke said.

"Blacked out," Lea said. "We say blacked out in English, but they say *redacted* in Nerdish, right Ryan?"

He ignored her, transfixed by the information unfolding on the screen in front of him. Since Sophie's murder in Tokyo, Ryan had gotten a lot less interested in sparring with Lea, or anyone else for that matter. He had gone back inside himself again, back to where he had hidden after his divorce. Now, all this seemed to be dragging him back to life.

"So all her research was pointing to Egypt?" Hawke asked.

Ryan nodded. "She seems to have followed a path from Poseidon back from Greece to Ancient Egypt, which isn't that surprising."

Lea frowned. "Why not?"

Ryan nodded. "The ancient Egyptians were very big on anything to do with immortality. They believed that eternal life was possible in the sense that their souls could be reincarnated in the next world so long as they led an honest, good life and never offended the gods."

"Sounds simple enough," Lea said.

"Not really. Like I said, they took it very seriously. There was a specific ritual of mummification that you had to go through if you were to going to be successful in reaching the next world."

"Like what?"

"For one thing, their internal organs were removed, dried out, and placed in Canopic jars."

"In *what*?"

"Large pottery jars with lids moulded into likenesses of the gods. Placing the *viscera*..."

"Ryan!"

"Sorry, Lea... placing the *organs* inside these jars after a process of drying them in salts was an important part of ensuring the soul would be reincarnated in the next world, thereby achieving immortality, so to speak. The stomach went inside the jackal jar, the liver went inside the human jar, the lungs went in the baboon jar and they put the intestines inside the hawk jar."

"Someone say my name?" Hawke said, turning to face them.

"No, I said…"

"I know what you said, mate," Hawke said, smiling. "But something's bothering me."

Ryan scratched his head. "What?"

"All this talk of taking people apart as part of the mummification process…"

"Yeah?"

"It's not quite the same kind of immortality that we're searching after, is it?"

Ryan turned in his chair to face Hawke. "How do you mean?"

"The stuff you're talking about here is about the immortality of the soul, but that's not what Hugo Zaugg or Sheng Fang were risking their lives to get hold of, and I doubt that it's what's motivating whoever's kidnapped Nightingale to get their hands on her knowledge of all of this stuff."

"I see what you mean."

"Those nutcases were trying to achieve immortality of the body – the power to live forever in their bodies, as they live and breathe *now*. They weren't seeking some kind of eternity in the spirit world."

Ryan looked a little deflated. "I guess."

"So what's the connection between the two?" Lea said.

"It's possible the gods were immortal in both the spiritual way and the way you've described here, and…"

"And everyone hold it right there!"

Hawke and the others looked up to see a man in the door. He was in a serious black suit and firmly pointing a Sig Sauer P229R in their faces. Worse, two other men in similar suits with guns were standing right behind him.

"Who the hell are you?" Hawke asked.

"I'm Agent Dempsey from the Bureau of Diplomatic Security."

"Yeah," Hawke said. "And I'm…"

"You're coming with us," Dempsey said flatly, cutting Hawke off. "Right now."

CHAPTER FIVE

Scarlet Sloane switched off the Passat's engine and watched the hotel for any signs of Lexi Zhang. This was the place where the renegade Chinese assassin had told Eden she would meet Scarlet – the Waldorf Astoria on Berlin's Hardenbergstrasse, but the Englishwoman wasn't taking any chances. She wanted to take a good look at things before stepping into any trouble – that was how she'd survived all these years.

Beside her, the former American Seal Bradley Karlsson dipped a bear-like paw into a bag of potato chips and jammed them into his mouth before snapping open the ring-pull on a can of Vanilla Coke.

Scarlet shifted over in her seat and brushed the crumbs from her leg. "It's like watching a gorilla at feeding time."

"Hey!" As he spoke, he exhaled a shower of potato crumbs over his lap.

Scarlet gave an exasperated sigh and stared at him. "Do you think you could try and get at least a quarter of them in your mouth next time?"

"Well, you know what you can put in *your* mouth…"

"I don't even want to know what that means. I presume something vulgar and American, but if you think… hey – there she is!" Scarlet pointed to the unmistakable figure of Lexi Zhang as she walked along the sidewalk outside the hotel. Their view was blocked for a second by a man walking with his young daughter, who was holding a bright red helium balloon on a little string, but then she was back in view for a second before stepping inside out of sight.

"That's the Dragonfly all right," Karlsson said, placing the bag of chips into the foot-well and pulling out his gun.

"Put the shooting iron away, Bradley. Do use your loaf."

"Use my *what*?" he said, confused.

"I'll explain later, darling," she said. "*Americans...*"

They left the car and jaywalked across the wide boulevard. The temperature had dropped below freezing, allowing them to see their breath as it condensed in the frozen air around them. Karlsson belched loudly.

"Was that strictly necessary, Brad?" Scarlet said reproachfully. "Any louder and they'd have heard you in Frankfurt."

"What can I say?" he said, grinning. "I'm a big guy and I don't hold back, as you well know."

Scarlet rolled her eyes. "Oh *please*, do spare me the innuendo. You weren't *that* good."

"I'm not going to say that doesn't hurt, Scarlet."

"You'll get over it, He-Man. Now, shall we do our thing?"

They linked arms and entered the lobby, pretending to be just another couple staying in Berlin for the weekend. They held back while Lexi crossed the floor to the elevators. She was the only one to enter, so they watched the lights above the door to see at which floor she got off. They had already been told, but they wanted to make sure nothing funny was going on.

A few moments later they were in the elevator, shooting up to her floor. When they arrived, the corridor was quiet and plush, and Scarlet wasted no time in tapping on Lexi's door, gun in hand.

Lexi Zhang opened the door and raised her arms. She took a tentative step back and beckoned them inside. “Please, come in,” she said quietly. “I was expecting you.”

“Yeah, right,” Scarlet said, and waved the gun in Lexi’s face. “Ladies first.”

Lexi turned and stepped back into the luxurious hotel room.

“And hands up, if you please.”

Lexi obliged them, and sat on the edge of the bed. Scarlet and Karlsson sat opposite her on comfortable leather chairs. Several moments of silence followed until Karlsson spoke up: “Well, this is *awkward…*”

“We heard a nasty rumor that you stole our map,” Scarlet said, her eyes glancing over the large room. “And then pretended to be dead.”

“Well…”

Scarlet scowled at her. “If I had my way you wouldn’t have to pretend.”

“I’m sorry about all of this… like I said to Richard, I was blackmailed. I never *stole* the map!”

“Save it, Lexi,” Karlsson said.

Lexi stared at Scarlet, imploring her to believe what she was saying. “It’s the truth, Scarlet, I swear it. Sorokin was blackmailing me – he said he’d kill my parents if…”

“I’m not buying any of it,” Scarlet said, “so stop wasting your breath.”

“But it’s true,” Lexi insisted. She held her phone up and showed them the photo of an elderly couple being held at gunpoint. They didn’t need to know it was taken less than an hour ago by two of her colleagues just to give her a cover story. That was the way this business rolled – deceit and dishonesty for the greater good.

Scarlet took the phone and stared at the image. It was dark, but she could easily make out an older Chinese man and woman sitting on plastic chairs. They were blindfolded and gagged and seemed to be in what looked like a kitchen.

She sighed and handed the phone back to Lexi . "It's *possible* you're telling the truth," she said, reluctantly. "But I've never trusted you in the way Hawke does, so any funny business and you can expect trouble from me – all right, darling?"

Lexi looked like she wanted to say something, but thought better of it, and simply slipped her phone back inside her jacket without saying a word.

"Hawke's too soft on you," Scarlet continued, still not entirely convinced by Lexi's story. "Don't make the mistake of thinking I'm like him."

"You know I won't," Lexi replied in an ambiguous tone.

"And where's the map, hun?" Karlsson.

"It's in a bank."

"How very convenient."

"It is! After I had time to think, I realized how vulnerable I was."

"You?" Scarlet said in disbelief. "You're about as vulnerable as a cobra."

"Listen," Lexi said, trying to calm the situation. "It's true… after they killed Sorokin I knew I would be next – you didn't see the hit outside the airport. Whoever did it was incredibly professional, totally ruthless."

"It was Ekel Kvashnin," Scarlet said coolly.

Lexi gasped. "Kamchatka?"

"The very same," Scarlet said, "or *Kodiak*, if you're an American like Bradley darling, here." She smiled at him.

"She loves me!"

"I wouldn't go *that* far, Brad," Scarlet said. "Let's say you're on probation."

"Ouch," Brad said, smirking, but Lexi was unmoved by the banter, her face deadly serious.

"It was really Kamchatka?"

Scarlet nodded. "Yes."

"Then I was right to be so concerned and take the map to the bank." Her words seemed to trail into nowhere.

Scarlet didn't reply. She was too busy thinking about the next strategy. Lexi had looked surprised enough when she had told her about Kodiak being the hit-man who had killed Yevgeny Sorokin in the botched attempt to secure the map, but who Kodiak was working for was still a mystery to them.

She hoped Hawke had made progress with retrieving Nightingale, and like the former SBS man she too had presumed early on that her kidnapping must be related to the search for the elixir of life. It was just too much of a coincidence for it to be anything else, but she did allow for the fact that Nightingale was a former CIA agent and would certainly have made many serious enemies over the years – the kind of enemy more than capable of orchestrating a successful snatch from a New York apartment and making someone simply disappear.

Scarlet Sloane tried to focus. It would be easy to see things as spinning totally out of control right now. First, as far as she was concerned, Lexi Zhang was now even less trustworthy than she was before, and that really was saying something. She had faked her own death and stolen the map, and was now claiming that all of this had happened while she was under the coercion of a Russian criminal by the name of Yevgeny Sorokin. The image of her hostage parents had looked real enough, but it would be simple to fake such a scene, especially if you had the experience, contacts and morals of the Dragonfly – and she'd certainly had the time to cook it up as well.

Then there was the fact that their team was dangerously divided again. Joe Hawke was chasing ghosts in New York City, and Lea Donovan and Ryan Bale had insisted on going with him to give him back-up. While Nightingale's disappearance was almost certainly connected to the map, Scarlet never counted her chickens until they were running around her garden.

Her SAS training kicked in as usual – bang on time. She knew what she had to do – retrieve the map from the safety deposit box while keeping a cautious eye on Lexi at all times, and then contact Sir Richard Eden and report her progress. He was the center of operations and would brief her on the next phase. The risks were high – she knew Kodiak was out there somewhere in Berlin, and that a man of his particular talents would be closing in on them fast.

When she spoke, her tone left no room for debate. "All right, we're going to need that map now, Lexi, and you're going to take us to it."

*

The man known to the Russian underworld as Kamchatka, but more familiar to Western intelligence agencies under the codename Kodiak, pushed back in his seat and stretched his arms. It had been a long wait, but as the old Russian proverb went, patience and labor will grind everything, and that was certainly the case now as he watched the beautiful Chinese woman leave the lobby of the Waldorf Astoria and make her way along Hardenbergstrasse.

The only problem was that she was no longer alone. Now, she was being accompanied by two others – a large man who looked like he knew his way around a gym, and someone whose role-model he presumed was Catwoman. Neither looked like they could stop Kamchatka from completing his mission. They walked to the road where someone from the hotel parking service pulled up in a BMW 7 Series and handed the man the keys.

Thanks to the laser microphone on the lap of the dead taxi driver beside him, he knew they didn't have the map on them, and that it was in a safety deposit box at a bank, but unfortunately they hadn't given the name of which bank, so he would be obliged to follow them all the way to the precious treasure. He couldn't risk any more mistakes after failing to kill the Chinese woman the first time and securing the map back at the airport. He knew his failure would have been reported by now, and he also knew only too well the folly of failing his leader.

Now, his targets climbed into the BMW and pulled gently away into the Berlin traffic.

Kamchatka pushed down the window and flicked his cigarette butt into the icy air. A moment later he fired up the Merc's ignition and rolled the heavy car out into the traffic a hundred yards or so behind his targets. They would lead him right to the map and then he would have redeemed himself.

CHAPTER SIX

The holding room was small and uncomfortable. Typical government hospitality, Hawke considered philosophically. They were sitting around a table in handcuffs and their only distraction was two small windows, one of which looked out on a brick wall a few yards away – which Hawke had already dismissed as a potential egress point – and the other was an internal window through which they could see part of a long corridor.

On the other side of this narrow window, a man in uniform was standing with his back to them, presumably their guard.

"Hey," Lea said. "Check that out – we have company."

"I'm not checking anything out," Ryan said. He was leaning back in his chair with his eyes closed. "I don't care who it is. They're all tossbags."

But Hawke followed Lea's gaze and immediately saw what all the fuss was about.

"Woah! I didn't see that coming," he said.

"Me neither,' said Lea, leaning forward in her chair. "I haven't been this excited since our divorce came through, Ry."

"I'm not opening my eyes," Ryan said. "I know you're just trying to get me to open my eyes and I'm just saying that I'm not going to."

"I really think you should, mate."

"Joe's right, Ry. You should definitely open your eyes."

"Nope."

Lea gave a frown. "I'm guessing this means we're in deeper shit than we thought."

Hawke laughed. "I would say you're a good guesser."

Lea nudged Ryan playfully in the side with her elbow. "Are you absolutely *sure* you don't want to know who's about to walk into your life, Ry?"

"As I said, you're just messing with me, so no. You two losers probably have a bet going or something. I open my eyes and the freaking janitor's coming, *and so on*."

"Have it your way, mate."

Lea bit her lip as she cast her mind back. "I'm also guessing this means the big boys had Nightingale under some pretty chunky surveillance."

Hawke nodded. "Another good guess, I'd say, but then not massively surprising since she was a former CIA asset and had done more hacking than a coal miner."

Lea shook her head in amazement. "But *this*…"

Hawke shrugged. "Just goes to show, you never know."

"Looks like it's show-time," Lea said. The group in the corridor were now at the door to the holding room. The guard snapped to attention and saluted. "Last chance, Ryan."

He sighed dramatically. "Nice try, but no cigar. Eyes are staying shut."

Hawke rolled his eyes.

The door opened.

Agent Dempsey walked in first and a second later several men in suits were standing in front of them, imposing, unsmiling.

"You already know me," Dempsey said, businesslike, "and I'm sure you know Jack Brooke, the US Secretary of Defense."

Ryan's eyes opened wide like saucers and he nearly fell off his chair.

"We know the Secretary," Hawke said.

"And now I know *you* all," Brooke said firmly, with no hint of a pleasantry in sight. "Especially *you*, Mr Hawke. Former SBS, British Special Forces, and now some kind of globe-trotting action-man wannabe, am I right?"

Hawke suppressed a smile and kept his cool. "And you're Jack Brooke, former Delta soldier, and now some kind of pen-pushing President wannabe, am I right?"

Agent Dempsey and the other BDS men looked to Brooke for a reaction, but when the Secretary cracked half a grin and nodded in appreciation of the response, they relaxed and took a step back.

Brooke sat down opposite Hawke and put his hands on the table. "Mr Hawke, I want you to tell me why you were in Agent Nightingale's apartment."

Hawke looked at the man. He had seen him enough times on the television news but he looked different up close and personal – older, more wrinkles, and a cast-iron slate-gray stare.

"Because she called me and asked for help just before they took her."

Secretary Brooke frowned deeply. "I see. And how does she know you in the first place?"

For a short moment, Hawke thought about spinning the Pentagon chief some kind of yarn. They weren't just talking about Joe Hawke, he contemplated, but also Agent Nightingale. For all he knew she didn't want the details of her relationships spilled all over the floor, no matter who was asking, but this was one of the most senior men in the American Government, and at this point Hawke was fresh out of ideas about how to save his friend. He knew his best play was to try and get Brooke onside as soon as possible, and you didn't do that by kicking things off with a bunch of lies.

"She saved my life when she worked for the CIA. As I say, I was in her apartment because I was trying to help her. That's all – and it's the truth."

"I believe you," Brooke said,

"You'd take our word just like that?" Ryan said, still shocked that one of the most powerful men on the planet was now sitting opposite him.

Brooke stared him down and fixed his eyes back on Hawke. "Of *course* I wouldn't take your word for it." He produced Hawke's phone from a pocket, confiscated from the Englishman earlier when they were arrested back in Tribeca. "But I would take Agent Nightingale's word for it."

Hawke looked down at the message she had sent him. The image of the man with the knife was right there again, mocking him, enraging him. He raised his eyes from the phone back up to Brooke.

"For this reason, I know you're legitimate and not lying to me, so I'm prepared to hear you out and give you a chance."

Hawke nodded. "Good, but what I don't understand is what any of this has got to do with you. Just what do you know about all of this?"

Brooke hesitated for a moment before replying. It looked like he was debating with himself just how much information to give them, and Hawke guessed that was exactly what was going on. After a few seconds of heavy silence, Brooke responded.

"I know more than you can imagine – I'm the US Defense Secretary, Mr Hawke."

"I understand that, but why were your men at Nightingale's apartment?"

Another pause. "She was under surveillance."

"Some great surveillance…" Lea said, but shut up immediately when Brooke turned his slate gray eyes to her.

"Who took her?" Hawke asked.

Brooke got straight to business. "We think a Russian citizen named Maxim Vetrov is behind the kidnapping, and that it has something to do with some work the agent was working on in relation to you."

"Me?" Hawke was stunned – his fears had been confirmed. He had put Nightingale's life in danger.

"Yes, you and your team working under the British politician, Eden."

"You know about Sir Richard?" Lea asked, concerned.

Brooke nodded gravely. "This goes higher than you can possibly imagine, any of you, including Sir Richard Eden."

Hawke, Lea and Ryan shared a concerned glance.

Brooke continued. "Unfortunately what we're dealing with here is so highly classified that only a handful of people know about it in the entire world, so you'll understand when I tell you that I can only release certain information to you and no more."

"Of course," Hawke said. "Who is this Vetrov character?"

"Maxim Vetrov is the original Russian oligarch. He has everything you can think of and then ten times more – the luxury apartments, the private islands and the yachts. He's even been to space three times on the Russian Space Program just for the hell of the ride up there."

Lea sighed. "Sounds like he has money to burn."

"If he burned his money he'd have enough to power New York City…" Brooke said, still no hint of a smile. "Our profilers tell me he exhibits the classic signs of a sociopath and an egomaniac, and we know for a fact he has personally killed dozens of people, mostly enemies but some of his own just for recreation purposes."

"What an asshole," Lea said.

Brooke ignored her. "Of course, we always have people like Vetrov under surveillance, but things got more interesting very recently when he had another Russian businessman named Sorokin killed in Berlin."

"Who?" Hawke said.

"Yevgeny Sorokin was a drugs kingpin from Moscow. Not the kind of person we'd waste too much of our precious time on, but we started paying more attention to him recently when he started communicating with Sheng Fang, with whom I know you are acquainted."

"Don't remind me," Lea said.

Hawke looked at her and knew she was thinking about Luk. It had bothered him too that they were unable to take the Hong Kong psychopath down, but now wasn't the time to worry about it. He returned his gaze to the Secretary. "Go on, please."

"Sheng hired Sorokin to deliver our stolen Tesla device into Tokyo Bay, as you all know."

Ryan lowered his head and covered his eyes. Lea turned and put an arm around his shoulder.

"For that, Mr Bale, we all have a great deal to thank you for. I will tell you in confidence that the President of the United States is aware of the role you personally played in retrieving the device and is truly grateful to you – to you all. It's another reason why you're talking to me right now and not in Sing Sing waiting for your lawyers."

Brooke turned to Hawke. "To say Sorokin was a double-crosser is an understatement. He always planned on betraying Sheng right from the start, but unfortunately for him, Maxim Vetrov has had long-standing plans of his own to locate the source of eternal life." He looked at their shocked faces. "Yes, I know all about that, of course."

"I see… and that's why he killed Sorokin?" Hawke said.

Brooke nodded. "Yes, outside the airport in Berlin. His plan was to kill both Sorokin and the Chinese agent Zhang Xiaoli, but she got away with the map."

Hawke frowned. It was beginning to sound like Dragonfly wasn't the traitor he had thought she was. "But what I don't understand is why Vetrov kidnapped Agent Nightingale – it can't be just for her research into the map, surely."

Brooke cleared his throat and glanced around the room uncomfortably.

"Agent Nightingale calls herself Alexandra Reeve."

Hawke looked at the Pentagon Chief and almost smiled. He'd known the enigmatic former CIA agent for many years and in all that time she'd played many games with him about her name. Now, at last, he knew. "I didn't know that," he said. "I never knew her real name."

"I said she calls herself that, it's not her *real* name, Hawke."

"I don't understand."

"Her real name is Alexandra Brooke."

"You mean…"

Secretary Brooke's eyes narrowed with emotion for a moment and the silence in the grim holding room grew heavier. "That's right, Hawke. Alex is my daughter."

The news hit Hawke like a sledgehammer. All those years and Nightingale had never told him her name or anything else about her personal life, and yet her father was the American Secretary of Defense, and a serious contender for President at the next election. For a second he had a hard time believing any of this was really happening. "But she never said anything to me..."

Brooke sighed. "My daughter and I are estranged. She never forgave me for divorcing her mother – Katie. She turned her back on me after that day and never said another word to me. It tears me up. That's why she uses her mother's name. I'd do anything to get my baby back, Hawke."

"I don't believe in any of this… this is getting mad." Hawke's voice trailed to a whisper.

"You'd better believe it," Brooke snapped, and returned to business. "After you contacted Alex about this Poseidon affair, she started looking into it in her usual extremely competent and determined way."

"How do you know that?" Lea asked. "I mean, if you were estranged and all?"

Brooke levelled his eyes at Lea. "I had her computers hacked."

"That is just terrible!" Lea said.

"That's between me and my daughter, Miss Donovan, and when it comes to my family I'll thank you to keep your opinions to yourself in future."

Lea blushed with embarrassment. "I'm sorry…"

"The point is she used her considerable skills, and exploited her relationship to me, to get hold of some information that she should never have seen."

"That only a handful of people know about, you mean?" Ryan said, recalling the Defense Sectary's mysterious earlier comment.

Brooke stared him out with the frown from hell and returned to Hawke. "She managed to get the details of a man who will be instrumental in translating the map. His name is Dario Mazzaro. He's reclusive and writes under the name Mercurio, and now he is in grave danger, just like my little girl. If Vetrov gets this man's details, he will not only secure the only way to decode the Map of Immortality, but he will no longer have any use for Alex."

"Why can't you send some people out to protect Mazzarro?" Ryan asked.

"As I say, he's a recluse and we have no idea where he is. I'm guessing my daughter knows which is why Vetrov took her."

"I understand," Hawke said.

Brooke's lips tightened and the slightest glint of a tear welled in his eyes. A second later he snapped back into the moment. "Anyway… the fact is she has knowledge she shouldn't have and this is the reason why Vetrov took her."

Hawke looked Brooke in the eye. "We shall just have to get her back again then, won't we?"

Lea frowned. "Excuse me, Mr Brooke, but the way you just talked about the map and the handful of people with this mysterious knowledge…"

"What?"

"There's more to this than we know, am I right?"

A long silence. Now, Brooke turned his attention on the Irishwoman. "Yes."

"And what would that be?" Ryan said.

"That would be what only a handful of people know," Brooke said. "And it's going to stay that way. All you need to know is that Vetrov has Alex, and is currently arranging to kill Agent Dragonfly, after which he will have not only my daughter and her knowledge of how to get to Mazzarro, but the Map of Immortality. The US Government is not prepared to allow that to happen, so we're organizing a team to put an end to it."

"Sounds fun," Lea said.

"There is nothing fun about any of this, Miss Donovan," Brooke said, ashen-faced. "Another comment like that and you're on a one-way trip to an early retirement in Dublin."

"Sorry…"

Ryan lowered his voice to a whisper and leaned closer to Lea. "You sure do spend a lot of time saying sorry these days."

"Who's on the team?" asked Hawke.

"Mack Dempsey, here, a former Green Beret, and two of his best men. Also, I know a former SEAL named Bradley Karlsson is working with your people in Berlin – I presume you're familiar with him."

"I wouldn't go that far," Hawke said.

Brooke ignored him. "And they will be putting their own people together. Given how much experience you've had in this, I want you to work with them. As I say, Karlsson is already in Germany working alongside an agent named Scarlet Sloane."

"I'd still like to know what it is you're keeping from us about all this," Hawke said.

"I bet you would, Mr Hawke, but that's never going to happen. Just you focus on getting my girl back from that asshole. I want her safe. After that, stop the asshole from getting to the source of eternal life, wherever the hell that is."

Ryan laughed. "Easy to say, but where the hell do we start?"

Another stony glance from Brooke. "A few hours ago I had a briefing from the CIA on the whereabouts of my daughter. We re-tasked a satellite watching the Baltic States and used it to track Vetrov's snatch squad. After landing in Domodedovo Airport in Moscow they flew out of the city in a private helicopter belonging to Vetrov."

"These egomaniacs sure do love their helicopters..." Lea whispered.

"It landed a short while later in the grounds of a private residence to the west of Moscow in a village called Barvikha. It's where much of the Russian elite own their second homes. Now we know that's where they're holding Alex, I want you on it right away. You'll have all the clearance you need, and there's a jet at your disposal waiting at La Guardia."

"We have our own transport," Lea said. "Our boss sent a plane over. It arrived in New York an hour ago."

"I see, then there's nothing stopping you."

Hawke nodded. He was already putting together a strategy for what was looking like his most complicated mission yet.

"One thing still bothers me," he said. "Why wasn't this all done when she was first kidnapped? I flew here as soon as I got her message but, you could have acted on this hours ago."

"As a matter of fact, we only just found out three hours ago. As I said, my daughter and I are estranged, Mr Hawke, but she's very close to her mother, whom she speaks with every day. They share a great deal. When Katie called Alex earlier today and there was no reply she grew fearful and contacted me. You'll understand now you've see the wheelchair – Alex has the mind of a genius, but she is physically frail and vulnerable, especially in a place like Manhattan, not to mention whatever hellhole Vetrov is keeping her in."

Brooke stopped to light a cigarette and blew the smoke out hard. He stared at the ceiling for a few seconds. Then he looked back down and saw Lea was watching the tiny burning embers, and she began to cough. “Excuse me, Miss Donovan,” he said, raising his cigarette hand. “Bad habit I picked up in the Delta Force before I went into politics.”

“Please, I understand. This must be very stressful for you.”

“You could say that.” He drifted for a second then fixed his eyes on Hawke. “Anyway, Katie asked me to look into it so I sent Dempsey and the others around to her apartment about three hours ago. That was when we found the place all smashed up and I feared the worst. If you had a daughter you’d know how I felt. I pulled every string at my disposal and had the satellite surveillance footage checked until we found who’d taken her.”

“We’ll get her back,” Hawke said, and raised his wrists. “Probably a bit easier with these off, though.”

Brooke waved at Dempsey and the BDS man walked forward with the keys to unlock the three of them.

They waited for the Pentagon chief’s lead, but for a few seconds there was nothing but silence. Then he sighed and closed his eyes. “I’ve been a terrible father, Hawke. When my daughter was kidnapped the first person who sprang to her mind was you, and not her father. You don’t think that kills me? I want a chance to put all these years of hurt and pain behind us. You got that?”

Hawke looked at Brooke’s anguished face. He got it.

CHAPTER SEVEN

Moscow

Maxim Vetrov watched dreamily through the window of his luxury dacha as the snow fell in heavy sheets over the countryside. He contemplated with something approximating pride that this was the landscape that destroyed Hitler's Panzer Armies. Behind him he heard the familiar deep, belly-growl of Osiris, or was it Anubis? Vetrov had trouble telling the difference sometimes, but after a short period of weighing up the probability he settled on Osiris. Osiris, after all, hadn't been fed for a very long time.

He turned his back on thc blizzard tearing through the pine forests of Barvikha, and cast a warm smile on the crocodiles as they lay on the artificial island in the center of the enormous enclosure. There were six in all, and all named after an ancient Egyptian deity. His favorite was the young female, Sekhmet, the goddess of fire and vengeance. He watched with pride as Anubis slid down from the island and disappeared into the salty brine with nothing left behind him other than a faint trail of bubbles, and then he was gone from the world again.

"*Crocodylus porosus* is a miracle of nature, Kosma." As he spoke, the giant Kosma was dragging a young man into the room. He hurled him on the floor a few yards from Vetrov and took a step back, keeping an evaluating eye on the surface of the water.

"The largest reptile alive in the entire world, the saltwater crocodile is truly the greatest predator on earth." He stopped talking for a moment to study his own reflection in the window with a mix of weariness and hope. It was true he was going gray, and the lines around his eyes were deepening every day, but unlike other men, Vetrov knew he wasn't going to grow any older. He knew, for a fact, that not only would he not grow old, but that he would never die.

Which was more than he could say for the young man now cowering opposite him.

He gave himself one last narcissistic glance and turned to face Kosma, whose seven-foot frame was towering over him. His number two was nervously explaining about the fiascos in China and Berlin.

"And you lost them?" Vetrov drawled, and then sipped a glass of chilled mineral water. His eyes crawled to the sweating man on the floor.

Kosma nodded unhappily. "At Xian. Two of my men let her get away with Sorokin."

"But he is dead now?"

"Yes. Ekel killed him in a cab outside Tegel in Berlin, but the woman got away with the map."

Vetrov sniffed sharply and walked away from his chair. Ekel Kvashnin was the very best in the business. He was not a man to mess with, but failing to kill the Chinese woman and secure the map was sloppy. His next failure would be his last, no matter what his reputation.

Once again, he watched the snow falling across the bleak landscape in thick white waves. "So Ekel killed Sorokin, but the little Dragonfly still *flutters…*" He made a casual, rising gesture with his hand to mimic a butterfly.

"Not for long. Ekel is tailing her to a bank somewhere in Berlin where she has stored the map. When she retrieves it he will kill her and take the map."

"And our American friend upstairs is still refusing to give up Mercurio?"

Kosma nodded in a businesslike manner.

Vetrov looked up at the giant man standing before him and considered his options. He wandered casually over to a large plastic box positioned by the fence surrounding the enclosure as Kosma dragged the man by the scruff of his neck closer to the water. "We call them hyper-carnivores because most of their diet is pure meat, but they are so much more than that. They are beautiful apex predators, to be respected, to be feared. Wouldn't you agree, Anatoly?"

The young man crawled up to his knees and clasped his hands in a show of desperate supplication. "Please, Mr Vetrov, sir." He broke down and began to cry without shame. "*Please*… I have children…"

Vetrov ignored his pleas. "In Ancient Egyptian bestiary, the crocodile was respected totally, for the entire economy was based on the Nile – the crocodile's territory. They wrote poetry about them, they worshipped them." He paused and raised his chin to look into the enclosure. "I wonder if Sebak will play today?"

"Mr Vetrov… please, I *beg* you…"

"Sebak was the crocodile god…" Vetrov opened the plastic box and the room was instantly filled with the sound and smell of chickens. "My darlings deserve a starter before the main course, naturally."

Vetrov pulled a chicken from the box and without a second thought tossed it live over the enclosure fence. It squawked and flapped but before it hit the water a male crocodile fired through the surface like a ballistic missile and snapped its wide jaws with a thunder-crack. The chicken was gone, the only remnants a small cloud of white feathers drifting through the air like snowflakes.

Vetrov gave an evaluating nod. "Ah! Anubis is faster today."

Anatoly turned white and began to tremble. Kosma took another step back.

"These beautiful specimens are from the Northern Territory of Australia, and they are the most formidable crocodiles on earth. They have the most powerful bite of any creature on the planet and can crush a buffalo's skull as if it were paper, as you will discover for yourself as soon as you tell me why you passed my research to Yevgeny Sorokin."

"I… I never…"

"Shhh," Vetrov gently stroked Anatoly's head. "Please, don't tell lies, Tolya. You, a humble research assistant from Volgograd, were entrusted with the greatest research secrets the world has ever known. I offered you more money than your family has accumulated in five centuries, and yet you pass critical information to my rival – who is now dead, by the way. I want to know why."

"I never even heard of Sorokin, Mr Vetrov, sir, *please…*"

"There are many ways to be killed by a crocodile, Tolya. If you are in the water, without a ripple on the surface, the next thing you know your head is crushed in its jaws. You wouldn't even see it coming. Less than a second and your skull is crushed and he is propelling you deep beneath the waves..." Vetrov waved his hand forward to simulate the path of a crocodile.

Antoly's reply was drowned in tears.

"And that is the good way, the fast way. Another way is Kosma here hangs you over the water from the rigging above the enclosure. That way my darlings will leap from the water and snap at your legs, each trying to make the kill. Now, how and why did you pass the information to Sorokin?"

"I swear, I never…"

Now bored with the game, Vetrov sighed deeply and snapped his fingers to bring matters to a close. Kosma moved reluctantly forward and took hold of Dr Anatoly Ivanov by the scruff of his neck and lifted the sobbing, broken man as if he were a simple cloth doll.

"One more chance, Tolya, and then you die."

"I do not know anyone called Sorokin!"

With a casual nod of his head, Vetrov gave Kosma the signal. The giant man raised the screaming man effortlessly above his head like he might lift a twenty kilo barbell and hurled him into the water beyond the fence.

For a second, or maybe two, the professor of Egyptian hieroglyphics tried to swim for the shore, driven by the most primal of instincts, but even he knew it was pointless. In the blink of an eye the enormous jaws seized him, and as the yellow teeth of Anubis sunk into his flesh, he disappeared beneath the foam and froth, now turned a startling crimson by his own blood.

"The girl knows more, I know it…" Vetrov murmured.

In the enclosure, a ferocious battle was unfolding. Water splashed all over the paving and occasionally a man's screams could be heard. Then a few short seconds later, Anubis dragged the still, silent Egyptologist into the brine and there was silence.

Vetrov chuckled and applauded as the water grew still again.

"Shall I get her?" Kosma was replying to his boss, but his eyes were firmly fixed on the horrendous scene that had unfolded in the enclosure.

Vetrov nodded his head and replied calmly. "Yes."

*

Still tied to the chair with the bag over her head, Alex Reeve strained to hear if anyone else was in the room with her. She thought she was alone, and her mind turned to escape. From somewhere below her, she heard the sound of splashing and the most terrified screams of a man she had ever heard in her life. After a moment of silence there followed the sound of a man laughing, and then applause. She strained at the duct tape holding her to the chair but it was no good. She wasn't going anywhere.

Then she heard the door open and a man walked in. Since being trapped in her new world of darkness behind the sack, she had learned to tell the difference in the sound of the footsteps. This was the footfall of the giant, and it was confirmed a second later when she heard his heavy breathing and felt his broad hands on her as he lifted her, still sitting in the chair, and carried her from the room.

*

The Gulfstream V cruised smoothly forty-thousand feet above the Norwegian Sea. On board, Lea and Ryan sat opposite each other and played poker, while Dempsey and his men sat up front and talked among themselves.

Hawke laid himself down on the long leather couch and painfully walked himself through the deaths of Hart and Durand for the thousandth time. Then, when that hell was over, he tortured himself some more over the kidnapping of Nightingale, a woman whose name he now knew was Alexandra Reeve, the estranged daughter of no less than the head of the Pentagon. All of this was starting to feel way above his pay grade and he wanted answers more than ever.

Lea's contagious laugh shook him from his thoughts and he glanced over to see her pulling a pile of dollar bills to her side of the little conference table. Ryan sighed and folded his hand, and then turned in the leather swivel chair to look out of the porthole at the ocean far below. Somewhere ahead he would soon see the Kjølen Mountains of Trøndelag on the western horizon.

Inwardly, Hawke was still finding it hard to deal with his responsibility for the deaths of Olivia Hart and Sophie Durand, and seeing Ryan as a mere shadow of his former self made things a thousand times worse. The smart-mouth kid-genius was gone – replaced by a sad, bitter cynic. Hawke had seen it happen before, but that didn't make it any easier to handle. Despite himself, he broke into a smile when he watched Lea take the money and crack some jokes – she was trying to make Ryan laugh, but his face was stone.

It had been no more than hours since the Chinese criminal kingpin Sheng Fang had fallen to his death in the hidden tomb of the Emperor Qin. Hawke could still see his terrified face as he plunged through the flames and crashed into the dirt beside a river of burning oil. Now, that was all tied up, except for Mr Luk… but they weren't out of the woods yet – a new monster had risen and was threatening to seize the elixir for himself. He had to be stopped.

Lea got a text, and she swivelled in the chair to face the front. Either side of the aircrew cabin were two large television screens, and the Irishwoman activated them with a flick of the remote. A second later the lean, sharp face of Sir Richard Eden appeared on the screens. Dempsey and the other American soldiers turned to look.

"Lea, how are you?"

"All good, Richard."

"Hawke?"

Hawke paused before replying, and rubbed the stubble on his chin. "*Well…*"

"Excellent, I want you all to listen carefully. I've had intelligence that the Russian hit man known as Kodiak, the man we now know killed Sorokin and attempted to kill Dragonfly, is on the trail of our people in Berlin. Presumably he has orders to kill them and retrieve the map."

"We know…"

"You're aware of this information?" Eden asked.

"Yes, you could say that," Hawke replied. "We just got a briefing by Jack Brooke about the guy behind all this – his name is Maxim Vetrov."

"Jack Brooke – you mean the Defense Secretary?"

Hawke nodded. "The very same. Agent Nightingale is his daughter."

Eden was stunned. Hawke saw for the first time that Sir Richard Eden's intelligence network obviously didn't extend quite as far as he would have liked.

"Well, I'll be buggered," Eden said. "Didn't see that one coming."

"Neither did we, Rich," Lea said. "But Jack Brooke knows all about us – and that includes you, too."

"I see…" Eden was silent for a few seconds but quickly regained his composure and returned to the matter at hand. "All right, then we know for sure Nightingale's kidnapping and the attempted murder of Dragonfly are connected – the link being Maxim Vetrov. He's obviously our man so get after him."

"We're already on our way," Hawke said.

Eden ended the call and Hawke gathered everyone for a briefing on the assault on Vetrov's dacha. Now wasn't the time for half-measures, and for the first time in a long time, he couldn’t wait until the shooting started. It was payback time, and he had a big score to settle with Maxim Vetrov.

CHAPTER EIGHT

Alex Reeve knew there was no point in struggling as the giant Russian plucked her out of her chair, took the sack from her head and heaved her over his shoulder. In broken English he had explained what would happen to her if she made a fuss, and her sense of self-preservation told her it was better to live to fight another day.

A few moments later Kosma kicked open a door and walked her into an enormous atrium. It was dim considering the size of the glass roof – but then she saw it was covered in fresh snowfall and that explained the lack of light. There was something else about the place that was wrong – an odd smell of salt which reminded her of the ocean. Somewhere to her left she heard a strange growling sound.

Kosma lowered her to the ground and placed her awkwardly on another chair. Now, she was sitting behind a high metal fence, beyond which was a large area of dark water with some kind of artificial island in the center of it. Above the enclosure was a substantial black metal rigging with a series of chain hoists attached to it.

"Good day, Miss Reeve."

She looked over the water to see the man who had spoken with her earlier. He was walking casually toward her. She could tell by the sound of his voice that this was the man who had been laughing. "Allow me to introduce myself more formally. I am Maxim Vetrov, and this is my assistant, Kosma Zhuravlev, an old associate of mine."

"You bastard! How dare you do this to me?"

"How do I *dare*, you ask? I dare to do so many things that the common man would shy away from. But before we talk, I must introduce you to my darlings."

After a brief moment of confusion, Alex looked with horror as Vetrov gestured toward the water, and saw for the first time what he meant by darlings – *crocodiles* – and lots of them. She could hardly bring herself to believe what her darkest fears were already beginning to see.

She watched one of the crocodiles crawl through the vegetation on the artificial island and slide effortlessly into the murky water. Another behind it, lost somewhere behind the plants made a deep, gurgling sound. She noticed floating on the surface what looked like a blood-stained shirt, now torn to rags, and her mind started to put together what she was now seeing with what she had heard a few moments ago.

"Now, Miss Reeve – or is it Miss Brooke? We have business to discuss, and I do hope you can be accommodating or…" he glanced at the enclosure.

Alex followed his eyes and saw the exoskeleton of another monstrous crocodile as it joined the other one and slipped beneath the slimy water a few yards from her. She flinched as a wave of disgust and terror crawled over her body. Now, at last, she knew her fate.

"What do you want, Vetrov?"

"You know what I want," he replied. As he spoke, he snapped his fingers and Kosma began to fix her chair to the load chain of a hoist. She followed the chain up from her chair to where it was attached to the rigging, which she now saw spanned the entire length of the enclosure, high above the water. Her first thoughts were that it was some kind of structure built with the maintenance of the enclosure in mind, but then she realized its purpose was for an altogether bleaker reason.

Vetrov saw the look of fear in her eyes and beamed. "Ah! You see, this is just my way of having fun. The crocodile is not treated with the respect it deserves by most people, but I know the truth – I know they are divine. This is my way of righting these wrongs. In making these offerings to the crocodile I restore a sense of balance to the universe."

Alex's breathing speeded up and she began to see stars. She could hardly believe what was happening to her. This man – this Maxim Vetrov, was clearly completely insane, and yet here she was trapped in his madness, and totally at his mercy. She had known danger in the CIA, but nothing like this.

She grew almost unable to control her fear. As far as she knew, the one man she had asked for help – Joe Hawke – was now in New York with nothing to go on but her trashed apartment. How he could he rescue her when not even she knew where she was? Maybe she should have contacted her father, but then the thought simply hadn't occurred to her. As far as she was concerned, she had no father. He probably didn't even care about her.

"You look scared, my dear… please – there is no need. I simply want information, and then you will be released, like a bird from a cage. I am not a monster, after all. Raise her!"

Kosma's massive arms heaved on the hand chain and the sound of the steel links sliding taut filled the otherwise silent room. She felt a jerk as the chain tugged against the weight of her chair, and watched the giant Russian heave harder to compensate. A second later she felt herself lift slowly off the ground and begin to sway slightly as Vetrov's henchman grunted with the effort of lifting her over the enclosure fence.

"My good man here will be lowering you into that water in a few moments. He will do this as a matter of course and he will not stop until I tell him to. I will not tell him to stop until you tell me the true identity of the mysterious Mercurio."

"I…I…"

Her head began to spin as she swayed back and forth above the water. Was all this really happening? A few hours ago she had been safe in her Manhattan loft apartment, researching what she had first thought was harmless esoteria. Then she had begun to realize that maybe there was something to it… then came her contact with Mercurio and now this. Her cozy world of disco albums and ice cream and romantic movies had been replaced by this terror – a Russian giant heaving her over a crocodile pit – the stench of chain lubricant and the sight of Maxim Vetrov smiling as her worst nightmare became real.

She thought once again about Joe Hawke, and how far away he was. She thought about all the times she had talked him through hells like this while she had been so safe back in her mission control, surrounded by the things that comforted her and made her feel secure while all the time he had been on the ground risking his life. The swaying of the elevated chair started to make her feel sick.

"As you can see, Kosma is now lowering you into the water. I estimate you have less than sixty seconds until you become acquainted with the crocodiles, and sadly for you, you have not been prepared for entry into the afterlife. This is your end-time."

She began to hyperventilate. "Why are you doing this to me?!"

"Mercurio's real identity, please. Thirty seconds."

She knew this was the end unless she gave him what he wanted. She had heard stories about CIA colleagues going to their graves before giving top secret information to enemy agents, but she knew she couldn't do it. She just didn't have it in her, and a wave of shame crossed her mind.

She thought about her mother back in New York who probably didn't even know she had been kidnapped. She would never know the truth about her daughter's disappearance… she thought about her father once again, the man she had loved more than anyone when she was growing up, but whom she hadn't spoken to for more years than she could remember. The last thing she had told him to do was go to hell… She couldn't leave the world like this.

"Mazzarro!" she screamed, her bulging eyes staring down past her feet at the circling crocodiles a few yards below her. "Mercurio's real name is Dario Mazzarro. He's an amateur Egyptologist from Venice, in Italy. Please! Please don't do this to me!" She broke down in tears at the thought of selling out Dario Mazzarro like this, but she knew she had no choice.

Vetrov smiled and spoke in rapid Russian to Kosma. A second later the giant ceased lowering her and tied off the chain, leaving her suspended a few yards above the enclosure.

She gasped in terror at the betrayal. "What are you doing?! I gave you what you wanted! You said you'd release me!"

She swung helplessly back and forth above the circling crocodiles.

"My dear, it is now necessary for me to check the quality of the information you have given me. I don't know about the CIA, but in the KGB we are taught never to trust information until it has been verified. You will remain where you are until I have checked out this Dario Mazzarro of Venice." As he spoke he made a phone call and began to speak into his phone.

Below her, Alex saw a slight ripple in the water and then two black nostril holes emerging from the dark surface. Less than a second later a gigantic crocodile was propelling itself from the water with startling velocity toward her. She thought it was going to reach her as its vile jaws snapped shut with a terrifyingly heavy crunch that made her jump. She screamed and began to spin around in tiny circles in the suspended chair.

"Don't worry so much, Miss Reeve. They are just playing with you. Seeing who can jump the highest. Take the time to study their beautiful form." He continued speaking on the phone for a few more moments and then disconnected the call.

"It seems you were being truthful, young Alex. There is indeed a Dario Mazzaro in Venice, and according to my people he is heavily engaged in researching ancient Egypt. Even better news – that was my man Kamchatka. After the egregious error of killing only Sorokin at the airport, he has redeemed himself and located the Chinese assassin who is, unless I am very much mistaken, in possession of the Map of Immortality."

"She'll never let you get your filthy hands on that map, Vetrov."

"Your invaluable naming of Dr Mazzarro, plus the map, my dear, means only one thing – I will be able to find the source of eternal life, wherever it is in this world, and the elixir of immortality will be mine!"

"You're just as crazy as all the others."

He shot her a devilish glance. "I think not, Alex. Where countless men before me have failed, I am succeeding. You see, I have a greater knowledge than any of the others. Where they fumbled in the darkness with only the faintest glimmer of vain hope to light their way, I know the darkest truth of all, and it is that very darkness which will lead me to the elixir."

"What the hell are you talking about?"

"I know *they* are real."

She stared at the Russian billionaire in despair and confusion. "*Who* are real?"

Vetrov laughed, pushed his hands into his pockets and walked casually to the window. "You'll be gone soon enough, so I suppose I can tell you, if you will only indulge my vanity. I'm talking about the *Athanatoi*, Miss Reeve."

"The *who*?"

Vetrov laughed again, but this time a much deeper, belly laugh. "I see I have the advantage! But then that is a pleasure enjoyed by many senior ranking former KGB men."

Alex fought hard to control the tears. "What the hell are you talking about, Vetrov?"

"No, I have said enough…"

He spoke in Russian to Kosma who punched some numbers on a keypad. A second later she heard the whine of hydraulics and felt a jerk as the chair began to lower toward the water. At first she thought she was imagining it – it was so slow it was almost imperceptible.

"It's on automatic now," Vetrov said, smiling. "A facility I installed to increase my pleasure because this way it takes my enemies so long to reach the hungry jaws of my darlings. I asked Kosma to set it to the slowest setting, so you have plenty of time to suffer – in your case, two or three hours. Now you will forgive me but I must also turn into a nightingale and fly to Venice, but for you, the struggle is almost over. *Do svidaniya*."

"You bastard! You *bastard...*" she began to sob as the chains lowered her torturously slowly toward the crazed crocodiles a few yards below.

CHAPTER NINE

Lea awoke to see a blanket of clouds stretching out above the Baltic Sea and on the horizon a faint gray-green line that was the northern coast of Estonia. She wondered how so much misery and terror could exist in a world so beautiful. She thought about why anyone would even want to live forever – what made life so precious was its transience, she thought, and then when she realized that sounded like something Ryan might say she smiled. Maybe she listened to him more than she thought.

Snapping out of her daydream, she rubbed her eyes and checked the screens on the aircrew partition at the front of the private jet. They were now at thirty-six thousand feet and had been in the air for a little over seven hours. They would be in Moscow in less than sixty minutes.

She turned to see Hawke was still asleep on the couch and watched him for a moment – the way his broad chest heaved up when he breathed, the shape of the muscles on his arms, and yet… when he was asleep like this there was a strange kind of vulnerability about him that made her love him even more. She worried that one day his luck might run out, that one of these days he was going to get himself killed.

"You want a drink?"

She looked up to see Ryan standing to her left holding a large tumbler of whisky in each hand.

"Um…" Lea checked her watch. "Sure, why not?"

"In that case there's a bottle in the cabinet at the back. These are both for me."

Lea thought about telling him not to be such a dick, but then she remembered why he was behaving like one and cut him some slack. Less than forty-eight hours ago Ryan Bale had watched one of the Lotus's men brutally kill his girlfriend. The fact she was trying to save his life at the same time made everything he was feeling ten times worse.

"I think maybe I'll leave it for now anyway," she said.

Ryan coughed and took a long drink from the tumbler, seeing off at least three fingers of the Scotch. "Suit yourself."

"What are the Americans doing?" she asked, peering over her seat.

"The Yanks are asleep," Ryan said flatly.

"Ryan…"

"Listen, don't even go there, all right?"

"Go where?"

"You know where. That little speech you were about to give me. You know – the one where you tell me it's not my fault and I'll get over it in time and *bla bla bla*."

"Well, it's not your fault, and you will."

Ryan didn't reply, but instead drank the rest of tumbler number one.

Lea watched him with concern. "Seriously, you can't get loaded right now, Ryan. I need you – Hawke needs you. Hell, someone's life is riding on this."

"Don't tell me what to do."

Lea decided to leave it and instead got ready for the landing. The aircraft had begun to descend and Dempsey and his men were awake and checking they were ready for the mission in Moscow. Hawke woke up and smiled at her, and then started his own preparations. He had his war face on.

She watched silently as the jet touched down at Domodedovo and taxied gently to the gate, and moments later they were going through customs. They quickly found themselves emerging into the freezing cold Moscow air and a crowd of people outside the airport. Hawke blew into his hands and smiled at the string of curses emanating from Lea's lips.

"Cold, Lea?"

"You could say that! It's cold enough to freeze the nuts off a brass monkey."

"Never deployed to the Arctic then?"

"Nope."

As she replied to him, a woman collided with Hawke and moved inside the airport without apologizing.

"Welcome to Russia…" Dempsey said.

Hawke ignored Dempsey's comment and turned to Ryan. "What about you – cold?"

Ryan shrugged his shoulders and pushed his hands into his pockets before turning to Lea. "And I think you mean it could freeze the nuts *on* a brass monkey."

"Don't tell me what I mean! I meant off so I said off."

"But that doesn't make sense," Ryan said. "The point is that it's so cold that it would freeze the balls currently on any given brass monkey."

"What? No! I'm saying it's so cold it could freeze its damned balls right off, you *eejit*."

Hawke opened his mouth to throw in his contribution, when Lea gave him one of her patented warning looks, a look which in this case was cold enough to freeze the balls either on or off him, depending on your preference. He shut his mouth without saying a word and they made their way to the car park.

Behind them, Dempsey, and his two men Dave Phillips and Frank Zimmerman tried to make themselves look like ordinary tourists instead of a trio of former

Green Berets on a covert operation deep inside Russian territory.

As Jack Brooke had promised, there was a black Audi Q7 SUV waiting for them in the car park, and Dempsey used the remote to blip open the doors. Without a second glance he opened the rear hatch and nodded appreciatively as he inspected what Hawke could see was a mini-arsenal of weapons. Apparently, being the American Defense Secretary opened doors shut to the rest of the world.

The Audi pulled away and Hawke watched the sad Soviet-era concrete and glass architecture of Domodedovo recede into the distance as they headed toward the Moscow Oblast.

A short drive later they were pulling up outside the perimeter fence of Vetrov's dacha and Hawke couldn't wait to start shooting. It was time for the fight-back from hell.

*

Scarlet watched Lexi closely as she filled out the paperwork and accessed the safety deposit box in the Berliner Bank. The Chinese assassin opened the box and Scarlet and Karlsson got their first view of the notorious map.

"I was disappointed when I saw that portrait back in Shanghai," Scarlet said. "But this is even more boring. I can hardly believe all the trouble there's been over it."

Karlsson agreed, and nodded his head. "I was expecting a treasure map, not… *this*."

Lexi smirked. "That's just what I thought. I also expected…well – a *map*, so you can imagine my disappointment when I first saw it."

"Just as well you couldn't read it, eh?" Scarlet said. "Or you'd be halfway to the elixir and we'd be twiddling our thumbs in London."

"That's not fair!" Lexi said. "I told you, they forced me to hand over the map."

"Save it for someone who gives a damn, darling," Scarlet said, as she studied the map. She was looking at a small document made from some kind of papyrus. It was covered in what looked a little like Egyptian hieroglyphics and other strange symbols which she thought *could* denote some kind of territorial position, but deciphering squiggles wasn't her thing. That was what the boy was for.

Karlsson glanced at his watch. "I hate to break up what could be an interesting little cat fight, ladies, but we're going to need to get back to the car and get out of here."

Scarlet nodded. "Brad's right. We need to report to Eden and get this thing somewhere safe."

They made their way through the bustling lobby of the bank and to the car park, where they climbed into the big Beamer and belted up. Brad drove out of the car park and into the Berlin traffic.

"Something's not right," he said, checking the rear-view mirror.

"Oh *great*," Lexi said. "A tail?"

Karlsson nodded.

"Easy, darling," Scarlet said with a smirk. "I'm sure we can persuade whoever it is to go and find someone else to play with." As she spoke, she opened the glove compartment and pulled out a box of nine mil bullets. "I suspect it's the chap who almost got the better of you at the airport." She began to load the bullets into her gun.

"That's what I'm afraid of," Lexi said, as Brad checked the mirror again.

"We're off," Brad said, and accelerated across into the left-hand lane.

"They're closing?"

"Uh-huh. Big Merc."

Scarlet laughed. "How original. Do these guys have a contract with Mercedes or something?"

"It looks like a hijacked cab, actually, but it sure as shit ain't driving like a cab." He turned to Lexi. "I'd say this Kodiak guy has been on our tail waiting for a chance to snatch the map and I guess some local cab driver just got unlucky today."

Karlsson tucked in tight just in front of a large removals truck and kept an eye on the Merc taxi that was now trailing only two or three cars behind them. He pulled out a little to get a better view and saw the driver of the Merc was loading what looked like a pump-action shotgun.

"Better get ready for some action," the former Seal said.

Scarlet raised an eyebrow and gently ran her hand down his thigh. "Why, are you feeling horny, Brad?"

"If I were, *kitten*, you'd already know it."

Lexi rolled her eyes. "Now? Really?"

Scarlet ignored her. "In that case, I guess our tail is upping the ante…" She leaned forward and looked in her side mirror. The removals truck signalled to exit the road and now the Merc raced up behind them.

"Ah *shit!*" Karlsson muttered.

A white muzzle flash behind them was followed a second later by the sound of the car's rear being peppered with shotgun pellets. The rear window shattered into thousands of pieces and Karlsson swerved hard into the adjoining lane to avoid a second shot. With his heavy hands gripping the wheel, the American floored the throttle and changed up through the ZF eight-speed box.

"Listen to that three liter turbo," Karlsson said. "Purring like a lioness."

"If we get out of this, Brad, we must make sure you and this car get some alone time."

"Very funny…"

"We're like sitting ducks on this damned street!" Lexi said, ignoring the banter.

Scarlet leaned out her window and fired three well-aimed shots from the Sig.

"Thanks for the warning!" Karlsson said, rubbing his ear.

"Don't be such a baby, Bradley," Scarlet said, and fired another shot. The Merc saw it coming and ducked in behind traffic.

"Damn it!" she said. "Lexi's right. We need to get off this street so they have nowhere to hide."

Karlsson weaved through the traffic with an ease and confidence that impressed Scarlet, not that she would ever have told him that. "I think we're going that way!" He pointed to a side-street and skidded dangerously over two lanes to make it.

A quick check in the rear-view and it was clear more action was needed. The Merc was also leaving the main street and closing the gap on them. Worse, the driver with the shotgun was reloading and preparing to take another shot. They were now in a more built-up area with people walking along the sidewalks, exercising dogs and jogging with their iPods.

"What now?"

"Keep going," Scarlet said. "There's a quiet stretch ahead without any people on the pavements. I'll take them out then."

"You're pretty confident."

"I'm pretty *and* confident, darling," Scarlet said, sliding around in her seat and leaning out of the window once again. She coolly aimed the Sig at the Merc, compensating for the drift of the cars and the uneven road surface as best as she could before firing a single shot at their pursuer.

Karlsson turned his head to check the mirror just in time to see Scarlet's shots hitting the pursuit car. The Merc's front tire blew out and sent the car screeching uncontrollably all over the road.

Scarlet smiled as she watched the man struggling to bring his vehicle back under control. He fought against the drag of the blown tire for a few seconds but lost the fight, plowing uncontrollably through a stack of boxes being delivered to a local store and spraying oranges and lemons into the air like confetti.

Scarlet put the gun in the side pocket, sure her work was done, while Karlsson took advantage and accelerated hard along the street.

Behind them in the chaos, the car-jacked Merc came to a juddering halt, skidding so its side was now facing the traffic. Undeterred, Kodiak lowered the window, leaned the barrel of the shotgun on the top of the door and fired.

A second later Brad was fighting was for control of the BMW. They mounted the sidewalk and a woman walking two cockapoos on sparkly pink leashes leaped for her life to avoid the Beamer. After a few seconds Brad brought the powerful car back under control.

"What the hell just happened?" Lexi asked, nervous.

"Bastard got us," Karlsson said. "Feels like the rear tire's out."

The wounded Beamer squealed to a noisy, whining stop, its rear driver's-side panel spinning around and smashing into a parked Honda and setting its alarm off.

Customers at a near-by café screamed and ran for safety, while one of the waiters made a call on his cell phone.

"Everyone okay?" Brad asked, taking a quick look at the others.

"Fine," Scarlet said, smacking the dashboard with the heel of her palm. "Damn it!"

"What about you, Lexi?"

"I'm okay, but you should know Kodiak is walking toward us and loading his shotgun."

"And matey-lad over there's probably calling the rozzers," Scarlet said, nodding at the waiter.

Brad turned to Scarlet and smiled. "This is just like our first date!"

She rolled her eyes and opened the door. "We have to get the map to safety, Bradley, darling. Do stop trying to be funny."

"Got it."

A terrific explosion behind them signalled that Kodiak had fired the shotgun once again. Scarlet saw a cloud of smoke rise from the sawn-off weapon in the Russian's hands and then shot-pellets sprayed over the side of the BMW. She ducked behind the front of their car and returned fire from the Sig while Brad and Lexi clambered out and took up defensive positions. Over their heads they heard the sound of a chopper approaching from the north.

"Police?" Karlsson asked.

Scarlet shook her head. "I doubt it. They'll respond in cars first – listen." She pointed in the direction they had just come from. Over the sound of the traffic and the screams of frightened pedestrians was the sound of police sirens.

"Which means…"

"Exactly," Scarlet said. "Kodiak's got back-up."

CHAPTER TEN

Hawke popped the trunk and climbed out of the Q7. It was freezing cold and snow blasted into their faces as they armed themselves from Brooke's mini-arsenal in the back. They selected from a range of weapons including assault rifles, automatic pistols and finally Hawke pulled out a Remington 870 Magnum shotgun for the internal doors, weighing it appreciatively in his gloved hands.

They put the final touches on their assault tactics as they marched through the snowstorm toward the dacha. Latest intel from Washington told them no one had left the complex and that Alex was still inside, but beyond that neither Jack Brooke nor anyone else knew what sort of danger she was in. They knew time was of the essence.

Now, Hawke moved forward through the snow and led the others closer to the enormous dacha complex, partially obscured by black Siberian pines and the swirling blizzard. They used the harsh conditions to their advantage and moved through the trees in the heavy snow to keep themselves out of sight.

Somewhere ahead of him was Agent Nightingale – the woman whose name he now knew was Alex Reeve, and she needed his help. Beyond that, he thought he might finally be nearing the truth that had evaded him since all this started – the truth about Scarlet Sloane never having been in MI5 – the truth about what Eden and Lea had kept from him.

He stared at the outline of the building in the snowy distance and was amazed by its size. He hadn't expected anything quite like this. "When they said 'holiday home', I wasn't exactly expecting all this – it's like a sodding castle."

"And who says crime doesn't pay?" Lea said.

Phillips opened the fence up with a pair of collapsible bolt cutters and a moment later the six of them were inside the grounds of the dacha. In front of them was a narrow stream, which ran freely in the summer but was now frozen solid. They stepped on the ice and climbed up the far bank to find a small clearing. They were now no more than fifty yards from the west wing of the dacha.

"Look over there!" Lea said, pointing to their right. "Looks like they're preparing to clear out."

Hawke looked to where she was pointing and saw several men in thick black coats and ushanka hats readying a sleek silver helicopter for flight. It was parked on a landing pad beside a hangar a hundred yards or so from the main house, and a second chopper was parked behind it.

Hawke sighed. "Not the best news I've had today…"

"Maybe they got what they wanted from Nightingale," Ryan said with a shudder. Ice was forming in his eyebrows.

"Let's hope not," Hawke said. "If they don't need her any more there's nothing to stop them killing her."

Zimmerman raised his rifle and squinted through the sights.

"No!" Hawke said, pushing the barrel away and down toward the snow. "Are you crazy?"

"I could take them all out right now!" he replied.

"No, Zimmerman! He's right," Dempsey said. "You could take those guys out, sure, but then our cover's blown and the Secretary's daughter is dead. You want to be responsible for that?"

Zimmerman lowered the rifle but said nothing. Hawke knew the tension was running higher than usual on this mission. The failure to rescue hostages always made the news, and a bungled attempt to save the life of the American Defense Secretary's daughter would make headline news on every network for weeks. It wasn't the sort of publicity any of these Special Forces operatives would ever desire.

For Hawke, nothing mattered except saving Alex's life. He couldn't give a damn either way what the press said, but the thought of failing Alex at her moment of need – when she had saved his life back in that Balkans hellhole – just wasn't worth contemplating.

They drew closer to the hangar and Hawke stood on a disused engine block to look through one of the windows. He pulled himself back to avoid being seen by an aviation mechanic who was whistling to himself and working casually inside the small building. Luckily, he hadn't seen him, and Hawke took a second look. The interior of the hangar was brightly lit by strip-lights and mostly empty now that the helicopters had obviously been rolled out ready for Vetrov.

"We need to get to the house, fast," Hawke said.

They moved toward the house and in line with their plan, they used grappling hooks to ascend to the roof where they moved low and cautiously until they found the atrium.

Hawke cleared some of the snow away and peered down through the thick glass.

"What the hell is this place?" he said, confused. "Looks like some kind of swimming pool."

"I don't think so," Ryan said.

"What do you mean?"

"I might be mistaken, Joe, but I think that's pretty much the last place you want to go swimming – look carefully over there by the artificial island."

Hawke followed where Ryan was indicating with his gloved hand and saw to his horror what had to be at least a twenty-five foot-long crocodile submerged a few inches below the surface of the brown water.

"Bloody hell! It's some kind of enclosure."

Ryan nodded. "Unbelievable. Who the hell has a crocodile enclosure in their house?"

"I'm learning more about Maxim Vetrov with each passing minute," Lea said. "And I don't like it…and just what the hell is that?"

Hawke looked closer and saw a woman suspended over the enclosure.

"Could that be Nightingale?" Ryan said, squinting through the snow.

"Holy crap, that's the asset," Dempsey said, and began radioing information into a concealed headset.

Hawke gave him a look. "It's not an *asset*, Dempsey, it's a person, and she happens to be an old friend of mine."

"Sorry…"

"Forget it," Hawke said flatly. "Listen up, here's the plan."

*

Alex Reeve had spent an agonizing length of time being slowly winched down toward the crocodiles. As each link in the chain had clunked in the housing, inching her ever closer, she had felt sick as her death drew ever nearer. In that time, Vetrov had been busy preparing to move out – mocking her as he gave his men orders and loaded his gear into the helicopters. Now he was ready for the short chopper flight to Moscow where his private jet was fuelled and ready to go.

She watched Vetrov and Kosma move to the door for the final time as the chain hoist lowered her slowly toward the snapping crocodiles, but then she heard the sound of smashing glass and glanced up to see something fall from the atrium roof into the water. A second later there was an enormous underwater explosion which sent a colossal wave of spray into the air, followed by flying bloody chunks of what she could only presume were crocodile, blown apart by the force of the grenade.

Vetrov staggered backwards and stared upwards at the roof in horror, the smile officially wiped from his face. Another grenade came down into the water and a second explosion made an even more lethal impact inside the enclosure.

The Russian called out with his arms wide open in shock. "Anubis! Osiris! My darlings!"

The calm, controlled madness of the enclosure room had now turned to chaos as Vetrov began to scream orders at his men, starting with Kosma, who snatched up a closed-bolt Uzi pistol and began spraying nine mil parabellums in a lethal arc across the glass-roofed atrium.

The other men followed suit and discharged their weapons in the direction of the atrium, spraying the glass with lead and shattering it into thousands of pieces. It fell through the air like crystal, followed by tons of the snow which had been accumulating on it since the start of the blizzard. The snow blew into the expansive room and added a further degree of confusion to the chaos.

"Kill them all!" Vetrov screamed hoarsely as his enraged eyes searched the destroyed enclosure for any signs of life.

Then the main doors blew off their hinges in a cloud of dust and splinters and a second later a man in a black Special Forces mask rushed into the room. He slung a shotgun over one shoulder and pulled a submachine gun off the other, firing in controlled, short bursts at the men in the room. His aim was lethally accurate, and he took out three of them with only six bullets in less than ten seconds.

He hit the reverse gear on the rigging and Alex began to rise back toward the shattered atrium as the fighting intensified. He directed the chain hoist to bring her back down outside the enclosure and she landed with a thud on the paving.

As the bullets flew over their heads, the masked man wordlessly ripped off her duct tape and freed her, but was then gone into the fray, stopping only to fire two rounds into a man running toward them. His bullets struck the man in the skull and sprayed high-velocity spatter all over wall behind him.

Alex took advantage of her new freedom and dragged herself away from the water with her arms in an attempt to hide behind Vetrov's depraved viewing platform, but at that moment she watched with stomach-turning terror as the head of a crocodile emerged from the depths and headed in her direction, crawling through a hole in the enclosure fence made by one of the grenades.

Vetrov saw what was happening and smiled with a mixture of relief and amusement. "Sekhmet, my darling… kill her!"

She jumped with fear as the bullets traced over her head, the terror of her vulnerability coursing through her veins like never before. Back in the CIA, when she had been on active operations all over the world, she had known the feeling of adrenalin rushing through her system, and she had known gun fights where her own survival was at stake, but she had never seen anything like this. This was total war – an all-out, open fire-fight with dozens of machine guns and hand grenades. It was total chaos, far-removed from the world of covert intelligence and computer surveillance she had trained for. And now a crocodile was hunting her.

Other masked men stormed the room, rappelling down through the atrium and pushing deeper into the fight. They took out two more of Vetrov's goons as the lead man drew closer to the panicking Russian. Alex was now beginning to wonder just who the hell this guy was, but her thoughts were disrupted by the sight of Darling Sekhmet crawling out of the water and moving slowly toward her.

She raised her weight up on the strength of her arms and started to pull herself back, dragging her powerless legs as fast as she could, cursing them for failing her as the crocodile's jaws began to open and revealed dozens of hideous yellow teeth, much larger in reality than they had ever looked in the pictures she had seen.

Slowly it gained on her until it was a matter of inches from her legs. It stopped for a second and she looked deep into its reptilian eyes. It was looking back at her, studying her weaknesses, and then it lunged forward, its jaws opening faster than anything she had ever seen in her life. She screamed and instinctively shut her eyes tight as she prepared for the attack.

Then she heard three sharp cracks from her left, close by and deafening. She opened her eyes and saw the masked man had returned and fired three shotgun rounds into the crocodile's head and exploded half its skull into oblivion. It now lay motionless and dead less than an inch from her legs. Slowly its jaws closed in response to the lethal attack.

The man wasted no time with pleasantries and shouldered the shotgun before snatching her up in a fireman's lift and hurling her over his shoulder. With his arm wrapped tightly around her legs, he ran from the room. Her head hung down behind his back, and the last thing she saw from her new upside-down perspective was Maxim Vetrov ordering Kosma and the surviving men to retreat as another man in a black mask rappelled through the atrium room and descended into the chaos of the enclosure.

The masked man carried her along the same corridor Kosma has used to take her to the enclosure, only now she was being rescued instead of taken to her execution. Behind her, she heard the screams of dying men as the battle raged on. They turned a corner and went into what looked like a library, inside which were two people – an attractive woman with her hair tied back and a slightly younger man with messy hair and a Superman t-shirt.

"Take care of her," screamed the man, and then he placed her down gently. "I'm going back to find Dempsey."

The man slipped through the door and disappeared into the smoke.

"Hi," the woman said. "I'm Lea, and this is Ryan."

Ryan gave her the slightest nod and an awkward wave, but no smile.

"You must be Nightingale?" As she spoke, she and Ryan moved her to a soft chair and tried to make her comfortable.

"Er… sure, but you can call me Alex, I guess."

"Sure thing, Alex. Good to meet you at last. Joe's told me a lot about you."

"Joe Hawke?"

Lea nodded. "Holds you in the highest of regards, he does."

Alex's head was still spinning from the action of five minutes ago. "That's good to know. Is he here? When can I meet him?"

Ryan smiled and pushed some hair away from his face. "I hate to be the bearer of bad news, but you just did." He nodded at the door where Hawke had brought her into the room.

Alex watched their faces, and then glanced back over her shoulder at the door she had just come through. "Oh… *got it.*"

"You'll get used to it," Ryan said.

Lea raised an eyebrow. "Or not."

"I'm sure I will, but I have to tell you something. It's really important."

Ryan sighed. "Most things seem to be these days."

"Vetrov kidnapped me to get information – he wanted the name of someone I've been working with on the map – Dario Mazzarro. The thing is…" she looked down, ashamed. "I gave it to him. I was scared, I thought he was going to kill me. We have to get to Venice to warn Mazzarro before Vetrov gets to him."

"We can do that," Lea said.

"Hell yeah," Ryan said. "I've always wanted to go to Venice."

"There's more than that, Vetrov also mentioned something about how he couldn't fail like all the others because he knew the darkest truth of all."

"Standard evil genius waffle," Lea said. "Heard it all before."

"No, he said he knew about the existence of a group called the *athanatoi*. I don't know what that means but I have a feeling they're behind all of this hell."

Ryan jerked his head up and stared at Alex. "Say that again."

"About the darkest truth?"

"No, the last thing you said – the people Vetrov said he knew existed."

"The athanatoi."

Ryan frowned.

"What's the matter, Ry?" Lea was unsettled by the look of concern now crossing Ryan's face like a shadow. "What does it mean?"

"It's Greek – it means *The Immortals*."

*

Scarlet, Karlsson and Lexi fired a ferocious volley of return fire at Kodiak, and forced the Russian to retreat behind a parked Nissan, but now the beating of the chopper's rotor blades was louder than ever. A moment later it drifted into view above the towering Europa-Center building complex on the Breitscheidplatz just off Budapester Strasse where they were currently taking cover behind the thrashed BMW.

"That doesn't look good," Lexi said.

"Seconded," Karlsson said.

"Thirded," added Scarlet, craning her neck to look for an egress point. "Over there!"

She pointed to a large gatehouse complex on the other side of the street. It looked Chinese in its construction, and two large stone elephants stood silent guard either side of the gates. A large sign said *Zoologischer Garten Berlin.*

"You want to take us to the zoo?" Lexi said.

"Hey, don't knock it till you've tried it," Karlsson said, smiling. "Can I have an ice cream when we get in there?"

The chopper came down into the center of Budapester Strasse and Kodiak clambered inside. As it rose up into the air, Scarlet saw at least three police cars racing up the street behind it in their direction, and then the chopper moved closer and made a ninety-degree turn so its side door was facing them.

"Incoming!" Karlsson shouted, and the three of them raced away from the BMW as an RPG tore through the air from the hovering Bell and hit their car, sending a gargantuan explosion of metal, glass shards and burning petrol into the air.

The police cars skidded all over the road, the confusion of their drivers obvious as they slammed on reverse and moved away from the carnage unfolding in the center of their capital city.

In the chaos, Scarlet Sloane and her sub-unit slipped away with the map into the Berlin Zoological Gardens, but behind them, the newly airborne Kodiak gave chase.

CHAPTER ELEVEN

Lea and Alex shared a concerned glance and looked back at Ryan. The London hacker dropout was starting to look increasingly anxious about things since Alex had mentioned the word *athanatoi*.

"The *immortals*?" Lea asked. "That sounds pretty ominous, Ry."

"Thought you'd be used to all things immortal by now, Lea."

"Sure, but what's freaking me out is that it's plural – how many of these people are we talking about?"

"Who said they were people?" Ryan said, smirking.

"Now you're just freaking me out!"

"Hey, don't shoot the messenger!" Ryan said, and pushed his glasses up on the bridge of his nose. A few rooms away the sound of machine gun fire and screams filled the air. He turned toward the noise for a second and then looked back at Lea. "I'm just telling you what *athanatoi* means, that's all."

"But what does the existence of such a group mean?" Alex said, flinching as another explosion went off in a nearby room.

Lea offered an empty sigh. "I'm guessing it means all of this damned mess goes a lot deeper than we thought."

"I'll say," Ryan added. "I thought we ended this when we stopped Zaugg getting the trident, but now it looks like there's some kind of secret group behind things. I think I just want to go home and get into bed."

"Just calm down, Ryan," Lea said. "It might not be as crazy as all that."

"Only if our luck changes, Lea. I'm starting to wish you'd never called me, back when you wanted my help on that bloody trident mission."

"Yeah… *about* that. The trident really is just the beginning of all this," Alex said with a nervous smile.

Lea fixed her eyes on Alex. "I think you need to start talking, Agent Nightingale."

Alex nodded and pulled her hair back. Outside in the corridor the sound of gunfire made her jump once again. "I hope Joe's okay…"

"Joe'll be just fine," Lea said flatly. "Start talking – I think you need to start tying some loose ends up."

"Sure… I'd used my Dad's passwords to get into some pretty heavy stuff at the Pentagon, and it wasn't long before I started reading some very interesting information – but always very vague. After a few hours I got hold of a list of names – Gottardo Ricci, Anton Reichardt, Felix Hoffmann, Giovanni Mazzarro and Dario Mazzarro."

Lea and Ryan shared a concerned glance.

"I'm guessing that's not your Dad's Christmas card list, right Alex?"

Alex flicked an anxious look at Lea. "You can say that again. All the names on this list were academics involved heavily in the search for the elixir."

"I don't recognize the last two names," Lea replied.

"The Mazzarros? Italian Egyptologists – Giovanni was the father and Dario is the son. Giovanni, the father, disappeared while on a dig in Egypt many years ago, but he'd dedicated his life to finding what he called the *white drops*."

Ryan pushed his glasses up his nose and blinked. "A common term used in ancient Egypt to describe what we today would call the elixir, or the water of life."

"Right," Alex said. "But like all the others he died before he discovered the truth."

"And his son?"

"Dario Mazzarro. He took up where his father left off. You have to remember all of these men knew what's at stake and tried to keep themselves totally under the radar. Their names only wound up on the DoD list because of an extensive hacking and tapping program by the CIA. But I got closer… I impressed Mazzarro with my research and I got to know him. Anyway, this was the research that Vetrov wanted from me, and I'm ashamed to say it, but I just handed it over to him. I gave him Mazzarro's name."

"Are you crazy?" Lea said, eyes wide with disbelief. "He was going to feed you alive to crocodiles! If he did that to me I'd do anything to play for time."

"She'd even sell me out," Ryan said.

Lea nodded. "I'd *especially* sell him out."

"Maybe," Alex said, sounding unconvinced. "But the CIA trained me better than that."

"You're being too hard on yourself," Ryan said.

"Either way," Alex said with a deep, sad sigh. "Vetrov now has Mazzarro's name, so now he's in grave danger and we have to get to him before the Russians do." Alex jumped yet again as a grenade went off in an adjoining room. "I can't explain it all here, in *this*, but if we get out of here there's a lot more you need to know."

*

Scarlet, Karlsson and Lexi sprinted though the ornate gates and disappeared inside the zoo as fast as they could. It wasn't easy to outrun a helicopter, but it wasn't impossible, all you had to do was find a highly populated area and some cover. Unfortunately for Scarlet Sloane, the RPG attack on Budapester Strasse had changed the mood of the people visiting the zoo, and now they were all screaming and scattering for their lives.

They sprinted deep in the zoo and looked for somewhere to escape from the chopper, but the guns in their hands caused yet more mass panic and the fleeing crowds only highlighted their isolation as they ran in the opposite direction.

"This way!" Scarlet shouted. "We need to get out of sight somewhere."

She pointed at some buildings a few hundred yards down a twisting path lined with monkey cages and lion enclosures.

"Is this shit actually happening?" Karlsson asked, incredulous.

"Yes it *is*, darling," Scarlet said. "What's the problem?"

"When I signed up I didn't realize it would end with crazy English women and baboons."

"But you're a Seal, Bradley. You should feel at home in a zoo."

Behind them, the chopper continued its deadly approach, and Kodiak fired at them once again with the assault rifle.

"He really does want this map!" Lexi shouted, as they drew nearer the safety of the buildings.

"What now?" Lexi screamed from the rear. "Those bastards are closing in fast."

Above her head, Scarlet heard the familiar *womp womp womp* of the chopper's rotors as it raced up behind them and prepared to attack again. She scanned the area for somewhere to hide and then she saw her answer.

Poking a little above the birch trees ahead of her was the strange wood and glass roofline of the bird house.

"There!" she shouted. "If we can get inside that building we can buy ourselves some time to think."

"What? Like the A-Team?" Karlsson said sarcastically.

"Huh?" said Lexi.

"Forget about it, honey…"

They sprinted past a couple of bemused polar bears and entered the bird house just as the chopper reached them. It raised its nose and raced over the top of the giant aviary as it overshot its quarry, now hiding inside the building below.

"What now?" Lexi said with a sigh. "Collect some eggs for lunch?"

Scarlet gave a sarcastic eye roll. "Listen, we had nowhere to run, and they're not going to waste ammo shooting blindly at us in here because…"

Before she could finish her sentence thousands of bullets drilled through the enormous glass roof of the bird house and sent millions of razor-sharp shards of splintered glass fragments showering over their heads.

"Run!" Scarlet said.

They ran along the twisting path of the bird house, flanked on either side by tall rubber plants and palms, now covered in the smashed crystal remnants of several tons' worth of reinforced atrium glass. Hundreds of terrified birds squawked and flapped and disappeared up into the sky in a shower of feathers. The icy air from outside rushed into the warm bird house.

Lexi spun around and fired off two or three rapid shots at the chopper but it was useless – a fast moving target obscured by the wood and steel beams of the roof.

"You were saying something about them not firing blindly at us?" Karlsson shouted as they finally reached the safety of the reception area and its solid roof.

Scarlet gave him a look but didn't rise to the bait. "There! I thought I heard submachine gunfire under the noise of Brad's whiny voice."

"From where?" Lexi said.

"Where we came in – down there."

She was right. Several men were now running toward them down the main room, crunching on the broken glass all over the path, and releasing short bursts of fire from what looked like PP-2000s.

"We're shit out of luck now," Karlsson said without emotion.

Lexi glanced at her gun and shook her head. "This isn't enough."

Scarlet took a deep breath and shook her head. "We have to get out of here – this is getting a little too real even for me."

Karlsson looked at her. "Do I need to remind you that there's a maniac with a machine gun in a chopper out there, and he's aiming for us."

"We have no choice," Scarlet said. "We can't take out half a dozen goons armed with subs in an enclosed space with these." She waved her pistol in the American's face.

He nodded in grim agreement and the three of them sprinted from the reception and into the open air.

"Where now?" Lexi said.

"We could try…"

But before Scarlet could finish, her heart sank as she watched the chopper appear from behind the atrium and descend into the paved entrance outside the bird house.

"Put your weapons down or we will open fire."

The voice came from the chopper, and was amplified through a megaphone.

Scarlet sighed deeply and reddened with anger. "Do it!" she commanded the others.

They lowered their guns.

"Put the map down and walk away with your hands up."

"Do it…I'm sorry, but do it," Scarlet said.

"You're the boss," Karlsson said.

Lexi lowered her bag to the ground and they walked backwards with their hands in the air.

The notorious Kodiak stepped out of the chopper and strolled casually to the bag. He looked inside, gave the thumbs up sign to the pilot, and returned to the helicopter. On his way back, he stopped and blew a kiss at Scarlet.

Scarlet's reply was wordless – the meaning conveyed in her narrowed eyes and clenched jaw.

The six men with submachine guns followed him into the chopper, and she watched with rage as it increased power and began to hover into the air, the mighty downwash of its speeding rotors sending ripples out across the surface of the polar bear enclosure and blowing a little ice cream cart over. Litter from the bins flicked up in the downdraft and blew around like snow. A second later it was high in the sky and turning away.

Then it was out of sight.

"Damn it all!" cursed Scarlet, and lashed out with her boot at the sign directing people to the café. An unusual failure for her, and she wished Kodiak dead for it. She didn't know if that made her a bad person or not, but that was just fine with her. In her view, anyone with a past like hers was allowed to think whatever they wanted about other people.

"Just cool it, honey," Karlsson said. "This isn't over yet. Not by a long-shot." He tried to put his hand around her shoulder but she pushed it away.

"But they have the map, Brad!"

"But they don't know how to decipher it," Lexi said.

"And you can shut up!" Scarlet snarled, still burned by her loss of the map and the thought of having to report her failure to Eden. "It's all your damned fault in the first place!"

"Hey, I told you they were going to kill my parents…"

"Yeah, *whatever*," Scarlet snapped.

She walked away, her head in her hands and her mind racing as problems and solutions fought in her mind. She didn't like losing and Lexi's parents being threatened with death brought back other raw memories. It had been a long time since Scarlet had watched those men gun her own parents down and kill them. She was no more than a child, and that was her introduction to the world around her.

Even now, she would wake in the night screaming, her dreams turned to nightmares once again as the agonized faces of her innocent parents rose up in her mind without warning. Her father had hidden her in their wardrobe and she had cowered there. She had done nothing to protect them or save their lives, and now she had failed again.

For this, Kodiak would pay the ultimate price.

"Listen, we have to regroup," Scarlet said at last, pulling herself together again. "We need to get our heads around this."

"We'll sort it out," Karlsson said reassuringly.

Scarlet scowled. "They have the fucking map and we don't. That's all I know."

"That's not strictly true," Lexi said, smiling.

"What do you mean?"

She pulled her phone from her pocket. "You think I'd have that map in my possession for all that time without taking a picture of it?

*

Alex and the others looked up startled as the door to the library smashed open and the man with the black mask stomped into the room. He tore off the mask and kicked the door shut behind him, shouldering a submachine gun as he moved into the room.

"Hi Alex, great to meet you. I'm Joe, by the way."

"Yeah, I got that…" she smiled for a second, not knowing what to think about a man she had spent years thinking about and now meeting him for the first time amidst such chaos and danger.

"Where are the others?" Ryan asked.

"Massive reinforcements out of nowhere, mate. No way can we fight them and me and Dempsey got cut off in the brawl. We're going to meet outside and try and take out Vetrov's chopper before he can get away."

Before Ryan could reply the library door was shredded by a savage burst of machine gun fire until a hole the size of a beach ball was in the top panel. A second later a grenade flew through the hole and landed in the center of the library.

Hawke snatched Alex up and screamed at the others to dive for cover. The grenade exploded and sprayed its lethal, twisted cast-iron shrapnel around the room in a burning fireball which set fire to the drapes and bookshelves.

Hawke was dazed, but staggered up and crawled over to Alex.

"Are you all right?"

She nodded, but was also too dazed to answer.

Hawke strained to see through the smoke. "Lea! Ryan!"

Back in the hall he heard the hideous chatter of machine guns as Vetrov's reinforcements closed in on them. Hawke knew their orders would be to terminate him and the others without mercy and he had only seconds to execute a safe retreat.

He fired the shotgun at the window and blasted the stained-glass out of the frame and over the snow outside where it fell like diamonds. Then, he hoisted Alex over his shoulder in a fireman's lift and staggered over to the window, clambering through and laying Alex on the soft, cool snow.

Without a second thought, he climbed back through the window into the black smoke and began the search for the others. The smoke stung his eyes and for a second he was disorientated until the sound of Vetrov's assault on the library helped him get his bearings back.

In the hot darkness he saw Ryan dragging Lea along the floor. Ryan was coughing heavily and looked like he was about to go over.

Hawke ran to him.

"Get to the window and get out!" he screamed.

"I'm not leaving Lea!" Ryan shouted back, grabbing the top of a chair for support.

"I'll get her – just get out of here – now!"

Hawke watched Ryan flee from the burning room and then he lifted Lea over his shoulder in another fireman's lift. The two of them went through the window into the icy cold air.

Above them half the complex was now on fire. Hawke looked down at Lea and Alex, and saw that Alex was coughing her way back to life. Then, another grenade landed with a soft thump on the snow beside Lea.

This time, Hawke had time to react and snatched up the grenade. Ryan watched in horror as the former SBS man simply held the grenade in his hands.

"What the hell are you doing?" Ryan asked, taking a step away from Hawke.

"Lie down over Lea, Ryan. She's unconscious and can't protect herself."

"What?"

"Wait… *three, four, five…*"

Ryan did as he was told and Hawke threw the grenade back into the library. He launched himself over Alex and a second later a colossal explosion ripped through the library. After some savage screams from inside there was silence except for the sound of the flames.

"That takes care of those wankers," Hawke said, rubbing the soot from his face. "How's Lea?"

Ryan looked down at Lea and back up at Hawke. "I think… she's stopped breathing, Joe."

CHAPTER TWELVE

Hawke picked Lea up and ran from the burning building, screaming at Ryan to do the same with Alex. The rage flowed through him like molten lava as he made his way to safety, but he fought it back and kept his focus.

Now, he held Lea's limp body in his arms as he emerged from the smoky ruins, gripping her tightly as the building blazed behind him. To his right, Ryan Bale dragged Alex and staggered out of the smoke, coughing violently as he struggled to heave some fresh air back into his lungs. All around them the swirling Russian snow added an extra degree of chaos to an already terrible moment.

"Is she okay, Joe?" Ryan wobbled over to Hawkc, his face smeared with soot from the fire. He took off his glasses and wiped his stinging eyes.

Hawke didn't reply, but instead he lowered Lea gently to the ground and gave her the kiss of life.

Nothing.

He did it again. This was basic training to a man like Hawke. It didn't matter that he knew how bad the statistics were. He had to save her life. Again, he took a deep breath, pinched her nose and blew into her mouth, manually inflating her lungs. This was essential to cardiopulmonary resuscitation, designed to restore the flow of oxygenated blood to the unconscious person before they suffered any long-term effects from a lack of oxygen.

But still nothing.

He did it again. He pinched her nose and inflated her lungs, and then once again performed the chest compressions. Ryan looked on in horror, and then finally unable to watch any more he stood up and spun around, his hands on his head, lost, in shock.

"This can't be happening…" he mumbled.

"Focus, Ryan," Hawke said coolly. "Check on Alex."

Still coughing, Ryan lurched over to Alex while Hawke persisted with Lea, but she was still silent and motionless below him in the Russian snow.

He stared at her face, streaked with soot, and her blackened, tangled hair. One more time, he told himself, and went through the process of insufflation and chest compressions once again.

And then she came to life.

Coughing hard, and moaning, her head moved from side to side as she tried to sit up. Hawke gently pushed her back to the ground. "Take it easy…"

"We've got company, Joe," Ryan said.

In the distance Hawke heard the sound of more shooting.

"Sorry, but it's time for us to go," Hawke said. "Sounds like Dempsey's making headway at the hangar."

Ryan shook his head. "Joe… I'm sorry but I can't carry Alex…"

"All right, chill out."

Hawke considered the situation for a few seconds and then worked out he could carry both Lea and Alex in a double fireman's lift – one on each shoulder. He'd once seen an SAS corporal do it in the African jungle and he wasn't going to be outdone by someone from Twenty-Two.

"I'm going to carry both, but I'm going to need you to help support one of them, right?"

Ryan seemed unsure. "*Okay…*"

"Then we're going to shoot some more twats, yeah?"

Ryan nodded, and helped take some of the weight by holding Alex in place. With considerable effort, they made their way through the snow to the hangar's rear door. They looked cautiously through the open roller door at the front onto the expansive snow-covered lawns to the south of the house. Dempsey was there on his own, desperately holding back an assault by more of Vetrov's men.

Hawke lowered Lea and Alex, both of whom were starting to come back to life, and jogged over to the former Green Beret. "What happened to Phillips and Zimmerman?"

Dempsey clenched his jaw and looked Hawke straight in the eyes. "They didn't make it. Phillips got taken out in an ambush outside Vetrov's office and Zimmerman…"

"What?"

Dempsey shut his eyes as if he were trying to rub out the very idea of what he was about to say – to destroy even the memory of it. "Zimmerman was blasted into the water by the shock of a grenade. The last I saw of him one of those damned bastard crocodiles was dragging him under the surface."

Lea was on her feet now, and joined them.

Hawke took her by her shoulders. "Are you sure you're all right now?"

"Me? Sure I am. Just took a little nap back there but I'm right up in their faces again now." She mimed shooting people with her fingers.

Hawke looked at her, unconvinced, but knew there was no option but to press on.

"Look!" Lea shouted. "Looks like Vetrov has stopped enjoying our company."

Hawke looked and saw the Russian making his way through the snow to one of the choppers. He was flanked on either side by a handful of his goons, armed to the teeth with submachine guns.

"Look at those bastards," Dempsey said. "Looks like they're ready for the Battle of Stalingrad."

"They've got every kind of weapon under the sun!" said Lea.

Hawke frowned. "They've got more than that – they've got all of Alex's research on her flash-drive, and Mazzarro's details as well. With that, they'll be able to translate the map and get to the source of eternal life. Damn it all!"

"But they haven't got the actual map, right?" said Dempsey.

"Not yet they haven't, but I'm not going to bet against Vetrov right now. He's obviously well-connected and he knows Lexi and the others are in Berlin because we know he's the one who killed Sorokin."

"And that's why we have to get that flash-drive back and stop him from getting to Mazzarro," Lea said.

Ryan spoke next: "And we need to contact Scarlet and tell her to get Lexi and the map the hell out of Berlin before Vetrov's men catch up with them."

"So what's your plan?" Dempsey asked Hawke.

"We need to get out of here or we're fish in a barrel. We'll go around the back of the hangar through the office door over there and attack from two fronts. When we get there you take out the Bell and we'll use the Kamov as our escape route, leaving Vetrov with no way out of this blizzard."

"The office door is locked," Dempsey said. "I tried to blast through with this but it was no good." He showed Hawke the only weapon he had left – a small pistol.

"No fucking problem at all," Hawke growled, and cocked the pump-action Remington with one hand. He was still thinking about Lea almost dying back at the library.

"Here we go again…" Lea said.

Hawke aimed the Remington at the door and fired three Hatton breaching rounds into the heavy, locked door in just four seconds – top hinge, handle lock, bottom hinge, and booted the door out of the way. An old technique he'd learned back in his Special Boat Service days. Any locked door on the floor in seconds.

Leaving Ryan and Alex behind, they ran into the blast of icy air and were outside again, where they split into two teams, Hawke and Lea on one side and Dempsey on the other, each approaching the choppers from opposite ends of the hangar.

The fire-fight was short. Not expecting assaults from two different directions, Vetrov and his men retreated to the dacha to regroup and re-arm. Seizing the moment, Dempsey fired a burst of submachine gun fire into the Bell's fuel tanks and sent it up in a massive fireball. The smoke poured out of the wreckage and gave them a few seconds of cover.

"Now!" Hawke screamed. "Everyone into the other chopper!"

They climbed in the helicopter and fired her up. Hawke looked over the instrument panel display and made a quick check while Lea and Ryan helped Alex into the back seat. Dempsey started firing at the main entrance to the house while Hawke hovered the Kamov a few feet above the icy tarmac.

"Now, Dempsey! We have to go!"

"Those bastards took out two of my men!" screamed the American as he sprayed a vicious volley of submachine gun fire at Vetrov's grand entrance, taking out several of his men. He turned to climb into the helicopter when Vetrov carefully aimed a pistol at him and shot him through the throat.

Hawke watched in horror as Dempsey's eyes widened and then blinked maniacally as he took in what had happened to him. He raised his hands to clasp at the blood pouring from his throat, but it spilled out onto the snow, unstoppable. Hawke leaned over to grab his hand, but a second shot from Vetrov ripped through the former Green Beret's chest and blew his heart out. He collapsed into the snow like a matchstick man.

Now the smoke began to clear, and Vetrov screamed orders at his men to move forward and retake the remaining helicopter. With no time to think, Hawke lifted the collective, raising the Russian military chopper into the air amidst a barrage of machine gun fire from Vetrov and his men.

They gained altitude fast and a second later they were out of sight, flying up into the swirling snowstorm.

CHAPTER THIRTEEN

Venice

Eden's Gulfstream touched down at Venice Marco Polo Airport and trundled to a private gate on the southern apron. They took a taxi to the hotel that Eden had arranged for them in advance, racing through Triestina before crossing the Ponta della Libertà – the Freedom Bridge that separated Venice from the Italian mainland.

They rode most of the way in silence, the terrible image of Dempsey's brutal murder still fresh in their memories, not to mention what had happened to his two men. Alex took it particularly hard – all of this was, after all, part of a mission to rescue her.

They emerged from the car into a bright, cool Venice day and moments later they were climbing into a gondola and giving the driver instructions to take them to the Gritti Palace, where Eden had booked some rooms to serve as a temporary headquarters during the mission to save Mazzarro. Hawke and Ryan carried Alex, and laid her down on the rear seat while Lea told the gondola driver where they needed to go.

Less than half an hour later the gondolier was gently cruising toward the mooring area outside the luxury hotel and for the briefest of moments Hawke almost relaxed, turning his face to the warm Italian sun and grateful to be out of the Russian winter at last.

"One of these days," he said, staring at the impressive façade of the eighteenth century building ahead of them, "someone's going to tell me where Eden gets all his cash, because this isn't the kind of place Her Majesty's Government hires out for its lackeys."

Lea smiled, but said nothing. Moments later and with the help of the hotel staff, they were inside the hotel and swiping the card in the door of their room.

Inside, Sir Richard Eden rose from his chair by the window and offered a solemn nod as a greeting. He didn't look happy.

"You're late," he said, but offered a belated smile. He kissed Lea on the cheek and nodded at Hawke and Ryan before turning to Alex. "And you must be the infamous Agent Nightingale?"

"Please, call me Alex."

"Welcome, Alex," Eden said. "And I took the liberty of arranging this wheelchair for you," he pulled it from the bathroom and unfolded it. "It was all the hotel could rustle up in so short a time."

"That'll work just fine," she said. "Thank you. Thanks for everything."

"Not at all."

Hawke and Ryan lowered her gently into the chair. As she made herself comfortable the balcony door opened and Lexi Zhang and Bradley Karlsson stepped into the room. Behind them Hawke saw the unmistakable figure of Scarlet Sloane smoking a cigarette. She was just about as sociable as he expected her to be.

He ignored the others and approached Lexi.

"Joe, I'm sorry about what happened, but…"

Hawke stared at her wordlessly for a long time before speaking. "You're not lying to me, are you, Lexi?"

She shook her head.

"I mean, Sorokin really was holding your parents hostage?"

She nodded.

"And was going to kill them?"

Another nod.

"I need to hear you say it, Lexi."

"It's the truth, Joe – I swear. I was acting under coercion. I had no choice."

Hawke frowned. "You could have told me – us – and we would have worked a way around it. Sent a team over to get your parents."

"It seems easy to say that now, but Sorokin was very clear about my not involving anyone else. I thought I could take him out before handing over the map, but I should have spoken to you about it. I'm sorry, Joe."

Hawke was unsure how to react, but unlike Scarlet Sloane he was inclined to believe her story, even if he harboured a shadow of a doubt at the same time. Either way, there was no time for recriminations now. The bottom line was she had contacted Eden and handed the map over to Scarlet and Karlsson in Berlin. That alone showed him her heart was in the right place and that she was telling him the truth, if not the whole truth.

"All right," he said at last. "I'll accept your word, but you'd better not be bullshitting me, Lexi."

"I'm not, I swear…"

"So where are we?" Lea asked, changing the subject. "It really feels like we've been put through the wringer this time."

Eden frowned. "The situation is critical. As you can see, Scarlet and Brad here got Agent Dragonfly out of Berlin after a little trouble in the zoo."

"In a *zoo*?" Alex asked.

Eden opened his mouth to reply, but Lea cut him off.

"Forget about it," she said. "That's just the sort of thing that happens around here."

"Unfortunately we lost the map, and now Vetrov has it." He fixed his eyes on Alex. "Miss Reeve, I know you tried to explain things back in Moscow when you were under fire, but now you're safe you need to tell me the whole story about why Vetrov ordered Kodiak to take you, and don't even try saying it's because your father is the Secretary of Defense."

"No, it's not that... and there's a lot I couldn't tell you back in Moscow..." Her words drifted away into the heavy anticipation of the room. She looked at the faces of the others, now staring at her expectantly.

These were the people she'd heard so much talk about, and now she was sharing a Venetian hotel room with them – Sir Richard Eden MP, Lea Donovan, Ryan Bale and the notorious Chinese assassin – all of whom she'd got to know thanks to Hawke's inimitable descriptions. They were all here, including Brad Karlsson, and Cairo Sloane, whom she'd heard more about than all the others combined, and of course, there was Joe Hawke himself. He seemed taller than she'd imagined him, and somehow more thoughtful and deliberate in his movements that she thought he would be.

"We need to know, Alex!" Lea said.

"Of course... I'm sorry," Alex replied, shocked out of her daydream by Lea's voice. "Like I tried to tell Lea and Ryan back in Moscow, the reason Maxim Vetrov ordered my kidnapping is because of my research."

"Your research?" Eden said.

She nodded sadly. "About this damned map, and the elixir of life. I'm so *sorry*."

Alex rubbed her eyes. She looked stressed – she felt stressed. It had felt like forever since Kodiak had taken her from the apartment and drugged her. The nightmare of the Moscow Dacha and the crocodile enclosure was behind her now, but it had really left its mark on her.

"It all started when Joe texted me about Poseidon and asked me to run checks on you guys..."

Lea's eyes widened. "He *what*?"

"Oh, come on, Lea," Eden said calmly. "You can't expect a man with Hawke's background to work with someone without running at least a cursory check on their backgrounds."

Lea pursed her lips. "I *suppose...*"

"We did the same to him, after all."

Hawke smiled but made no reply.

"Anyway," Alex continued, "after that he had me researching all kinds of stuff about the ancient Greek gods – Poseidon, the trident – you name it. The thing is I started to get into it and I sort of went my own way."

Eden was inscrutable. "Go on."

"As you know, I have extensive contacts in American intelligence..."

Ryan chuckled bitterly. "Isn't that what they call an oxymoron?"

"No," Lea said. "But you're what they call an assy moron. Please continue, Alex."

Alex glanced at them all, unsure what passed for banter, and what was insult. "I'm good at what I do – I had to be after the shooting in Bogotá," she looked down at her legs. "I have time on my hands, so I devoted all that time to researching this damned map."

"And what did all this devotion reveal to you?" asked Eden.

"First, I wouldn't have been able to do any of my work without all the research Hawke already did."

"You mean me, but carry on." Ryan said.

"Sorry… I mean all of you – yes."

"Well, it's more *me* than all of us, but do continue."

Lea rolled her eyes. "Ignore it."

"Look… there's still so much I don't know, but the research led me from ancient Greece back to ancient Egypt."

"Egypt?" Eden said.

Alex nodded. "Sure. I was expecting that anyway, but it was a great moment when it was confirmed. You see, it all started when Sheng Fang had that Lotus creature kill Felix Hoffman on the Paris Métro. That was when I started digging around for real. We knew he had worked under the direction of Anton Reichardt, so I started asking more questions about Reichardt himself."

"I like where this is going," Ryan said.

"Anton Reichardt was an eminent scholar in his own right, but not without controversy. Back when he was starting out on all this immortality stuff, there were accusations of plagiarism made against him by an amateur Italian Egyptologist by the name of Professor Giovanni Mazzarro."

Eden looked at her, carefully following her every word. "Amateur?"

Alex nodded keenly. She was enjoying the conversation after so long spent on her own. "Amateur, sure. In fact Mazzarro was a curator at the Ca d'Oro."

"The where?" Lea asked.

"The House of Gold," Ryan said from the background. "It's a six-hundred year-old palace on the Grand Canal. Its real name is Palazzo Santa Sofia."

Alex gave him an admiring glance. "I'm impressed. Hawke said you knew a lot."

Ryan turned and beamed with pride. "He said I knew a lot?"

"Well… not in so many words, but that was the drift."

"I think I might have said something along the lines of big-headed twat," Hawke said loudly.

"Gotcha."

Eden frowned and returned to the point. "What kind of accusations were made against Reichardt, exactly?"

"That Reichardt had not only copied his ideas in an intellectual capacity, but had tried to steal some of Mazzarro's actual, physical research."

"Now that's what I call an accusation!" Ryan said. "I told you nerds could get nasty."

Lea rolled her eyes again. "What research did he steal?"

"*Tried* to steal, according to Mazzarro – but he didn't get his hands on it. That stayed under lock and key for the rest of Mazzarro's, and Reichardt's life. But here's the interesting thing – Mazzarro had a son who inherited not only his father's obsession with ancient hieroglyphics, but also his research and notes."

As she spoke, she couldn't help but smile a little when she saw the expressions on the others' faces.

"Shut your mouth, Ryan," Scarlet said, "You look like you're catching flies for fuck's sake."

"Sorry, but…tell us more!"

Alex grew more serious again. "What Mazzarro had put together was a vast collection of very ancient hieroglyphics – older than ancient Egypt, older even than Sumeria – and started working on a way to decode them – just to try and make sense of them, I guess. I'd never seen anything like them before, and neither had anyone else in the world if my Google searches were anything to go by."

Ryan leaned in closer. "This is better than sex!"

"It is the way *you* try and do it," Lea said, giving him a playful nudge with her elbow.

Alex laughed, but Eden was unmoved by the gag. "You made records of all these, naturally?"

"Of course, and more than that, I began to translate them. I started to create a sort of deciphering matrix, but I just didn't have enough to go on without speaking with

Dario Mazzarro, and it was around then I contacted him and we started working together."

"And how did that go?" Eden asked.

"Awkward at first, but when he got to trust me it was good. I really needed his work, and his father's work, to make any progress, so it was essential he agreed to help me, and in return I was able to offer my computer skills and contacts. Anyway, it was shortly after that when that Russian asshole kicked my door in and dragged me to Moscow, so that was where my research ended – and without Mazzarro I'm not sure how much progress I can make."

"You've done well to get this far," Eden said.

"Maybe," Alex replied. "All I know is what I've already told you – that the glyphs on the map are older than any other hieroglyphics on the planet, and that Mazzarro is the only man who can really crack them."

"I wouldn't be so sure about that," Hawke said, glancing at Ryan.

Alex looked at Ryan and then back to Eden. "I don't even know what Mazzarro was using as a reference for his own deciphering matrix, so I guess that's why Vetrov decided now was the time to steal my research – he wanted me to give him Mazzarro's name – because as I say, he's the only person who can translate the map."

"And now Vetrov knows he's in Venice," Lea said.

Alex nodded grimly while Scarlet lit another cigarette from the burning stub of her last one, undeterred by Hawke's disapproving look.

Alex continued. "So as I say, Mazzarro has the only real knowledge in the world of those particular glyphs and this is why Vetrov needs him. He didn't exactly have a great employee-rights scheme so I guess most academics capable of helping him out – supposing there are any – wouldn't go within a hundred miles of him. He threw his last researcher into a crocodile enclosure, after all. That's why I told everyone to come to Venice. It wasn't just for the ice cream, you know."

A subdued ripple of grim laughter went around the room, then Eden cleared his throat. "Where is this Mazzarro?"

"He works at the Doge's Palace," Alex said quietly.

Eden nodded. "Okay, good… Sounds like Vetrov must have been following you around the internet as you were doing your research. I guess when he saw the progress you'd made, he decided he wanted both you and your research, and more particularly that list of names, and that was when he must have decided to send that bastard to New York to get you."

Alex looked at the others in the heavy silence. The smell of Scarlet's cigarette smoke drifted into the room on a sea breeze. Lea smiled awkwardly, but Ryan just stared out the window. Karlsson shrugged his broad shoulders and felt around in his pockets for a cigarette even though he had quit ten years ago – it was an old habit of his to combat the silence.

Eden flicked the locks on an expensive Samsonite suitcase and revealed a small array of weapons.

"So this is the plan. I will go with Hawke, Lea and Bradley to the Doge's Palace and track down this Mazzarro character, while Ryan and Alex will stay here at HQ and start working on Lexi's picture of the map. Scarlet and Lexi, you're to remain here in case Vetrov has tracked us. The last thing I want is an assault on this hotel and Ryan and Alex vulnerable to attack." He turned to face them all. "Clear?"

"Clear as Irish crystal, Rich," Lea said, but no one else spoke.

Eden tossed her a brand new Glock 19 and a box of ammunition. "Hope for the best, plan for the worst."

"As always," she said, sliding the versatile black pistol into her holster.

Eden continued to hand out the weapons as he spoke. "There's no doubt Maxim Vetrov is the most organized and ruthless enemy we've faced and we all know he's got the best of us more than once."

"You can say that again," Ryan said.

Eden slid a pistol into a shoulder holster beneath his smart, linen jacket. "Well, this is our chance to turn the tables on him and get the map back into safe hands. We know he has the information about Mazzarro but we also know we're ahead of him thanks to your destruction of his complex. But the fact is he's probably in Venice as we speak and we can't let him get to Dario Mazzarro before us, because then he'll have both the map and the man who can translate it."

"Which is not good," Lexi said.

"All right, everyone," Eden said, looking each one of them in the eye. "It's time to bring this to an end. Let's go."

CHAPTER FOURTEEN

Eden, Hawke, Lea and Karlsson moved silently through the bustling crowd in San Marco's Square, each armed with concealed Glocks and with the clear goal of warning Dr Dario Mazzarro about the imminent danger he faced, and how his life's research and deciphering work could now at last be put to the test on the map – once it was recovered.

As they walked, Venice seemed to swallow them up. The Doge's Palace rose up from the square and Hawke could see why it was one of the city's most famous landmarks. Built over seven hundred years ago to serve as the residence of the Doge, or chief magistrate of Venice, the enormous Gothic building shone in the sun and cast its vast shadow across the busy lagoon.

Hawke and the others were anxious as they stepped out of the safety of the shaded colonnade and weaved into the relaxed crowd of tourists. Checking for threats, they walked across the famous courtyard on their way to the glistening red Verona marble of the Foscari Arch and the Giants' Staircase.

"Is this it?" Lea asked.

Eden nodded but made no reply.

"Looks like a giant wedding cake."

Passing the ancient Sansovino statues of Mars and Neptune, they shuffled up the steps on their way to Dr Mazzarro's office.

Eden knocked on the door and a moment later it swung open to reveal a middle-aged man in a raggedy tweed jacket and baggy moleskin trousers. His hair was black and silver and a mess of curls not unlike a bird's nest. A pair of tortoiseshell glasses balanced on the bridge of his prominent nose.

"Si?"

"Dottore Dario Mazzarro?"

"Si. Chi siete tutti?"

Eden spoke in rapid Italian for a few seconds and Hawke watched the Doctor's eyebrows gradually rise higher as the explanation went on.

Mazzarro looked at the foreigners outside his door suspiciously for a few moments and then went to close the door on them, but then the sound of gunfire and desperate, terrified screams emanating from below worked the magic that Eden's Italian had failed to do.

Eden tightened his jaw and stared down the long corridor. "The bastards must have worked out where we are!"

Without wasting a second Mazzarro stepped into the corridor and slammed the door behind him, fumbling the key in his lock.

Hawke grabbed his arm and stopped him. "These people don't need keys to open doors, Doctor Mazzarro, and we need to get you out of here right now."

"But how do I know you're who you say you are – you could be criminals!"

More gunshots and screams from downstairs.

Hawke looked him in the eye. "Your choice."

They ran downstairs away from the office, desperate to get away before any innocent people got hurt, but before they'd got a hundred yards the sound of more automatic gunfire reverberated in the ancient halls of the palace. It was followed by yet more terrified screams of innocent tourists and the sound of stampeding as they desperately rushed the fire exits to escape the terror.

"Damn it!" Eden cried as the gunshots grew closer.

"This way!" Hawke said.

They sprinted along a corridor before entering an enormous, highly decorative room with a beautiful coffered ceiling. Below, the walls were covered in grand, eighteenth century oil paintings.

"This is the Scarlet Chamber," Mazzarro said. "We need to go through that far door. It's the quickest way out of here – and then we must go straight to the police… But wait! We need to go back to my office – all my research notebooks are there and we cannot let these people get their hands on them."

"Where are they in your office, exactly?" Hawke asked.

"Hidden…"

After a few seconds of wrangling, the Italian eventually gave up the location of the notes as they moved toward the door.

Outside the chamber, it sounded like someone was spraying bullets up the walls just for the hell of it. A second later a man carrying a Russian submachine gun burst through the door beneath the vast *Paradise* painting which stretched across the entire far wall.

They all looked to Eden for his lead. This was the first time Hawke had seen Eden under fire in the field and he wondered how he would react. He knew he had spent fifteen years in the army as an officer in the Parachute Regiment, and the Paras weren't exactly known for running away from fights. They were universally regarded as the toughest regiment in the British Army – highly trained airborne soldiers whose only real rival were the Royal Marines Commandos themselves. They also had the proud distinction of supplying more soldiers into the SAS than any other regiment. But all that was a long time ago and Eden had lived the life of a pampered Member of Parliament for a long time now.

Maybe he's lost it, Hawke thought, reaching for his gun.

Then Eden pulled out the Glock from the shoulder holster beneath his Savile Row suit and dropped the man in less than two seconds with the classic double-tap.

Or maybe not...

Eden holstered the weapon before the man's body had even hit the floor and turned to Hawke and the others. "He was going to ruin this wonderful *Tintoretto* with that blood dreadful Vityaz," he said coolly. "I'm just not having it."

Mazzarro clasped his face with his hands in horror and began to mumble in Italian.

Karlsson looked from Eden to Lea and whispered: "Is this guy for real?"

"You'd better believe it, laddo."

Karlsson shook his head. "You kill the guy because he's an *asshole*, not to save the artwork…"

Eden looked him in the eye. "That artwork is over two hundred years older than your country."

"Hey…" Karlsson replied, totally untouched by the remark, "all I can say is you're one hell of a shot."

"It's time to leave, people," Hawke said.

As he spoke, several more armed men burst into the chamber, fanned out and drew closer to them. They were led by a man who was at least seven feet tall. The pistol in his hand looked like a little toy.

"Who the hell is that?" Hawke asked as they began to retreat.

Eden watched the men as they got closer. "His name is Kosma Zhuravlev, a former KGB agent. He's worked for Vetrov in one capacity or another for years. He's known to break necks with his bare hands. We don't want to talk to him today – let's go."

Outside, St. Mark's Square was buzzing with tourists as they made their way hurriedly across it.

"This place is heaving!" Karlsson said.

Eden frowned as they hurried Mazzarro along through the tourists. "My concern is that innocents are going to get killed if those maniacs decide to open fire on us."

"But what do they want with me?" Mazzarro mumbled in English. "I still don't understand…"

"You don't want to know," Lea said. "But it ain't a game of poker and a quiet glass of Amaretto."

As she spoke, Hawke turned to see where Kosma and the others were.

"They're keeping their distance, but still behind us," he said.

"We'll lose them up here," Lea said.

"Just keep moving, everyone," Eden said. "We need to lose them before returning to the hotel."

Then, the unexpected happened, taking even Hawke by surprise. In a fraction of a second a man stepped out ahead of them from behind a colonnade – he was armed with a knife and looked like he knew some moves.

It was Kodiak.

He moved in a flash, grabbing hold of a young American woman who was taking a picture of the Doge's Palace. He put the blade to her throat. A young child screamed, sending dozens of pigeons into the sunny air, and nearby tourists panicked and stumbled away from the man with the knife. A middle-aged man with an ice cream pulled out a camera phone and started to record. Lea watched Hawke move his hand slowly to his gun.

"Just let her go, Kodiak!" Eden said, quietly and in control.

Hawke cursed himself for not thinking about anyone being ahead of them, least of all this maniac.

"Give me Mazzarro or she dies," the Russian said. A wicked smile danced on his lips. "You know I'll do it."

Eden stepped forward, his hand now moving inside his jacket.

"Make another move and…" He drew his finger across his throat to simulate the method of execution.

Lea watched Eden freeze in his tracks and drop the gun. Hawke followed his lead.

"Now… give me Mazzarro."

Hawke looked at Mazzarro – he was sweating profusely and his hands were shaking. "I…I…" was all the Italian could manage as he stared at the horror right before his eyes.

"You have to go, Dario" Eden said. "I'm sorry, but we can't let an innocent young woman die like this."

Mazzarro saw the woman squirming in the assassin's arms, terrified, and immediately knew his predicament. He agreed to walk over to Kodiak.

Then in a flash the Russian assassin pushed the sobbing woman away and greedily grabbed the Italian, now holding the shining blade at the Egyptologist's throat instead.

"Now get back, or I slit his throat."

Eden and the others took a few steps back as Kodiak moved slowly away and climbed on board a motorboat moored beside the square. A second later he was steering the boat out into the Grand Canal.

Hawke spun around to confront Kosma and the other men but there was no sign of them.

"They've just disappeared into thin air!" Lea said.

"We need to split up," Eden said, thinking fast. "Lea and Brad – go after Mazzarro and do everything in your power to get that man back to us. It's imperative Vetrov doesn't get his hands on him because he'll torture him for what he wants and then kill him. Hawke and I will go to Mazzarro's office and retrieve the notes he told us about – presuming Maxim Bloody Vetrov hasn't got *there* first as well. Then we'll try and take out Kosma if we can find him."

Hawke wasn't too happy about watching Lea run after Kodiak and Mazzarro with Bradley Karlsson, but he knew she and Eden had a long relationship and lots of experience, so he followed her lead, stopping only to kiss her.

"Just make sure you get that bloody map back!" he said.

"That's the plan, Joe, and just *you* make sure you don't get your stupid *eejit* head blown off when you're going after that Russian oaf, right?"

Hawke agreed that was a good idea and watched as she and Karlsson sprinted toward the boats moored on the side of the square. He hoped it wasn't the last time he would see her, and turned to join Eden in their pursuit of Kosma and the notes.

*

The sun streamed through the blinds and cast striped shadows on the cornflower blue wall of the hotel room. Scarlet squinted in the glare as she disconnected her phone and turned to Alex and Ryan.

"Not great news, chaps."

"Oh *God*," Ryan said. "What now?"

"That was Richard. They've lost Mazzarro."

"Well, where did they have him last?" Ryan said.

"Don't be so bloody juvenile, Ryan," Scarlet snapped. "Those Russian bastards just took him. This isn't a game."

"Oh, it's not a game, eh?" he said, the anger in his voice rising. "Funny that, because I thought my girlfriend getting blown apart right before my eyes was exactly that, a fucking game."

"Guys!" Alex pushed her wheelchair between them, sensing the rising tensions in the room. "This situation is getting out of control, right? We all feel it. We lost the map in Berlin and now we've lost Mazzarro, but we're not going to let them win! You can't let them make us turn on each other and fall apart like this. We have to stick together."

Ryan and Scarlet stared at each other for a few seconds, and then each of them backed down.

"I need a drink," Lexi said, opening the mini-bar.

"Sorry, Alex," Ryan said. "It's just that we're really getting our arses kicked right now and we're not used to it."

"We've been here before," Scarlet said, sighing and clearly calmer now. "Back when we were trying to stop our man Zaugg from breaking the world in two pieces with that damned trident – remember?"

Ryan nodded. "I do remember, yes – I'm not a bloody goldfish."

"Easy there, tiger," Scarlet said. "Remember what Alex just said about you having to stay calm."

"Yeah, sorry… hang on – about *me* having to stay calm?"

Alex looked awkward again. "You two love each other really, right?"

Lexi smirked. "They do, I think."

"Nothing can love Scarlet Sloane," Ryan said sulkily.

"Right then," Alex said, ignoring him and trying to diffuse the tension. "So we know we're getting our asses kicked – fine. Let's get our shit together and start thinking. What have we got?"

"Without Mazzarro or his notes – not much," Ryan said, sighing.

Scarlet scowled. "Rich and Joe are going to Mazzarro's apartment to get his notes – but there's a chance Vetrov might have got there first – they say Kosma and his thugs slipped away while they were dealing with Kodiak."

"We're really going to need those notes," Alex said, unconsciously biting her lip.

"Well, we haven't got the sodding notes, have we?" Scarlet said, turning to Ryan. "What about all that bollocks about nectar you said you were working on earlier today, Ryan? Can't you start there or something?"

Alex brightened up. "What nectar thing?"

Ryan almost beamed, but pulled himself back. "I was looking at the picture Lexi took of the map and it occurred to me that one of the glyphs looks similar to the Egyptian one for nectar."

Alex smiled. "And we're talking about the food of the gods and not the flowers, right?"

"Right, the food of the gods – the substance that is mentioned over and over again in so many ancient texts relating to their incredible longevity – isn't restricted to the ancient Greeks, you realize."

Scarlet frowned. "As far as this shit is concerned, *boy*, I know only what you tell me, and that just about drives me insane."

"I know," Ryan said. "Great isn't it?"

"But he's right," Alex said, tying her hair back and rolling up her sleeves. "It's true that the main sources referring to eternal life being conferred by some kind of food are mostly within the Greek myths – and this is mainly described as ambrosia, but other cultures had similar myths and legends."

"Legends about custard..." Ryan said, his voice trailing away to a whisper as he thought about that day in Demetriou's Athens apartment. That was the day he first noticed Sophie. It all seemed like so long ago – an age away, but it was just a few short weeks.

Alex looked at him, confused. "Huh?"

"Forget it," he said, realizing that no one else understood the old joke.

"I don't know anything about custard," continued Alex, "but I know that the ancient Greeks believed ambrosia was derived from the horn of Amalthea, a goat who helped raise Zeus."

Scarlet smirked. "Zeus was raised by a goat?"

"It's a little more complex than that…" Alex said.

"Ah! What's this then?" Ryan said, studying the line of hieroglyphics along the bottom of the map.

Scarlet took a step forward. "What have you found?"

"Here on the map could be a reference to Kemet."

Scarlet sighed. "First custard and now the fucking Muppets!"

"*Kemet*, I said, not Kermit."

"And that means what?" she said.

"Kemet is the ancient native word for Egypt – what the ancient Egyptians called their homeland. This reference is yet more evidence pointing to Egypt, plus there's something else as well. If your excellent research work is right, Alex," Ryan said, smiling at the American, "this glyph right here *could* be referring to the drinking of liquid gold, and if so then this here *might* be describing mystical white drops that can make a man god-like. Both those references are about the elixir of life."

Scarlet shook her head. "A lot of coulds and mights in your vocabulary all of a sudden, boy."

"Like we just explained, these glyphs are not easy to translate and we could really use those notebooks. All we have to go on at the moment is the work Alex has already done with Mazzarro himself."

"Which is not that great, honestly. We'd only just started working together and I'm not sure he had really started trusting me yet."

"But," Ryan added optimistically, "if we're even half right, it means not only does the map specifically mention the elixir of life, but that we're sort of learning how to translate it."

"Slow progress though…" Alex said.

"So what we really need is those sodding notes," Scarlet said, lighting a cigarette and stepping out into the warm Italian day. "Let's hope Joe gets hold of them."

*

Hawke and Eden made their way across the square and returned to Mazzarro's office in the Doge's Palace. They breathed a sigh of relief when they saw the Egyptologist's notes were exactly where he had told them they were – safely hidden behind a sliding partition in the bookcase behind his desk. There were five of them in all – just simple yellow notebooks covered in inky scrawls and strange hand-drawn hieroglyphs. Clearly Vetrov was satisfied with Mazzarro – the first prize – and had ordered his men to retreat.

"These are going to lead us to the greatest secret on earth?" Hawke said as he looked at the notebooks.

"Whatever they might look like," Eden replied coolly, "Dario Mazzarro is the only man in the world who really understands the ciphers which will decode the glyphs on the map. If Lea and Karlsson can't get him back, these are all we have."

They shared a glance which was part excitement and part anxiety before pocketing the notebooks and heading back to the hotel. It was time Ryan and Alex got to work.

CHAPTER FIFTEEN

Lea reached the mooring area out of breath, and watched with anger as Kodiak's boat moved away up the Grand Canal at speed before disappearing into the water traffic of the busy Venetian day.

"What now?" Karlsson said.

"Over there, look!" She pointed at an older man mooring a sleek motorboat to the side of the square.

"Not just a pretty face, babe," he said.

"And I'm taken, so cut it out, *babe*."

"Roger that, but we're in love for the next thirty seconds, all right with you?"

"Sure is," Lea said, understanding at once what Karlsson was thinking.

They walked toward the man, arm in arm, and pretended to share an intimate conversation.

Lea approached him and started to ask for directions in terrible Italian, while Karlsson pretended to take in the view and walked around behind the man. He had his hands in his pockets and was whistling in an attempt to look as casual as possible.

As Lea distracted the man, Karlsson unhooked the mooring rope and stepped quietly into the boat, a thirty-three foot-long Aquariva Super with a polished mahogany deck which shone in the bright Venetian sun. He turned the key and the two powerful 370 horsepower Yanmar engines roared to life, causing the man to turn immediately and move toward the boat.

"Cosa fai?!"

Lea acted fast, pushing him into the water, where he landed with a mighty splash and screamed something about a *zoccola* while pointing at the boat-thieves. Lea wasted no time in leaping into the luxury sports boat. "Hit it, Brad!"

Karlsson pushed the throttle forward and at the stern, the twin bladed bronze propellers accelerated into a deep roar and drove them out into the Grand Canal to the south of San Marco.

Lea watched the commotion on the south bank of the island as the man clambered out of water and ran for help.

"Something tells me he's going to want his boat back, Brad."

"You think?"

"I *know* – look!"

Brad turned to see the *carabinieri* – the Italian police – speed out into the canal in a police motorboat, lights flashing. An enormous arc of sea-spray flew out behind it. "Oh joy," he said. "I was kind hoping that might happen."

"Just get after the map and forget about the cops!"

Karlsson took the advice and powered the Aquariva after Kodiak in the speedboat ahead of them. Behind, the police were slowly closing the distance, but he couldn't worry about that right now. Up ahead, he saw the Russian was now steering the boat off to the right in an attempt to lose them.

"Is he crazy?" Karlsson shouted.

"What?"

"He's getting off the Grand Canal and heading into the city!"

"Then yes," Lea replied. "He is crazy! Those canals are too narrow for a decent boat chase… what the hell's the matter with these people?"

Lea watched Kodiak's boat speed out of sight into a smaller canal ahead on the right, and a few seconds later they were making the same sharp turn. They threw out another colossal arc of canal spray into the air, only this time it came crashing down on the deck of a boat full of Japanese tourists and soaked them to the skin.

"Sorry!" she shouted, cheerily waving at them. "Why are they screaming?" she asked, frowning. "Some people! I was only trying to say sorry."

Karlsson glanced back and shook his head. "Next time maybe put the semi-automatic pistol down before you wave your apologies, yeah?"

Lea looked at the gun. "Ah… gotcha."

Now they were entering the Rio de San Moise, a narrow canal less than thirty feet wide, lined either side with towering eighteenth century hotels. The tremendous noise of the speedboats' engines reverberated in the enclosed space and caused several people to lean out of their windows to see what was happening.

"Can't you speed this thing up?" Lea said.

"Not in these little canals, I can't," Karlsson said. "Why do you think they brought us into this damn labyrinth?"

Behind them, they heard the sound of gunshots, and Lea turned to see the police firing warning shots into the air.

"They're getting closer!" Lea said.

Brad turned and saw the carabinieri closing in. He sighed and returned his attention to Kodiak and the boat in front. "And I bet they know this place like the back of their hands…"

Lea casually pulled her gun out. "Want me to sink 'em?"

"The police? Are you crazy?"

A second round of gunshots rang out, only this time they weren't going into the air. Karlsson glanced behind and saw a police marksman on the front deck of the police boat. He was aiming a rifle right at the Aquariva. Less than fifty yards were between them and the carabinieri now, and they were still hemmed in either side by the towering walls of some of the city's grandest hotels. Ahead of them, Kodiak was racing his boat beneath a low stone bridge, the Ponte San Moise. He fired a few shots at them over his shoulder while trying to navigate the speeding boat through the canals. Mazzarro was cowering in the back, covering his head with his arms and trying to dodge the flying lead.

The police shouted a string of commands in Italian through a megaphone, and then a second later fired at the Aquariva. The bullet hit the ridge of the maple inlay stretching around the stern of the boat and sent a shower of splinters flying into the air.

Karlsson took one look at the damage and saw the police marksman aiming for a second shot. "Yeah… on reflection, Lea, I want you to sink them!"

They raced toward the Ponte San Moise, ducking instinctively to avoid hitting their heads on the low stonework of the bridge. As they passed under the bridge the police's second shot struck the carved face on the bridge's beam and blasted it into shards of masonry falling into their wake in the canal behind them.

"All right, I've had enough of this!" Lea said, and crawled to the back of the boat. She raised the gun and rested her arms on the back seats as she lined the police boat up in her sights. A woman hanging some washing out screamed obscenities at them as they flashed past her and sprayed her with canal water.

Lea ducked to avoid a third bullet which hit the chrome edge of the windshield and pinged off to the left where it lodged into the soft plaster wall of an adjacent hotel.

"Holy shit!" Karlsson said. "That nearly put a hole right through me!"

Lea raised her gun a second time, and aimed for the police boat. "Sorry guys!"

She fired three shots at the bow and all of them hit home, blasting three holes in the fiber glass hull on the portside bow.

The carabinieri responded with more shots from the rifle, but their boat was losing speed. Lea planted another six shots in the port bow. The resulting hole was now so large that they began taking on water and moments later the police boat slowed and its nose sank slowly into the brown canal. What was once a threat was now an amusing scene of flashing blue lights and angry carabinieri trying to avoid a soaking in the water.

Lea spun the gun around her finger like a cowboy from a Western and pretended to blow smoke from the muzzle.

The marksman took one final shot but Karlsson steered the Aquariva around a shallow bend to the left, pausing only to give the police a big fat bird, and then return his attention to Kodiak and the rescue of Dr Dario Mazzarro.

"Wow, that was childish," Lea said. "They were only doing their job."

"*That* was childish, but you pretending to be the Bandit Queen was cool?"

"The who?"

"You don't know who the Bandit Queen was?" Karlsson shook his head in despair.

Lea smiled. "I know Calamity Jane. Was the Bandit Queen anything like Calamity Jane?"

Karlsson sighed and fixed his attention back on Kodiak who was now speeding as fast as he could through the narrow canals in the older quarters of the city.

"Forget about it, honey. We have work to do."

CHAPTER SIXTEEN

When Sir Richard Eden handed him Dario Mazzaro's notebooks, Ryan Bale smiled fully for the first time since Tokyo Bay. What had looked like nothing but illegible scrawl to Hawke looked like the answer to life, the universe and everything to Ryan and he wasted no time in getting stuck into them.

Since they had arrived in Venice and got their hands on Lexi's picture of the map, they had struggled to translate the glyphs even with the work Alex had already done back in New York, but with the notes they were certain they could make much faster and more accurate progress. Now he and Alex shared a glance which was neither optimistic nor fearful, but said: this is our chance to beat that bastard to the greatest secret on earth.

And the last chance.

Alex once again opened up the digital image of the map that Lexi had taken back in Berlin while Ryan pored over the notes, absent-mindedly tapping his fingers on the wooden desk.

Eden passed a nervous hand over his face as he watched Ryan. "You think you can work out Mazzarro's work, Mr Bale?"

"I bloody hope so," Ryan mumbled, without taking his eyes off the pages. "We've only translated a couple of glyphs without them, so let's have some peace and quiet and maybe I might get somewhere."

Eden raised his eyebrows but said nothing. Everyone was more than a little keen for Ryan to work his magic, and with Alex working alongside him the expectations were higher than ever.

As they worked, Hawke paced the room and waited nervously for word from Lea. Eden had sent her in pursuit of the notorious Russian assassin Kodiak, and now she had been gone a long time – perhaps a little longer than he would have expected – and he was worried. Lea could look after herself in most cases, but he was beginning to realize this Kodiak character was in a different league.

In the other room, Lexi was sleeping on the bed, while Scarlet dealt with the tension in her usual way – stepping out to the balcony and lighting a cigarette. There was nothing any of them could do but wait – wait for Ryan and Alex to crack the code in Mazzarro's notes and use it to translate the glyphs on the map, and wait for Lea and Karlsson to get in touch and tell them they had secured Mazzarro and were all safe.

Hawke grabbed a beer from the fridge and cracked it open. After downing half of it in a few seconds, he followed Scarlet to the balcony and stood with her while she smoked, looking out over the Grand Canal of Venice, now glittering in the bright Italian sunshine.

"She'll be all right, Joe," Scarlet said.

"Eh?"

"Lea – she'll be fine. She's pretty tough, you know – almost as hard as me. Plus Brad's with her. He's pretty hard as well, and not just when we're together in…"

"Please don't finish that sentence, Cairo," Hawke said, smiling. "But I appreciate the sentiment."

Scarlet smiled and blew smoke out into the air. Below them, gondolas and tour boats slipped back and forth on the water. A man selling ice creams from a cart called out his prices as Hawke watched a young couple kiss beside a red and white striped mooring pole.

"It's hard to believe all these people have no idea what's going on, really," he said, raising his eyes to the sunny horizon.

"What do you mean?" Scarlet stubbed her cigarette out and went to flick it in the canal, but Hawke grabbed her arm and gave her a look.

"I *mean*," he said, pulling the butt from her fingers and putting it in the ashtray on the table, "that they have no idea about the Vetrovs of this world, and what they want to do with it, or these *athanatoi* or whatever the hell they are."

"Not scared are you, Joe?" she said, smirking.

Hawke rolled his eyes. "Hardly – I just wonder if sometimes it would be better not to know the truth."

"Never. It's up to people like us to know the truth about the world and fight for it."

Hawke looked at her, his eyes narrowing a little. "You say that like this is just a day job, Cairo."

"Did I?" She went to light another cigarette but her lighter wouldn't work. "I didn't mean it to sound like that."

"Well, it did. Want to tell me anything?"

"Like what? I think maybe this bloody useless lighter's out of fuel."

"Don't change the subject, Cairo."

"I don't need to change subjects, Joe. If I didn't want to talk about something I'd just fuck off somewhere else. You know that, darling."

"Yes, I know that, but I'm still asking you why you just talked about how it's down to people like *you* to fight like this. What did you mean by that?"

"Nothing at all – you're imagining it."

"Like the way I imagined how after you left the SAS you decided to work for MI5, and yet you accidentally never arrived there?"

Scarlet looked at him sharply, cigarette still hanging from her lip. "What's that supposed to mean?"

"Come off it, Cairo. I know you never worked for MI5 and I know Sophie Durand never worked for the DGSE. You, and everyone else here has been lying to me from the start and I want answers or I walk."

She looked at him for a few seconds with the cigarette still hanging off her lower lip. "Yeah - bloody lighter's packed in. Got a light, Joe?"

Hawke sighed, and fished around in his pockets but found nothing.

"Are you going to talk to me or not?" he said as he searched.

"Just be a darling and get me a light?"

He sighed. "Wait a minute."

He went inside and pulled the coat he had worn in Russia from his bag and went through the pockets. He found a box of matches and a small slip of paper. He looked at it with confusion for a second and took the matches to Scarlet on the balcony.

"Thanks, darling," she said, lighting the cigarette. She waved the match until it blew out and then tossed it in the canal. "What's that you've got?"

"I don't know..." He opened the slip of paper and saw there was a message. It was written in black ink in English and the message read: *J. Hawke – Important information about your wife – contact me. Snowcat.* At the end of the message was a telephone number.

Scarlet looked up at him. "What is it, Joe?"

He frowned and handed her the piece of paper.

She read it and sighed. "A joke?"

Hawke shook his head. "No, I don't think so. I want the others to see this."

He and Scarlet walked back into the hotel room and joined the others where he showed them the note.

"Any idea where it came from?" Eden asked, intrigued.

"No. It wasn't in my pocket when we left New York, and no one who knows me, or anything about me, knew I was in Russia." He turned to the others and fixed a serious glance in their direction. "Unless, of course, it's one of you guys?"

All the heads shook at once. No.

"So when did this…" Scarlet took another look at the note. "This *Snowcat* have time to put the message in your pocket?"

"When we were at the airport," Ryan said calmly.

Hawke shot him a glance. "Eh?"

"After customs, we stepped out the front of the airport and that woman collided with you, remember?"

"Sure," Hawke said. "I remember that." He scratched the stubble on his jaw and slowly nodded his head. "She was blonde."

"To be honest, I thought she was a pickpocket," Ryan said.

Scarlet looked at Ryan. "You thought she was a pickpocket but you never said anything until now?"

Ryan shrugged his shoulders. "That's pretty much right, yeah. Sorry."

Hawke stared at the note, at a loss for what to do. His mind was filling with problems again – was Lea safe? Why was Scarlet refusing to tell him the truth? And now, why had a random stranger called Snowcat claimed knowledge about his wife? He knew it could be a trap, but at the same time he knew there could be something in it, and there was no way he could risk throwing away an opportunity to know the truth about his wife's murder after so long.

"I've got to contact this person."

"Do you think that's wise?" Eden said.

Hawke turned the paper over in his hand once again, staring at the handwritten note. "I have no choice, Richard. I have to know. I need to know the truth."

Hawke picked up his cell phone and left the room.

*

Karlsson rounded the bend and immediately saw they had driven straight into a trap. Ahead of them, Kodiak's boat was slowing to a stop. Worse, they could hear the sound of a helicopter approaching from behind them, and then half a dozen armed men appeared on either side of the canal, guns raised and aimed at their heads.

"We've been led into a trap!" Lea said.

"Dead end," the American said, crushed. "We have to stop the boat."

He slowed the boat down as fast as he could and narrowly avoided colliding with Kodiak, who was now standing on the rear deck of his motorboat with a gun jabbing into Mazzarro's neck.

Lea watched in despair as a Bell 212 now hovered directly above their boat, the powerful downwash lifting water out of the canal and spraying it all over them and splashing it up the sides of the motorboat. They were trapped and it would be fish in a barrel time if they tried to shoot their way out of it.

Moments later the chopper's side door swung open and the giant they had seen earlier – whom Eden had described as Kosma, a former KGB operative, leaned out of the door with a Groza assault rifle in one hand and a megaphone in the other.

"Put down your guns!" he shouted. His accent was thick and hard to understand.

"What do we do now?" Karlsson asked, still gripping his Glock. "Maybe we can still shoot our way out?"

"I think we have to do as he says," Lea said, shaking her head. "If he opens fire with that thing we'll be so full of holes we're going to look like a couple of cocktail strainers in less than ten seconds – and that's not to mention all these goons." She nodded at the men surrounding them on either side of the canal – they were obviously receiving orders though the small headsets they wore.

Without giving them any chance to think, Kodiak pushed Mazzarro onto Lea's boat and snatched Lea's and Karlsson's weapons and tossed them in the canal. Then he ordered Mazzarro to climb the rope ladder which came tumbling down from the chopper. Kosma's giant hands grabbed the Italian and hauled him inside the chopper.

"Your turn," Kodiak said, pointing the gun at Karlsson.

When the American was inside, Kodiak turned the gun on Lea. "Ladies last," he said, grinning.

Lea climbed into the helicopter, a look of defeat on her slim face. Her hair whipped around in the chopper's downdraft as she went inside the cabin. A moment later, Kodiak joined them and the chopper pulled up into the sky and banked sharply to the right. Kodiak and Kosma sat either side of Mazzarro, opposite Lea and Bradley Karlsson. Each of the men was armed – Kosma still held the Groza while Kodiak had picked up a compact Bizon submachine gun.

"What are you going to do with us?" Lea asked flatly, and trying not to give away how angry and humiliated she was for getting caught.

"They're going to shoot us and dump us in the sea, right?" Karlsson said with a fake grin.

"Oh no," Kodiak said with a snarl. "You two are coming with us. Mr Vetrov needs fresh meat for another sacrifice to his gods."

*

Eden disconnected his phone and turned grim-faced to the others who were waiting, expectant, for him to tell them what had just happened.

"That was a contact of mine from the Italian police. I'm sorry to say they just found the boat Lea and Brad were using to retrieve Dr Mazzarro."

"And?" Ryan asked, wide-eyed.

"And it was empty. Eye-witnesses report seeing men with guns forcing them into a helicopter. An MI5 contact of mine has just told me that the chopper went to the airport where they boarded a private A380. It looks like it's heading south but that's all they could give me for now."

Eden, like everyone else in the room was suddenly deflated, and deeply worried about Lea and Karlsson.

Then, Hawke walked back into the room, still holding his phone.

"Ah, the wanderer returns,' Scarlet said.

"Any news?" Eden asked.

Hawke nodded. "I believe her."

"*Her*?" Ryan said.

"Snowcat is a bit of a giveaway codename, boy," Scarlet said.

"Not necessarily," he replied.

"I suppose you're right," Scarlet said. "Yours would probably be something like Candy Floss."

"And what was yours?" Ryan replied with a smirk. "Iron-drawers?"

"Ha, ha… *ha*," she said in a sarcastic tone.

"Thanks everyone, but this is about Liz," Hawke said, bringing the banter to an end. "This woman clams she's in the FSB and says she has important information about what happened in Vietnam, so I'm going to meet her."

"Where and when?" Eden asked.

"To be arranged."

"And why is she doing this?" Lexi asked.

"She claims it has something to do with why we were in Moscow, but she didn't elaborate."

Scarlet sighed. "And you're taking the word of someone in the Russian Main Intelligence Directorate? I know you're SBS and all, but I thought you were smarter than that."

Alex gave him a look. "He's not an idiot, Scarlet. He'll be ready for anything."

"I guess," replied Ryan. "Plus this Snowcat chick sounds pretty sexy."

Scarlet rolled her eyes. "Oh *please*, this isn't 1971."

"What? It was just a compliment!"

Hawke looked at them all. "Why do you all look so upset? It's just a meeting with an FSB agent, and not my first time, either."

Eden cleared his throat and looked at Hawke. "I'm sorry Joe, but they've got Lea and Karlsson. They flew out of Venice a few minutes ago."

Hawke picked up a Glock and jammed it in his belt. "Then we have to get after them, don't we?"

"But where are they going?" Ryan asked.

"I'm not a betting man," Eden said. "But we know their flight is heading south, and we also know Mazzarro's research points heavily to Egypt. There's only one place that fits all of this."

Hawke agreed. "So let's get on instead of waffling and we might beat them to it."

*

On board Eden's Gulfstream, Hawke closed his eyes and tried to focus. Ahead of him lay not only the difficult and dangerous task of rescuing Lea and Karlsson and stopping Vetrov, but the truth behind his wife's murder.

More than a small part of him seriously thought it was the kind of stone better off left unturned. But a bigger part of him – the better part, the part that motivated him to get out of bed in the morning and do the right thing in life no matter the cost – understood that not knowing the truth wasn't an option.

Now he had the worst choice of his life – whether to rescue Lea first or meet Snowcat. The Russian had sounded like she might not suffer fools gladly, and had told him if he was late for their meeting she would be gone. His mind was torn in two and he agonized over the decision he had to make. And it was that final torturous decision that plagued him as drifted to sleep.

CHAPTER SEVENTEEN

Airborne

The first thing Lea saw when the bag was removed from her head was the enormous, hairy hands that had taken it off. She blinked in the bright light and tried to focus on where she was. She was staring at the same man she had seen in the Piazza San Marco – the man Richard had named as Kosma Zhuravlev. The smaller one – the bastard from the boat they called Kodiak – was nowhere in sight.

While she was blindfolded she'd been busy trying to get her bearings, so she already knew she was in an aircraft, and a very large one by the sound of the thrust at take-off. Judging by the time it took to reach cruising altitude she presumed she was at around thirty-five thousand feet. She also knew they weren't going anywhere – the plane was just executing its tenth right-turn since reaching cruising height.

The giant padded over to Karlsson and snatched the bag from his head a moment later. Lea's eyes widened when she saw the man looming over the American SEAL. Bradley Karlsson was one of the biggest men she had ever met but he looked pretty fragile beside this other guy.

"You get up now," the man said in a deep, bass growl. "We see boss."

The man sloppily pulled an old Makarov from his belt, waving them through the door and out into the corridor. He ordered them to a lift. They ascended for a few seconds before a gentle ping alerted them that they were at their destination and the doors opened to reveal a plush lounge.

"Hey," Karlsson whispered, looking down at the carpet. "Don't get lost in the pile."

Lea smiled, but her mind was in no place for jokes. She knew they were being given the scenic route so they got a good idea of just how powerful their host really was. She peered out the windows and saw they were above water.

At the far end of the lounge was another room, which opened onto what looked like a very expensive boardroom. Lea had seen something similar when she'd watched a documentary on Air Force One, only this was much bigger and more luxuriously appointed.

"Wait here," said the giant, and left the room.

Moments later they were called into a private office. The far wall was lined with tropical fish tanks under-lit by a blue neon light which made the place look like an upmarket strip club. Behind the desk was an enormous tapestry. It was an image of an Egyptian god, but which one, Lea didn't recognize.

"You know who that is?" she asked.

Karlsson shook his head. "Nope. Went through college on a football scholarship then joined the Navy. You're asking the wrong guy, honey."

"Don't worry about it."

"I'm not. You don't know who it is either."

It was beautiful, but there was something sinister about it – something out of place with the modern world.

"Ah – I see you are admiring the greatest god of them all – Osiris!"

The heavy Russian accent left no need for an introduction, but they got one anyway. They turned to see a tall, lean man with greying hair and three long scars running down the right side of his face. Maxim Vetrov.

"Welcome to my little airplane – I hope you like it!"

"Not really, and the service sucks."

"Don't be too hard on Kosma," Vetrov said, his voice dripping with insincerity. "Here he is out of his milieu. He was hired because he can break a man's neck with his bare hands, not for his interpersonal skills."

"How very reassuring," Lea said, staring at his face.

"Oh, this?" Vetrov said, pointing at the three thick scars. "Attacked by a bear when I was a young man hunting in the woods. I'm not bitter. It taught me to respect nature, plus, the bear's head is on the wall of my Moscow apartment."

He stared at them both for a long time, but particularly at Lea. "You know, I was just reading about you, Miss Donovan."

"Interesting?"

"Not until the last chapter."

"And what's so fascinating about the last chapter?"

"You die, of course. That time is rapidly approaching."

"You know nothing about me or my life, weirdo."

He laughed. "You see, back in the good old days no one ever really *left* the KGB. Take me for example. I was a leading light at the academy, destined for great things, until *perestroika* and *glasnost* put me out of a job. But once a KGB man, always a KGB man, for better or worse – you make friends, you know?"

"It's hard to imagine you just chilling out with your buddies," Lea said. "Just you, some cold ones, a crocodile pit and a private, customized airbus."

"This?" Vetrov waved a casual hand at the aircraft. "This is nothing, just a trinket, bought by the proceeds of my many corporations. The real wealth I have yet to attain…" He narrowed his eyes and fixed them on her. It felt like they were burning a hole in her. He began to laugh quietly, a sort of fiendish, suppressed chuckle. "You know of what I speak, no?"

"Well…"

"Don't be coy, Miss Donovan. As I said, I was just reading all about you. Your little trips all over America, Europe and China during which you just happened to be at the right place and the right time whenever the elixir of life was mentioned, you were always there… You were there when Zaugg tried to claim it for himself, and you were there when Sheng tried to take it for *himself*…but…"

"Just spit it out, Vetrov," Karlsson said.

"But now," Vetrov continued, never taking his eyes off Lea and ignoring Karlsson, "but now… this time you are in the wrong place at the wrong time. That is why the last chapter of your story is so interesting, because it is here that you and your friends finally meet your end, and I fulfil my destiny."

"That remains to be seen," Karlsson said, louder this time and stepping forward.

Vetrov nodded and gave the former SEAL the most cursory of glances. Kosma stepped forward and gripped the American by the shoulder before dragging him back a few yards.

"We have been tormented by the terrible bounds of mortality since the dawn of our species. For millennia, desperate kings and emperors sought to attain eternal life by any means at their considerable disposal, but all their attempts were in vain – pathetic alchemies that usually ended in their premature deaths… the irony!"

Lea sighed. "Not this again…"

"You heard this before then?" Karlsson said.

"You could say that…"

Vetrov was undeterred. "It was one of these grand failures that led to the theft of the Map of Immortality from Poseidon's tomb – when the Chinese Emperor Qin failed to achieve eternal life by consuming the *lingzhi* mushroom in a ridiculous concoction developed by his priests and doctors! After that was the mercury, and then his death – all because he couldn't translate the map…"

"This is madness, Vetrov!" Lea shouted, the cable ties cutting into her wrists.

"Wrong again. Madness is drinking mercury because you have mistranslated a reference to the ancient Egyptians consuming white drops or liquid gold! That is madness."

Lea watched a crazed look creep into Vetrov's eyes as his mind ran away with all the possibilities of harnessing the source of eternal life.

"Can you imagine what it would be like to live forever? The ancients knew the power we are talking about… they knew how to transport their souls to the Elysian Fields – the Sekhet-Aaru, or heavenly paradise fields where the mighty Osiris rules for all eternity."

"And you're going to challenge him?"

"Of course not! No one challenges the mighty Osiris, but Osiris rules in the reed fields of paradise, Miss Donovan – not here on earth. This is *my* kingdom…Imagine the knowledge and power I will accumulate, imagine the strength of my armies. Think about the things I will see in the far future, when you are no more than long-forgotten dust."

"In your dreams," Lea said angrily, but she was starting to feel nervous.

"A dream for me, but a nightmare for you – as you will discover when you are sacrificed to the gods… Did you know that if you are to reach Sekhet-Aaru, your soul must weigh exactly the same as the feather from the head-dress of the great Ma'at, the goddess of truth and beauty?"

"Fascinating," Lea said.

"But no *way* does she weigh that," Karlsson drawled. "You should have seen what she had for lunch."

A look of dark rage crossed Vetrov's face. "Silence! The deities will not be mocked, and that includes me!"

"Talk about an ego problem."

Vetrov calmed down and joined his hands as if in prayer. "Do you think, Miss Donovan, that your soul weighs more or less than that feather?"

"I wouldn't know how much anyone's soul weighs," Lea replied in disgust. "You can't weigh a soul."

"Not true... the ancient Egyptians found a way. They weighed the hearts of the recently deceased. Perhaps, I will weigh your heart against Ma'at's ostrich feather to see if your soul can enter the reed fields?"

"This guy is *totally* crackers," Karlsson whispered.

Vetrov stared hard at her. "Well, what do you think about that?"

"You're not there yet, Vetrov."

"We'll see about that," Vetrov said, and turned to Kosma. "Bring me Mazzarro. It's time for him to share his research with us."

CHAPTER EIGHTEEN

Cairo

The Gulfstream touched down into a bright Egyptian morning, and after a short moment in customs, Hawke and the rest of the team emerged from the airport and made their way to the taxi rank. Before checking into their hotel, Eden and the others went straight to the home of the British Ambassador, a personal friend of Sir Richard's, where he planned on apprising the British Government formally about what was going on.

Hawke, meanwhile, had other business to attend to – the note from Snowcat. He watched his friends drive away in a government SUV while he waited for the next cab to pull up. Moments later, he was driving from the airport in the back of a 1977 Mercedes 280SE and watching the city pass in a blur through the half-cracked window.

The atmosphere here reminded him vaguely of Kabul, only Cairo was much bigger and wealthier. He hadn't spent long in Kabul – just a couple of hours before flying out to Kamdesh in pursuit of the Taliban top brass. Kamdesh at the time was rumored to be the headquarters of the most senior members of Al-Qaeda, and Hawke's OP confirmed this. When they called the sighting of the notorious convoy into base they were told in no uncertain terms to hold fire and wait for a unit of US Rangers to come in and claim the prize. By the time the American forces arrived, the convoy had gone.

That was a long time ago, and he still wasn't sure if he missed it or not. Probably not, all things considered. The SBS had a habit of getting up at two a.m. and lying in frozen ditches for hours on end or diving under enemy corvettes and planting limpet mines on the hull, and Joe Hawke wasn't getting any younger.

A hot wind blew from the south, and the driver told him it was the *khamasin* – the desert wind which blew from the southwest, off the Sahara. It was early this year, the driver explained, but Hawke's mind was elsewhere. He was thinking about the day he met Lea in London, and his new career as a security guard had gone down the pan in royal fashion. After seeing what had almost happened to Alex back at the Moscow dacha, just thinking about Lea being held hostage by Vetrov was enough to drive him insane with rage, but that was an emotion he knew how to suppress. Revenge, after all was a dish best served cold.

He glanced through the windshield and saw some kind of obstacle ahead. According to the driver, a van delivering water to a corner shop had crashed into what he called a *toktok* – an auto-rickshaw – and knocked it over. They were used all over the poorer parts of Cairo instead of taxis because they were much cheaper, he explained. As they cruised past Hawke saw the toktok passengers climbing out with bleeding heads and an enormous argument erupted between their driver and the man behind the wheel of the van.

Hawke watched with casual interest as they passed by. It was his first trip to Cairo and he had no idea what to expect. He'd heard it was the biggest city in the Middle East, but it was only as the cab wound its way painstakingly through the heavy traffic that he really understood what that truly meant. They fought against an incessant tide of cars, buses and pedestrians ambling all over the streets as they nosed their way toward the address Snowcat had given him.

Progress was too slow for Hawke, but then most things were. He looked over the chaos around him as his driver proudly explained that the word Cairo meant the Place of Combat. He said nothing in response, but wondered just how true that would turn out to be for him – it would all depend on how things went with the Russian woman, he guessed.

They crossed the Nile and drove over Gezira Island before pulling south off of El Tahrir and arriving at the Sheraton. It was a more upmarket area than where they had just driven through – well-dressed people crossed the bridge over the river in the hot sun, talking into cell phones. A group of tourists in white shirts and sun hats gently moved out of the shade of a date palm on the bank of the Nile and stepped down into one of the many cruise boats moored on the west bank.

They pulled up outside the hotel.

"Your destination!" the driver said proudly and presented the building to his passenger with a gentle wave of his palms.

Hawke thanked him and paid. A second later he was staring up at the enormous white twenty-storey tower which loomed above the western bank of the Nile. If all of this was real, and not just a wild goose chase – or worse, a trap – then somewhere in this hotel was a Russian agent named Snowcat, and the final truth about his wife's brutal murder in Vietnam.

He took a deep breath of the warm air and walked toward the lobby.

The lobby lounge of the Sheraton was a large expanse filled with expensive furniture and the same kind of well-dressed people he'd seen back on the bridge. A man played some light jazz on a grand piano in the corner, his face only partially visible in the low light of the lamp beside him, while the pale marble floors reflected the neon blue of the strip light running around the edge of the room.

Hawke walked toward the bar, brushing against one of the many potted palms which decorated the place as he moved forward. It was busy here, and he ordered a sparkling water. He selected a seat which offered a good view of the room but at the same time allowed easy access to an egress point. It was an old habit he couldn't shake off, he thought, and besides, you never knew when it might come in handy.

As he waited, his mind turned to Eden and the others. He wondered what information Eden was passing to the British Ambassador and just how high all of this went in HMG. He now knew it went at least as high as the chief of the Pentagon as far as the US Government was concerned, and could hardly believe he was in the middle of it all.

Either way, they would be safely in the Four Seasons by now, hard at work on decoding the hieroglyphics on the map – they might have lost Mazzarro but at least they had his notebooks. With any luck, he could get the information he wanted here in the Sheraton and be back with them as soon as possible. After all, Lea was out there somewhere and he had to get her back. He had accepted a long time ago that getting to the bottom of his wife's murder was not much more than chasing ghosts, but Lea was alive, and needed him. The fact they didn't know where she was drove him crazy.

He saw a woman exit the elevators in the lobby. She wore a dark suit and her blonde hair was tied back. She had a slim, oval face, with powerful blue eyes. Could it be the woman who had left him the note outside of Domodedovo Airport in Moscow? He was unsure, especially from this distance, but he thought it could have been her. He'd only seen her for a second – she had left the note in his pocket in a heartbeat and was gone again, into the busy airport crowd.

He sipped the water and watched her as she walked from the elevators to the bar and ordered herself a drink – plain water with ice and lemon. Maybe it was her after all, but she could still be anyone, he thought. The place was heaving with business people from all over the world, all keen to exploit a basket-case government in crisis and get a piece of the sixth biggest oil reserves in Africa. For all he knew she was an OPEC executive flying in from their headquarters in Vienna.

But then he looked a little closer and his suspicions grew. He watched closely as she talked to the barman for a few moments. She held up her hands to convey to the barman something to do with the number six, and then they laughed and he pointed to the seats by the piano. Then, she started to walk toward him and by the time she was halfway to his table he knew this was no oil executive from Austria.

She sat a few seats away to his right and smiled at him before retrieving a cell phone from her bag and flicking the screen with her thumb.

Hawke cleared his throat and pushed back into his chair. "You must be Snowcat, then?"

The woman looked up at him sharply. For a second she looked startled, but then she smiled and relaxed a little. "Yes, but how did you know?"

"Easy. First, you counted something on your fingers."

She looked confused. "Yes – I was telling him my room number, sixty-six."

"And you used your little finger for the six, instead of your thumb, which told me you were Russian."

She opened her mouth slightly in surprise. "I never even thought…"

"Forget about it," he continued. "If you're going to worry about something giving you away then you should spend some more time on how you walk."

"On how I walk?"

"I can tell from the way you walked over here you have a small firearm in your right-hand pocket – am I right?"

"Well…" she looked a little embarrassed now. She nodded her head. "Yes, yes I do – but how did you know?"

"Simple – your right stride is shorter than your left, and your right arm is swinging less than your left arm. Both of these things tell me you have a weapon in the right-hand pocket of your trousers."

She looked confused. "My *what*?'

Hawke rolled his eyes. "Pants."

"Oh… then yes. If you mean pants then say pants."

"No, I meant trousers so I said trousers. Pants are what go *under* your trousers… Anyway, my guess is you're carrying something super compact like a Beretta Pico or maybe a Sig P238."

She smiled and looked in his eyes. "Well there, Mr Hawke, you are wrong." She flicked her eyes over the room to ensure they were alone and then pulled the weapon from her pocket for a second before sliding it back again.

"Ah – of course – the Makarov. Should have known better – Russian."

"Reliable, accurate and lethal."

Hawke nodded. "It's an excellent pistol, I agree."

Snowcat's smiled faded. "I was talking about *me*, Englishman."

Hawke made no reply, but stayed alert as she rose from her seat and wandered closer to him. She sat beside him, so close he could smell her perfume – foreign, exotic.

"Why did you ask me to meet you here in Cairo?" she asked.

"Because I'm working here," he said flatly.

"You mean you're tailing Maxim Vetrov, perhaps?" she said with a half smile.

Hawke thought about lying, but saw no point. "Yes. You know him?"

She nodded. "Of course. He is known to my government – he is a very powerful and dangerous man, and before you ask, yes I do know all about the Map of Immortality."

For a moment he was stunned and not sure how to respond. This woman had honey-trap written all over her in bright, flashing neon, and he knew he had to be careful about what he told her, on the other hand, no one was supposed to know about a map which had remained buried in a lost tomb in Greece for the last few thousand years.

Now he was confronted with a choice – be straight with her or be guarded. If she knew anything about his wife's murder he couldn't risk her walking, so he went with being straight.

"You know about the map?"

"Of course. We have Maxim Vetrov under more surveillance than an airport and we've known about his search for the map for a long time. We've also been watching you since you decided to turn Geneva into a rally track."

Hawke cracked a smile and nodded in admiration. "I should have known."

"Don't be too hard on yourself – you are a soldier, not a spy."

"Where is Vetrov now – do you know?"

She shook her head. "We don't know. He took off from Venice some time ago and is flying south, we think. We presume he is heading to Egypt."

"Have you heard of Dario Mazzarro?" Hawke asked her.

She shook her head, and Hawke smiled. For once he had more information.

"He's the only man in the world who can translate the map properly, and Vetrov snatched him from Venice before taking off. If that weren't bad enough, he took two of my people hostage, an American CIA man named Karlsson and a woman named Lea Donovan who means a great deal to me."

"I see... I will need to report this to my superiors and..."

Without any warning, half a dozen men burst through the revolving doors of the hotel lobby and opened fire with submachine guns. The bullets smashed into marble, wood and glass, and in seconds had turned a peaceful, relaxed place into a horrifying scene of bloody carnage where people screamed and ran through the dust and chaos for their lives.

Hawke and Snowcat immediately thought the same thing – a terrorist attack – but this changed when the men made an obvious move toward their table and fired on them personally.

They dived for cover behind the leather couch they'd been sitting on and Snowcat extracted the Makarov and took aim over the top of the cushions using a rubber plant for cover. She took out two of the men in a second, causing Hawke to raise an eyebrow of appreciation.

They turned to each other and at the same time said: "They must have followed you!"

"Hey, they never followed me!" Snowcat said. "This is an outrageous slur on a Russian agent…"

"Well don't look at me!" Hawke said in reply. "I didn't let anyone follow me here, either!"

"Oh, fine," Snowcat said. "Then we agree that the fairies brought them here, no?"

Hawke rolled his eyes.

"*However* they got here," he said firmly, "it's time we got *out* of here, agreed?"

Snowcat nodded and after firing a few more warning shots in the direction of the armed men, they slipped out through the door at the rear of the lobby. They searched for a way out, and after running along a utility corridor lined with elevator shafts they burst through a fire escape and emerged into a bright Cairo day.

"Which way now?" Hawke asked.

"Follow me," Snowcat said, pocketing the Makarov.

Behind them, the sound of enemy gunfire drew closer.

CHAPTER NINETEEN

Kosma Zhuravlev seemed to be enjoying his work as he dragged Dr Dario Mazzarro through the plush carpet of Vetrov's airborne office and dumped him like a sack of potatoes at the Russian billionaire's desk.

Vetrov stared at the Italian academic for a few moments with a look of cold contempt in his eyes before speaking.

"Welcome to my airplane, Dr Mazzarro. I apologize that we have not been properly introduced yet, but my man here was under strict orders to keep you safe from any interference that might be offered at the hands of these people here, or their friends." As he spoke, he pointed disrespectfully with his chin at Lea Donovan and Bradley Karlsson, both now gagged and bound on Vetrov's white leather couch.

Mazzarro struggled to his feet and stared at the horribly scarred face of the man behind the desk.

"Where are my manners..." Vetrov said, almost to himself. "Kosma, get our guest a seat, and a some refreshments... Dr Mazzarro, what would you like – whisky, perhaps, or wine – some water?"

"I...I – who are you?"

"Forgive me. My name is Maxim Vetrov, and we have more in common than you might think."

Kosma put a chair down opposite the desk as Vetrov swivelled in his seat and poured two big glasses of Scottish single malt whisky. He handed one to Mazzarro and took a large sip of his own.

"I don't understand what you want with me, Mr Vetrov," Mazzarro said, flicking his head nervously as Lea and Karlsson for a moment. Lea wanted to urge him not to help Vetrov but she was helpless to do anything.

Vetrov smiled at him. "Of course you do, Dario. As I say, you and I share a great deal in common. My father, like your father, spent his life in the search for the greatest secret our planet holds – a secret the planet has been keeping from us from the very beginning… a secret kept from us by not just Mother Nature – am I right?"

Lea saw the indecision on Mazzarro's face as he wrestled with what he should tell this man – the man who had kidnapped him by force, blasted the Doge's Palace and now had three innocent people held against their will on his private jet.

"I don't know what you mean," he said at last, immediately dropping his eyes into his whisky glass.

Vetrov nodded and smiled again, but colder this time. "I expected a little resistance, Dario. You are your father's son after all. Not that I would know, of course – I never knew your father." He sipped his whisky. "But my father knew him."

Mazzarro's eyes widened and he looked up from the Scotch. Kosma took a step forward and stood immediately behind the Italian.

Vetrov continued. "My father spent a great deal of time researching the elixir – like so many others, including Otto Zaugg, his great rival so many years ago. But Zaugg wasn't up to the fight. Zaugg never knew about the work your father did on the Phaistos Disc – but my father did. My father knew all about it, and worked with your father for many months in his pursuit of the elixir."

"You are a liar! My father never worked with any Russian named Vetrov in all his life."

Vetrov laughed. "No, no he did not. But if I say the name Wojciech Kowalski to you, then…"

Mazzarro's eyes grew yet wider as the name hung in the air between them.

"I can tell from your stunned silence that you recognize the name as the young Polish assistant who worked on your father's Egyptian expeditions for many months – a long time ago now, of course. This was my father."

"But Kowalski was a verified academic – a real person."

"Yes, he was a real person, right up to the moment my father killed him and assumed his identity."

"This cannot be true…"

"Why? Must the truth always be good?"

"My father would never have worked with him if he'd known the truth!"

"Your father was a fool who would not cooperate, which is why my father killed him too."

Mazzarro's mouth opened when he heard the words, almost hissed from Vetrov's mouth. He dropped the whisky tumbler to the ground and began sobbing. "No…no… my father disappeared on an expedition of the Upper Nile. His body was never found."

"I should think not. My father gave it to the crocodiles of the Upper Nile…"

"No… no! Brutto figlio di puttana bastardo!" Mazzarro leaped from his chair to attack Vetrov but Kosma gripped his shoulders and forced him back into it, where he collapsed, sobbing once again.

"Please, remain calm, Dr Mazzarro, or my man here will be forced to restrain you much more robustly next time."

Lea watched Mazzarro break down and cover his face with his hands. There was in his mannerisms something that reminded her of her father – something about the shape of his shoulders and the way he moved. Her father's death was a catastrophe to her, happening when she was still a young teenager. For a long time she was sure Dr Henry Donovan was murdered, but her theories were dismissed as the ramblings of a teenager scarred by the premature and tragic death of her beloved dad.

But it took a long time for her to see it that way, because she was there the day it happened. She was walking with him on the Cliffs of Moher in County Clare. It was a cool, fresh day, with no wind to speak of, and a bright sun in the sky. The two of them were walking along the path – Dr Donovan was hoping to take some pictures of the sea.

Then he realized he'd left one of his lenses in the car, and Lea ran back to fetch it for him. She had told him that when she grew up she didn't want to be a doctor like he was – she didn't like blood and guts, as she put it – but a photographer. She got the lens from the back seat and ran back to give it to him, but he was gone. They found his body an hour later on the rocks. A terrible accident, they told her. But she remembered the man in black running along the coast path afterwards, the man everyone told her she'd imagined.

Lea was shocked back to reality by the sound of Vetrov slamming his glass down on the desk. "It was a mistake, killing your father, of course," he continued. "My father believed he'd already ascertained the location of the elixir and all that remained was to eliminate any competition or other annoyances, such as your father's insistence on giving the United Nations the location so it could be protected for all mankind. Sadly, he had underestimated your father and was fooled. He died a broken man and I vowed to continue his struggle. I did much better, no?"

"You are a psychotic!" Mazzarro finally managed, his voice breaking from the horror of his father's unimaginably terrible death.

"Wrong, I am a genius, and now you will translate this map with the knowledge your father and you accumulated from your research into the Phaistos Disc, or I will kill you."

Lea listened carefully – that was the second reference to this mysterious Phaistos Disc. She had never heard of it before but it could come in useful if she ever got out of here and back to Hawke and the others.

As Vetrov spoke, he opened a drawer in the desk and extracted a neatly rolled parchment. He stared at it lovingly for a few moments and then carefully rolled it out on his desk.

Mazzarro's sobs receded as he beheld the Map of Immortality for the first time.

"This… this is amazing!" he said, reaching out with trembling fingers to touch it like a drowning man reaching for a rope. "This cannot be real… the myths were real – the disc was real! The map exists…"

Lea saw the amateur Egyptologist was immediately intoxicated by the strange papyrus before him, but then he sank back into his chair and began to shake his head, torn apart by cognitive dissonance – he could finally translate the map he had spent his life searching for, but it meant helping the man whose father killed his own beloved *babbo*. "No… non voglio aiutare. I will not help. Your father murdered my father. You will kill me as well – I know it. If I help you, you will kill me, if I don't help you, you will kill me. Either way I die."

"Your logic is sound, Dr Mazzarro, but perhaps you will be more helpful if it is not *your* life depending on the translation?"

Mazzarro turned his sweating face up to Vetrov. "I don't understand."

Vetrov clicked his fingers and Kosma padded over to the couch.

"Come now, Dario. There has been enough killing and my plane cannot stay up here forever. Tell me where we need to go and we will fly there – you can help me discover the elixir."

"Never!"

"In that case, I will kill Miss Donovan. If you still do not tell me, I will kill the American, and then I will have my people in Italy track down your family. Believe me when I tell you – you will translate this map."

Kosma heaved Lea up out of the couch and slung her over his shoulder.

"Tell the pilot to descend below pressurization altitude." Vetrov glanced out of his window. "The Adriatic Sea is beautiful today, Miss Donovan, and you will soon be flying toward it at terminal velocity."

CHAPTER TWENTY

Ryan increased the air-conditioning in the Cairo hotel room and moaned all the way back to his desk. They'd been working on the translation since first getting their hands on the notebooks back in Venice but were still getting nowhere fast.

From looking at the complex notes, Alex was beginning to realize just how little information Mazzarro had given her when they had worked together over the past few weeks. Now she was able to see the full extent of his and his father's research, she could see that the Italian had remained guarded and suspicious of her, and the information he had given her was very limited in its nature. Now, she and Ryan were side by side with their laptop screens flickering as they desperately sought anything that might point them in the right direction.

Across the room, Sir Richard Eden was calm and in control, reassured by his visit to the British Ambassador. He'd known Peter Henderson since their days in the Paras together and trusted him to deliver the news of their progress, or lack of it, to the relevant authorities in the British Government. Henderson had been the Ambassador in Egypt for over ten years now and knew the place like the back of his hand. If Vetrov touched down anywhere in the country, he would know about it in short order and tell Eden at once.

Scarlet and Lexi, meanwhile, were arguing about whether or not they should have gone with Hawke as back-up when he went to meet the Russian Agent Snowcat. Lexi thought yes, that he would need the help,

Scarlet said no, that Joe wasn't a big girl's blouse and could handle it himself. She had won the argument, but it was a Pyrrhic victory because Lexi had now made her start to worry about her old SBS friend.

She knew that despite his denials, Hawke had never really got over the murder of his wife and the deaths of Sophie and Olivia in the Far East would be taking their toll on him, however much he tried to fight through it. Now his mind was divided at a dangerous time, with part of him desperately trying to rescue Lea while another part of him was trying to lay the ghost of Liz to rest. She just hoped he could keep it together at such a critical time for the mission.

Ryan was still unhappy that he couldn't be more specific than Egypt, but it was the best he could do in such a short time. He thought about the broken fragments which helped him lead the others to the vault of Poseidon, and the stolen portrait in Hong Kong which had given him the clues to help the team find the map itself in the tomb of Emperor Qin in Xian. They were both child's play compared with this nightmare, and he knew he had the time it took Hawke to track down this Snowcat woman to come up with something better.

"How you going?" Lexi asked at last, brushing past Sir Richard as she walked over to the desk. She sat up on the desk and tied her hair back.

Ryan sighed and ran his hand through his hair. "Hard to say. Mazzarro's notes are all over the place and almost illegible in some places – and yet… some of the drawings he's done in here remind me of something, but I just can't work out what it is...."

Alex leaned forward and handed him some more notes. "Show them this stuff, Ryan."

"Oh yeah… shit. Forgot about this."

"What is it?"

"Seems like this Mazzarro was a big fan of Jean-François Champollion."

Eden stepped forward, coffee in hand. "Who?"

"He was a French scholar who specialized in ancient Egypt. He spent half his life exploring Egypt back in the nineteenth century – the Giza pyramids, the Karnak Temple, the Necropolis, the Valley of the Kings – you name it, he went there."

"He liked sunny holidays then?" Lexi said.

Ryan rolled his eyes. "Champollion was a specialist in hieroglyphics – in fact it's broadly accepted that back in his day he was the only person in the whole world who could read them."

"Talk about a skill in demand."

Ryan ignored her. "It all started with the Dendera Zodiac, a famous carving found on the ceiling of an ancient chapel. Today, the carving is in the Louvre in Paris, but it originated in Dendera, a small town on the Nile in central Egypt. Its function was to map the sky, and in fact even today it remains the only full portrayal of an ancient sky."

"*Fascinating*," Lexi said, "but… *what* all started with this zodiac thing?"

"Ah, yes. Champollion was the only man to date the thing correctly. When everyone else said it belonged to the New Kingdom, he claimed it was much earlier in the Greco-Roman period, and he was able to do this because of his incredible understanding of ancient Egyptian hieroglyphics. As I said, he was pretty much one of a kind. He discovered a cartouche which proved Egyptian civilization predated the Biblical flood story."

Scarlet sniffed. "I bet that went down well."

"Actually, no one ever knew – he kept it a secret for the rest of his life rather than publicly challenge the entire Christian belief structure."

"Heavy stuff."

"It gets better – Giovanni Mazzarro claims to have discovered some previously unknown work by Champollion about the City of the Dead at Saqqara, which was where they buried their dead in Memphis."

"We're not talking about Elvis here, are we?" Scarlet said.

"Hardly. We're talking about the place where the first pyramid was ever built – constructed by Imhotep."

"Oh – the guy from *The Mummy*?"

"If you *must*, Scarlet… Anyway, what really interests me now though is that according to Mazzarro he also found previously unknown information in the Valley of the Kings written in Coptic on a vase dedicated to Osiris."

Lexi leaned against the wall and closed her eyes. "And Coptic is what?"

"Oh, sure… It's the last version of the ancient Egyptian language. Anyway, as you know, the Valley of the Kings is basically the biggest graveyard in the world – all of the tombs of the pharaohs were put there to keep them safe from tomb raiders."

Scarlet sighed. "We tomb raiders always get such a bad press."

"So what was this new stuff Mazzarro claims to have found?" Lexi said, ignoring Scarlet's remark.

Ryan ignored her and pointed at the notes again, turning to Alex. "This one here is very similar to *akhmet*, the hieroglyph for the horizon, see?"

Alex nodded enthusiastically. "I see, yeah! Old Mazzarro must have spent forever on this."

"Ryan!" Scarlet said. "Lexi asked you a question."

"Oh sorry, Lexi – what did you say?"

"I asked what's the new stuff Mazzarro claims to have found?"

Ryan shook his head. "I'm not sure yet, but it could be the key to everything. He claims Champollion's undiscovered work contained similar glyphs to the ones on the map and that they seem to be referring to the death of Osiris and something called the Tomb of Eternity."

"That sounds ominous."

"Going by the sketches in the notes, the hieroglyphs in Champollion's mysterious, unknown work are definitely different from the rest of his stuff and Mazzarro claims that they predate the oldest glyphs ever found in Egypt."

"Impressive stuff," Eden said.

"That's only half the story – he makes a reference here, if my Italian is correct, to how the glyphs in question could well be older than Sumerian cuneiform."

Eden's eyes widened. "Hand it over."

Ryan gave him the notes and Eden read them for a few seconds. "Good God… the implications of this are astounding… and yes, your Italian is perfectly correct."

"And what are the implications?" Lexi asked.

Ryan took the notes from Eden and replied to Lexi. "The entire history of humanity is based on the fact that we started written communication around ten thousand years ago. It all started when the ancient Sumerians began making simple pictographs on clay tablets in order to communicate messages about trade goods. By around five thousand years ago they were using a reed stylus to make the symbols and this left a very particular wedge shape in the clay. Cuneiform is from the Latin *cuneus*, which just means wedge."

"Interesting, boy, but Lexi asked what the implications are. She wasn't just giving you a chance to prattle on aimlessly about old bits of pottery."

"I would have thought," Ryan replied haughtily, "that the implications for humanity were easily inferred."

"He means, I *think*," Alex said, stepping in to diffuse the tension once again, "that if the glyphs Champollion found are older than those found in ancient Sumer, all of human history just changed right before our eyes."

"Quite," Eden said coolly. "If it's true, then that raises further questions, not least of which who wrote them? What civilization were they from?"

Ryan took his glasses off and rubbed his eyes. "Well…whatever they are and whoever made them, they look like they're pointing to this Tomb of Eternity, anyway."

"And that sounds like a good place to avoid," Scarlet said. "The Tomb of Gold, I could get excited about, or even the Tomb of Emeralds, but the Tomb of *Eternity*… not so much. I can't sell eternity on the black market."

"I wouldn't be so sure of that," Alex said. "I think maybe this tomb has the greatest treasure of all within its walls."

"As far as I can tell," Ryan said, "it's called that because some kind of ancient god predating even Osiris and Poseidon was buried in secret there. They called it the Tomb of Eternity because the buried god would be launched into eternity from it into the night sky – the same principle as the pyramids."

Lexi sighed. "The pyramids? I thought that was all still a mystery."

"Nope. The pyramids were basically like giant submarine torpedo tubes aimed at the stars. They built tunnels leading from the burial chamber at the heart of the pyramid all the way to the outside wall where they were lined up with the Indestructibles."

"The what?"

"Ikhemu-Sek in Egyptian – it means 'those who do not know destruction' and referred to what today we call the circumpolar stars, as in those stars around the Little and Big Dippers."

"Why those stars?" Scarlet asked with genuine interest.

"Because the other stars revolved around them, which is why we call them the circumpolar stars. The ancient Egyptians believed that because the other stars circled these particular stars that they must be heaven itself."

"I see… now it's beginning to make sense."

"Right – and that's why they built the pyramids to align north in this way – so the *ka*, which was what they believed was the soul, or the vital spark, could be reunited with the *ba*, or personality, and transmute into the *akh*, and enter the afterlife as a kind of reincarnated, or immortal being.

"Is he still speaking English?" Lexi said.

Alex smirked. "Sorry, but yes."

Scarlet stepped up, less amused. "So what does all this mean, Ryan? You're starting to give me a headache."

"Sadly… it means we still don't know enough about these glyphs to translate them properly."

Alex sipped her coffee. "But it also means that we're probably talking about Thebes."

Lexi looked confused. "Was Thebes another god or something?"

Ryan offered a condescending smirk. "Hardly, Thebes is a place – or *was* a place, more like."

"I don't understand."

"Today it's called Luxor," Alex said.

"Luxor is a city in Upper Egypt, and back when it was Thebes it was the capital. It's where they buried the kings during the New Kingdom."

"I know where Luxor is, Ryan," Lexi said.

"Sorry, but you don't look like you'd know," he said, straight-faced.

Lexi looked at him sharply. "You want a slap, is that it?"

"Hey!" Scarlet said. "No one talks to Ryan like that except me."

Ryan ignored the comment. "Our only clue so far is the reference to Osiris. Over the last few years there have been several tombs discovered supposedly connected to him, one in Giza at the turn of the century, and one more recently in Thebes where they found a large underground complex with a wall relief of a knife-wielding demon and an impressive carving of Osiris himself."

Lexi looked concerned. "Demons?"

"They're to protect the body."

"Body? So Osiris really was real, just like Poseidon?" Scarlet asked.

Ryan nodded. "Ancient Egyptian legends have long told of Osiris having a tomb, and the one located in Thebes is a miniature version of the temple dedicated to the god in Abydos. Considering all available evidence, I would say Thebes – or Luxor was our best bet, but first we need to know what we're looking for when we get there, and that means back to the drawing board with these damned glyphs."

"But this tomb you say they found," Scarlet asked. "that's not our place?"

Ryan shook his head. "Nope – it was actually just a kind of initiation chamber."

"What about the Temple of Osiris at Karnak?" Alex asked. "That's in Luxor."

Ryan sighed and shook his head. "Sorry, but I don't think so – this glyph here specifically says *tomb* not temple – I don't think it can be referring to the temple you're talking about."

"So like you say, back to the drawing board, right?"

"Sorry, but yeah."

Eden sighed and ran his hands through his hair. "We need to go faster on this, everyone. We don't know what the hell Vetrov is doing to Lea or Brad at the moment and the only way we can get to them is by getting to the tomb before those bastards get there."

The words hung in the air like smoke. Everyone knew what Vetrov had done to Alex, and now he had Lea and Karlsson. The pressure to save their lives was building.

"I'm sure Lea's fine," Scarlet said. "She can look after herself. She's probably already killed Vetrov and is escaping as we speak. Pretty soon she'll just be hanging around somewhere, chilling, and waiting for us to pick her up."

"Let's hope you're right," Eden said. "But she hasn't made contact, so I don't share your optimism."

CHAPTER TWENTY-ONE

From her position over Kosma's shoulder, Lea could do nothing as the giant carried her out of Vetrov's office and down the long, plush corridor running outside it. He opened an internal door and began to descend down a metal staircase into another corridor. There was a low-light and it was much colder down here.

She realized they were taking her into the hold of the enormous aircraft and when they got there she saw where they had kept Mazzarro just a few moments ago – ropes and a blindfold left on the floor beside a large metal crate. From her upside-down view of things, she could see Vetrov himself behind Kosma. He was holding a gun on Mazzarro who he was forcing to walk a few yards ahead of him with his hands raised.

They stopped and she was spun around and dumped on the floor. She landed with a loud crack on the cold metal sheeting and rolled on her front. She tried to spin over, but Vetrov put his boot on her back where her hands were tied and pushed down on her wrists, making her cry out.

Ahead of her she watched the heavy boots of Kosma Zhuravlev as he diligently followed out his boss's commands and yanked something off the wall. It took her a few seconds to realize what it was, but then she saw – a parachute.

Kosma opened it up and stretched out the rigging. He pulled the canopy away and then laid out the steering lines and risers in neat lines. He worked with the casual diligence of someone erecting a tent, but she knew whatever he was doing would have a much grimmer purpose.

Some more Russian followed between the two men, and then a short burst of laughter from Vetrov. Kosma was unmoved by the joke, and simply plodded on, arranging the parachute for some purpose they had not yet shared with her, but she knew it was coming and she started to feel sick about it.

Another command from Vetrov and Kosma picked Lea up and lowered her into the harness, tying her into the steering lines and risers so she was completely unable to move. Then he lashed the other end of the steering lines and the canopy haphazardly around the heavy metal container.

There followed a few moments of discussion where Kosma tugged on the knots and tested the lines. Her fate was clear when Kosma slowly opened the front port cargo hatch opposite the container box and pushed Lea over to the edge with his boot.

Mazzarro looked on, horrified.

Cold air rushed into the hold, but the lack of altitude meant the aircraft was no longer pressurized, and there was no danger of being sucked out.

Only pushed out.

At last, Vetrov spoke.

"Dr Mazzarro. You see what your intransigence has driven me to. You will now start work on the map translation or Miss Donovan here goes over the side. Let me remind you we are cruising at a little over eight thousand feet, doctor. That is two and a half kilometers. If she falls from here she will hit the surface of the ocean at two hundred kilometers an hour just thirty seconds after leaving the aircraft. She will have just enough time to consider her fate, but not enough time for anyone to do anything about it." He laughed again, proud of his ingenuity.

"You're a monster!" Mazzarro cried out, reaching desperately for something to cling to as he staggered away from the open door.

Lea's eyes bulged as she strained in the ropes, unable to cry out because of the gag. She was good at getting out of tricky situations, but this time she knew she was out of luck.

"A monster who will kill everyone you have ever known, starting with this pathetic Irish troublemaker. Will you translate the map?"

"I…I already told you that I can't…"

"Wrong answer!"

Vetrov snapped his fingers and Kosma booted Lea in the ribs, sending her flying out the open cargo hatch. She felt her stomach turn as she tumbled out of the aircraft and began to plummet toward the water, but then the steering lines lashed to the container inside the plane went suddenly taut and arrested her fall.

She swung violently beneath the aircraft and smashed into the underside of the main body. Then she swung back again like a human pendulum before the force of the aircraft's forward motion swept her back in mid-air where she stayed, hanging behind the cargo door just a few dozen meters in front of the inner port engine. It growled hungrily in the distance. The blades raced at over three thousand revs per minute, and the white spiral painted on the fan hub was now just a blur. She felt sick and confused.

"Oh my *God!*" Mazzarro screamed, pointing at Lea. "Bring her in! Bring her in now, please."

"The map, Doctor Mazzarro. You will begin translating it, or…"

He nodded at Kosma, and the giant pulled an old Soviet combat knife from his belt and began to hack away at one of the steering lines.

"What are you doing! She will fall to her death!"

Vetrov peered out the cargo door. "I hope so, Dario, because if she goes into engine Number Two I'll have to get the pilot to shut it off."

The academic recoiled with fear as he watched Lea suspended in the parachute canopy.

"Please, Dr Mazzarro," Vetrov said gently. "I beg you to reconsider your position."

The line Kosma was cutting broke, and twanged violently apart under the pressure. Lea slipped a little closer to the whirring engine's fans blades.

Vetrov beamed. "There are not many more lines to cut through, as you see."

Mazzarro broke. "All right, all right – I can't stand it any more… bring me the map."

Leaving Lea dangling from the aircraft, Vetrov ordered Kosma to fetch the map, and when he returned Mazzarro got to work. He translated the first few glyphs in less than twenty minutes.

"Well, doctor?" Vetrov asked.

"Yes… yes! I've done as you ask – please bring the girl back in!"

"What have you found?" the Russian asked him,

Mazzarro looked nervously from Lea to Vetrov. "The hieroglyphics on the map tell a story… They tell a story… it's about Poseidon and Osiris warring over the source of eternal life. They tore the map in half – what you have in your hands is the half Poseidon kept for himself. Without the other half it is useless…"

Without Mazzarro explaining another word, a crooked smile spread on Vetrov's lips. "Of course… and the other half is buried with Osiris!"

Mazzarro looked once again at Lea, lashed in the steering lines of the chute outside the plane. "Please, will God and the world forgive me…"

Vetrov turned to leave the hold. "Kosma, order the pilot to fly on to Luxor. We're going on an excavation…oh, and pull our Irish friend back into the plane. She can die later on, the way the gods intended."

CHAPTER TWENTY-TWO

Hawke and Snowcat emerged from the hotel on the eastern side and found themselves opposite a busy marina on the west bank of the Nile. The sun shone powerfully on the river's broad surface, and the smell of exhaust fumes hung heavy in the air. The street was quiet with only a few taxis and the occasional delivery truck, but this was the up-market part of the city where the authorities liked to sweep any trouble out of sight.

"This way!" the Russian agent said, pulling on Hawke's arm.

"Oh *please*, no more rivers!" Hawke said, thinking about Venice.

She looked at him, confused. "No! You think I'm crazy? No, this way!"

Hawke followed her south along the road running parallel to the Nile for a few hundred yards until they reached a building of peach and white plaster rising from behind a high wall.

"What the hell is this place?" he asked.

"Russian Embassy – here we will be safe."

They moved along the road until they were at the entrance, and Snowcat rang the buzzer on the enormous white gates. Back at the Sheraton, the armed men were now spilling out onto the street and heading in their direction. Hawke watched as Snowcat stared at the intercom speaker, desperate, her heart beating hard in her chest with the breathlessness of the chase.

A man answered through the intercom. He spoke Russian, and his voice was muffled and hard to hear.

Snowcat spoke with him for a few moments, but the gates stayed shut.

Hawke watched the men advancing on them. “I hate to tell you this, Agent Snowcat, but our friends are getting rather too close for comfort.” As he spoke they had to duck behind the wall at the side of the gate for cover as the men fired in their direction.

“Shut up! I’m trying to speak.”

“All right, take it easy. *Russians...*”

More conversation followed in rapid Russian, totally incomprehensible to Hawke, who was now starting to have serious doubts about this particular exit strategy.

“What’s the deal?” he said urgently.

Snowcat turned to him, confused. “They won’t let me in.”

“What?”

“They say they don’t know who I am – I gave them my full name and codename and some other information we use to identify ourselves, but they claim not to know me and they say I must go away or they will call the police.”

Closer now, the men’s shooting had begun to cause a general panic on the street outside the embassy. “I think that ship’s already sailed, to be honest,” Hawke said, grimacing as another bullet traced over his head and thudded into the plaster of the gatehouse.

“I don’t know what to do,” Snowcat said, shaking her head in bewilderment.

“Then it’s over to me,” Hawke said, grabbing her hand. “Come on!”

They sprinted away from the men, turning right on Ibn Al Akhsheed Road and running up the street toward a high building at the end. “Looks like this should give us some time to think,” Hawke said as he pulled Snowcat into the Pyramisa Casino.

They entered a plush, expansive casino with lights built inside the ceiling that glittered like diamonds over the busy room beneath them. Everywhere they looked they saw people throwing money away on roulette wheels and backgammon boards.

"What now?" Snowcat said.

"We could play poker, but I've always preferred blackjack," Hawke said, as he scanned the room for another exit.

Snowcat rolled her eyes and stared at the Englishman. "Now is the time for jokes, really?"

"I guess not," he said, noticing the look on her face. "This way!"

They ran down the carpeted steps into the busy room and weaved through the hundreds of people crowding around baccarat tables and pachinko machines, all hoping to win a million, or at the very least, watch someone else win a million.

Hawke knew they'd all be focussing on something other than their odds in a few seconds' time, but that was the plan. If anything could give them good cover and slow down the armed men, it was hundreds of terrified gamblers desperately clutching their chips and running six ways from Sunday.

Then the armed men burst into the casino and fired a few rounds from their guns into the ceiling, bringing the chaos Hawke had wished for.

Shouts and screams rose from the casino floor as the horror of what was happening dawned on the guests, but Hawke and Snowcat had the advantage. He surveyed the area and realized they were still a hundred yards from the nearest steps to the upper level where the exits were. Then he saw another option.

"Can you run?" he asked.

"Of course!"

"No, I mean really *run*."

"I think so," she replied, narrowing her eyes in confusion.

"Good, then let's go!"

He sprinted forward and drawing on his parkour training he vaulted over the brass bars that separated the casino floor from the raised area where people ate and drank. Snowcat watched with respect as the Englishman's powerful body sailed over the bars and he landed with the agility of a cat on the upper level. He stopped and automatically crouched down for cover before turning back to face her.

"You can do that?"

"Of course..." she said, and sprinted forward, copying the manoeuvre Hawke had just completed and nearly pulling it off, but her right foot caught the top bar and pulled her upper body down hard into the carpet of the upper level.

"Nearly, I can do it..."

"You're doing fine."

Behind them the men had located them from the far side of the room and were now spreading out and running down both sides of the casino on the upper level, firing occasional shots in short, professional bursts which were designed to keep Hawke and Snowcat pinned down.

"We need that exit!" he said, and they dashed toward a fire escape with all their might.

Hawke kicked the panic bar so hard he nearly tore it off, and they were once again shielding their eyes from the savagely bright Cairo sun.

"These guys just don't give up!"

"They will never give up," Snowcat said, an eerie knowing look on her young face. "Trust me, they will not stop until you are dead, and now me too."

"Too bad they picked a fight with me then," Hawke said. "Because I never give up either."

Behind them they heard the men shouting as they cleared the casino and made their way toward the rear fire escape.

"They're talking in English!" Hawke said.

"Of course they are, Joe! You haven't worked any of this out yet?"

"Worked what out? Those bastards are British and they're trying to kill me! I thought they were Russians – no offense."

"Hey," Snowcat said, and shrugged her shoulders. "None taken, but we have to get out of here, right now."

"You read my mind."

As the men crashed through the fire escape and Hawke and Snowcat sprinted away into the Cairo sprawl, his mind buzzed with a thousand thoughts. Clearly the men were professionals – either Special Forces or former Special Forces guys – and now he knew they were British... but why were British soldiers trying to kill him?

His heart pounded as he raced through the back streets of Cairo with no answers, and the only person who could give them to him was a Russian woman he barely knew, running beside him into nowhere.

CHAPTER TWENTY-THREE

They ran along two more streets until Snowcat began to slow down. He could see that she didn't want to admit it, but she was flat out knackered. He looked around for another way and saw what he was looking for just a few yards ahead outside a small shop selling oranges and other fruit out of wooden crates.

"Hey! There!" Hawke pointed at a motorbike chained to a rank outside the shop.

"This is a joke, yes?" said Snowcat, staring at Hawke in wonder.

"Eh? What's wrong with it?"

Snowcat sighed and shook her head. "Fine, but don't complain to me if falls apart and we get killed on it." Without even glancing around, she pulled out her Makarov and blasted the chain off the forty year-old Kreidler Florett.

As the bullet echoed around the street, passers-by screamed and ran for cover, while Hawke nodded with casual appreciation. "Good shot."

"Is it safe?" she asked. "There's rust all over the fuel tank and the tires looked like they've seen better days."

"Yeah, like back when Reagan was president. Now give me some of that gum you're chewing and leave the rest to me."

"My chewing gum?"

"Just hand it over – it's a filthy habit anyway."

"Hey!" Snowcat said as she handed him a piece of the gum.

Hawke slung the gum and kept the wrapper, rolling it into a thin tube like a wire and holding it in his lips as he traced the bike's ignition wires back to a small plastic connector. He decoupled the connector and placed the foil wrapper into the connector and bridged two of the open ports. A second later a low clicking noise told him it was ready to start up, which he did with a smug nod of his head. "Not bad even if I do say so myself."

"Not a lot of room on this thing, is there?" Snowcat said as she straddled the bike. "Coming?"

They climbed aboard. Hawke sat on the front and Snowcat sat behind him, her hands around his waist. Moments later they were skidding out into the traffic. The tinny rasping of the fifty cc engine filled the street as they sped away from the armed men, and Hawke watched with undisguised alarm as their pursuers clambered into a jet black Cadillac Escalade which had skidded to a halt a few yards behind them.

"These blokes are good..." Hawke said. "And they've already got back-up from somewhere!"

Snowcat turned to see. "How are we supposed to get away from them on this? I've got a hair dryer with more power."

"You need a little faith, Agent Snowcat," Hawke said, and revved the Kreidler.

"People have faith in God, Hawke. With you I'm beginning to think it's more like despair."

Hawke laughed and revved the ancient German motorbike for a few more seconds before accelerating faster down the street.

Snowcat turned and tried to aim at the approaching Escalade but Hawke was weaving the Kreidler in and out of the traffic in an attempt to put some distance between them and the goons behind.

He jumped a red light and speeded west along the broad El Tahrir boulevard.

The driver of the Escalade floored the throttle and sent a plume of burned rubber smoke into the air. The giant Caddy lurched forward even faster and began to close in on them.

"Time to speed up, Englishman!"

"Hold on!" he shouted, and then turned a sharp right. He almost tipped the bike over and had to use his right boot to maintain some stability.

Snowcat grasped him tighter and screamed as they flew around a street corner in a hail of dust and more burning rubber.

"Thanks for the warning…" she screamed in his ear.

Hawke shrugged his shoulder. "Sorry… I *did* say hold on!"

On the straight now, Snowcat spun around and aimed the Makarov once more at the windshield of the enormous Escalade. She fired two shots, the first missing and the second pinging off the front driver's side wing and ricocheting up into the air.

"They're gaining on us, Hawke!"

Hawke already knew. He'd checked the mirror and seen how close the Cadillac was getting – its Vortec V8 easily overpowering the Kreidler's ageing 50 cc which was now smoking like a destroyer as it screamed in and out of the dense Cairo traffic.

"We have to get off the road!" Hawke said, and steered the bike into the Cairo University Gardens. "They won't be able to get that bollocking thing through here."

He revved the bike to keep the dying engine alive and drove at speed along the central pathway which was an ornate water feature surrounded by star flower plants and date palms. Students dived for cover as the foreigners raced along the walkway, but all that mattered to Hawke was that they were getting away from the Escalade.

They emerged the other side of the gardens and jumped the kerb into King Faisal Street. They landed with a barely controlled skid and a puff of smoke and Hawke powered the bike toward the western edge of the city.

"Any sign of them?" he called over his shoulder.

"No, I don't think so…" Snowcat searched behind them. "Yes – sorry, and they're closing on us again!"

Hawke cursed and headed toward the busy ring road, hoping to lose them in the dense traffic. "How could they have known where we are?" he said, confused. "There's no way they could have known which way we were going to drive through the university gardens."

"We'll worry about that later, yes?" Snowcat said. "For now we have to stay alive!"

Eyes focussed ahead as the ring road rapidly approached them, Hawke checked his mirror and saw the Escalade was once again closing in on them, and this time one of the goons was emerging from the rear sunroof and assembling what looked like a bazooka.

"Um… we might have a slight problem, Agent Snowcat."

"Like what?" As she spoke, the Russian instinctively turned to look at the Escalade. "Holy fucking shit! Drive faster, Englishman!"

"Yes, thanks… I had mulled the thought over…"

Hawke increased speed and at the same time weaved dangerously through the traffic on the ring road, almost clipping a taxi which would have sent them both flying over the handlebars, but it was their only chance. The Caddy had more power and they were clearly better armed, but they had the advantage over them as long as they kept in dense traffic.

Then Snowcat screamed. “Incoming!”

Or not, Hawke thought, as the goon fired the bazooka and sent a rocket speeding through the air toward them. At over three hundred meters per second, it took less than three seconds for the rocket to reach them, but in those three seconds Hawke hung a sharp left, almost sending themselves flying off the bike once again.

The rocket slammed into the side of a falafel truck and exploded into a massive fireball. Seconds later the ring road traffic was in chaos as panic gripped the drivers and sent them in all directions.

“That should slow them down a bit,” Hawke said.

Snowcat shook her head. “A perfectly good day in Cairo totally ruined. Is it like this wherever you go, Mr Hawke?”

“Pretty much.”

Behind them the Escalade was trapped in the carnage of its own making. One of the men inside tried to fire an automatic rifle into the air to scare the drivers out of the way, but this was Cairo and the passengers inside a nearby police van tumbled out and returned fire with submachine guns and carbines and merely increased the disarray.

“I think we did it,” Hawke said reluctantly as he skidded off the ring road and into a side street.

“Then think again,” Snowcat said. “Look over there.”

She pointed the muzzle of the Makarov to his right at another Escalade – this time a white one.

“This can’t be real,” he said. “Are these guys telepathic or something?”

“Just get us out of here, Englishman!”

Hawke looked at the almost-empty gas tank. “Sure thing.”

He revved the 50 cc engine and took off in the opposite direction of the white Escalade, which now gave chase. He didn't know what was going on, but he knew something was very wrong with this situation – these guys knew where he was at all times, and no way was anyone *that* lucky.

They accelerated away from the white Escalade but then the engine began to sputter.

"What's going on?" Snowcat asked. She looked over his shoulder at the bike's instrument panel.

"Slight issue with the fuel situation, I'm afraid."

Snowcat screamed and kicked the side of the bike with her heel. "Damn it!"

"It's not a horse, Snowcat… that's not going to help us go any faster."

As the engine began to lose power, the men in the Escalade fired at them, one round hitting Snowcat in her upper arm, and a second bullet striking the rear tire and blowing it into shreds. Hawke fought to maintain control of the bike but with no power it spun out from under him and crashed into the gutter, sending the two of them crashing into the dirt.

Behind them the Escalade rapidly approached.

*

Lea peered through the window as the A380 lined up for final approach at Luxor Airport. They were flying in from the north and through the window she could see the endless Sahara desert as the plane descended toward the runway. Her ordeal outside the aircraft had left her shocked and battered, but she consoled herself with the thought that Vetrov made a big mistake in letting her live.

When she had told him, Karlsson had found it hard to believe what they had done to her – and he'd seen some torture techniques in his time, for sure. He too had vowed bloody revenge on Vetrov, but now was not the time. They were still bound with cable-ties and helpless as the plane screeched onto the runway and rapidly decreased speed.

Before the plane had come to a stop, the door opened and Kosma was looming over them once again, Makarov in hand. He forced them along the corridor to the door where they descended a flight of steps pushed up against the side of the aircraft. Lea felt the hot air blowing around her neck – it was hard to believe she was watching snow fall just a few hours ago.

Kosma pushed Karlsson hard between the shoulder blades and almost knocked him over. Karlsson turned to hit him out of instinct, but with his hands secured behind his back he had to make do with a snarl and a mumbled threat, neither of which seemed to concern the enormous Russian. He simply waved the gun toward a black Humvee idling on the apron a few hundred yards from Vetrov's flying palace and shouted at them to get moving.

CHAPTER TWENTY-FOUR

Sir Richard Eden was starting to feel nervous. He paced the length of the hotel room in silence while Ryan and Alex continued their work with the notebooks and the photo of the map. He stopped occasionally to look at his watch. Things were falling apart at the most critical time – Vetrov had the map, Mazzarro plus Lea and Karlsson, and Hawke was off the radar somewhere in the grimmer quarters of Cairo.

"Mr Bale, we need some progress now please."

"I'm sorry, but I'm just not getting anywhere with this." Ryan took his glasses off and rubbed his eyes. Even with the air-conditioning on, the unusually hot weather in Cairo made the hotel room uncomfortably warm and he was sweating in the heat.

"All right," Alex said calmly. "Let's start at the beginning. What have we got?"

Ryan sighed and cracked open a beer. "We have a slightly blurred photo of the Map of Immortality taken in a hurry on a camera phone."

"It's better than nothing, nerd," Lexi shouted from the other room.

Ryan ignored her. "We have a heap of notebooks belonging to Giovanni and Dario Mazzarro, some of which look like they're older than the actual pyramids."

Alex was determined to keep him focused. "And what do those things tell us?"

"The symbols on the map pointed us to Egypt, and now it looks like they're referring to the ancient Egyptian god Osiris."

"And what do we know about him?"

"The same as everyone else – ancient Egyptian god of the afterlife and the dead, usually portrayed as having green skin. The oldest son of Geb, bla bla bla."

"Or Ra, depending on who you read."

"Sure."

They heard a tongue-click from the bed. "Relevance?"

"The relevance, *Scarlet*, is that he was right at the top of the tree of gods in Egyptian culture, just like Poseidon, and…"

"Wait!" Alex picked up one of the notebooks and showed it to Ryan. "Look at this!"

Ryan stared at the page for a few seconds, open jawed. "No way!"

Eden moved forward. "Mr Bale?"

"Surely not…!"

"Ryan!" snapped Scarlet, spinning her legs off the bed and joining them at the desk. "Stop being a silly little tit and tell us what's going on. Our people are missing."

"These notes here seem to be indicating that…"

"What is it?" Eden asked keenly. "What have you got?"

"The Phaistos Disc."

"I'm sorry?"

Alex smiled and turned to Ryan. "Do you want to tell them or should I?"

"The Phaistos Disc," Ryan said again, ignoring her. "It was discovered in Crete in 1908 by the Italian archaeologist Luigi Pernier."

Scarlet frowned. "And why do we give a damn about this, Ryan?"

Eden looked annoyed. "Let him get started, Scarlet, at least."

"Thanks, Rich. Now, Pernier was a close friend of Giovanni Mazzaro later in life. And according to this they worked together on the disc, which according to history, no one's ever been able to decipher."

"But...?"

Ryan was hungrily reading the notes as he was relaying them to the others. "But Dario Mazzarro claims his father did so, and that it made references to a war between Poseidon and Osiris – a war over a map."

Scarlet smiled . "What a surprise – another shagging map!"

"You betcha. He claims his father's translation is accurate, and that it refers to the elixir of eternal life."

"The source of the gods' immortality?" Eden asked.

Alex shrugged. "Who knows? Now we're getting into whether there's a difference between an immortal man and a deity, and that's way above my pay grade."

Ryan sighed. "Well, actually…"

"Ryan, no time," Scarlet said. "Alex, please continue."

Alex laughed and took the notebook from Ryan. "Sure… Anyway, according to Mazzarro here, the map was even older than the gods of ancient Egypt and Greece, a kind of precious relic handed down to them from an older time. He claims they couldn't agree on who would own the map, so they tore it in two and kept half each. Half was buried with Poseidon in his tomb in Kefalonia, and the other half disappeared into mythical history."

For the first time since Sophie's death, Ryan leaned back in his chair and laughed. "What's so funny?" Eden asked.

"Nothing, really," he said. "Just that all that effort by Emperor Qin just to raid Poseidon's tomb and get the map and he only ever had half of the thing. Even if he'd been able to translate it he still wouldn't have got anywhere."

"So where's the other half?" Eden asked.

"In Osiris's tomb, I presume. That's where Mazzarro comes in."

"So we still need Mazzarro to find the tomb of Osiris?" Lexi said.

"We can find a bloody tomb without Mazzarro!" Ryan said, suddenly indignant.

"Sure we can!" Scarlet said. "I can find any tomb in the world, so long as the golden incentive is there…"

"But what does all this mean for us right now?" Lexi asked.

"It means we can do it – not only do we now know that Osiris was real and that he and Poseidon fought over the map, but we also know for sure that there are two halves of the map and that we – and Vetrov – only have half of it. If we can cross-reference Mazzarro's research with the Phaistos Disc we should be able to translate the map faster."

"But we still need Osiris's half of the map if we're going to find the Tomb of Eternity, right?" said Scarlet.

Alex nodded. "We can start translating the map we have right now thanks to this new information about the disc, but we only have half the map. Without the other half we're never going to find the tomb, no."

"So we raid the tomb, simples," Scarlet said.

"If you're *sure* Osiris was real," Lexi said.

Ryan nodded. "If this is right, then it strongly suggests Osiris was real."

"You mean like Poseidon?"

"Exactly – not a mythical figure but really here, in Egypt."

"Woah!" Alex said, staring at the map.

"What is it?" Ryan said, turning toward her.

"This glyph right here – it's the same as one on the Phaistos Disc that Mazzarro claims means *Ipet-isut*."

Ryan's jaw went slack. "No way!"

"Ryan!" Scarlet shouted.

"It means *the most selected of places* – it's a reference to Karnak."

"I don't believe it." Alex said. "So obvious, now..."

"I'll say," Ryan added. "The Hek-Djet – of course!"

Scarlet leaned in close to Ryan and tweaked his ear. "Stop talking in riddles and tell me what all this means, *boy*, or I'm going to take you outside."

Ryan looked up at her and smirked. "You can take me in here if you like."

"Ugh," Scarlet said, and pushed him away. "In your wildest dreams that would still not happen."

Alex looked on, bemused, before speaking. "It's the Osiris Hek-Djet if the lecture's going to be formal. It means Osiris, the Ruler of Eternity. Karnak is regarded as pretty much one of Egypt's most important sites for archaeological artefacts. The thing is, if Mazzarro's decipher matrix is right, then these hieroglyphics aren't directing us to the Osiris Hek-Djet exactly, but *beneath* it."

"Beneath it?" Lexi said, surprised.

Alex nodded. "Now we know how to translate all this it's pretty obvious when you look at it. If Mazzarro's research is right, then the Phaistos Disc makes a clear reference to the map being torn in two, one half going to Poseidon in Kefalonia and the other half going to Osiris – in the Hek-Djet. This is ancient knowledge."

"And this means?" Scarlet asked.

Eden stepped forward. "It means we're going to the Temple of Amun Ra in Luxor, right?"

Alex and Ryan nodded.

"Good," Eden said flatly. "Start packing the gear up – we leave as soon as possible."

"But what about Joe?" Ryan asked.

"Hawke has for as long as it takes us to pack up. After that he misses the boat and he's on his own." Eden looked at Scarlet and they shared a glance. "We can do this without Joe Hawke if we have to… we've done so plenty of times in the past, after all."

CHAPTER TWENTY-FIVE

Hawke scrambled up from the wrecked motorbike and sprinted over to Snowcat, who was now lying in the gutter and surrounded by a mix of concerned and angry street traders. He pushed his way through the crowd and saw she was clutching her arm and wincing in pain. He could see blood just above the elbow of her suit jacket.

He moved down to her while keeping one eye on the street behind the bustling traders, who were now beginning to shout in Arabic at them. The white Escalade had slowed down to navigate through the bustling crowd. The crowd parted and the Escalade drew nearer like a lion about to make its death blow.

"Are you all right?" he asked.

She turned and screamed something in Arabic, sending the crowd running for their lives, and then she fired the Makarov at the Escalade, hitting the gas tank and exploding the vehicle into a massive fireball. "I think so," she said. "It's just a flesh wound."

"Er...*all right then,*" Hawke said, seeing the Russian's no-nonsense approach applied with such good timing. "Good, because I think we've outstayed our welcome – that fireball is going to have every cop in Cairo here in a few short minutes."

He helped her stand. By now another large crowd of passers-by had formed to see what all the fuss was about, and Hawke tried to push his way through them but there were just too many.

Suddenly he heard another gunshot, close and loud. He ducked as the crowd broke apart and people screamed and ran for cover all over again.

"Get down, Snowcat!" he shouted, turning to pull her to safety, but as he did so he saw her standing behind him, smoking Makarov held aloft.

"What the..?"

"Russian way of dispersing a crowd," she said coolly, and slipped the gun back inside her pocket.

"The Russian way, or *your* way?" he asked smiling, and pulled himself back up from the dusty street.

"A little of both, I guess." He saw a sparkle in her blues eyes that he hadn't noticed before, and guessed that just like him, she was happiest when in the field, on the edge of things.

"Well, in that case…" he stopped in his tracks.

"What is it?"

He pointed behind her and she turned to see what he was showing her.

They watched in horror as a fully-armed Boeing AH-64 Apache helicopter emerged from the Cairo smog and turned in their direction. Hellfire missiles, Hydra 70 rocket pods and, sitting right up front, a 30 mm M230 chain gun.

"This is turning into a really bad day," he said, shaking his head in disbelief at what he was seeing.

"Tell me about it – that bullet just put a hole right through my best jacket."

Hawke went to reply, but stopped when he saw the expression on Snowcat's face.

"So what do we do?" she asked, pointing at the bike. We can't out run it on that – it's totally wrecked."

She was right. The Kreidler had definitely polluted its last day, and was now nothing more than a pile of rusted metal and burned rubber with a badly bent front axle. Worse, the helicopter gunship was getting closer.

"No, we run over there," he said, pointing at the Giza pyramid complex.

"Run into the pyramids?" she said, her eyes widening. "You have to be crazy! This isn't *The Spy Who Loved Me*… I hope you realize that."

"Yes, funnily enough I had realized that, but now it's our only chance of surviving this."

She shrugged her shoulders. "Okay, crazy Englishman. Let's do it."

With no other choice and a fully armed Apache on their backs, Hawke led Snowcat out of the labyrinthine stacks of houses and across a wide boulevard shaded with beautiful flame trees.

The scene changed fast as they turned the corner. Behind them was the everyday life, junk and clutter of the Giza suburbs, but now they were in ancient Egypt. They stared right into the eyes of the Great Sphinx which sat in the bright sunshine a few hundred yards ahead of them.

Hawke watched as a large tour bus pulled up beside them and he turned to Snowcat.

"Follow me."

"What are we doing?"

"We're about to go on honeymoon together." As he spoke he offered her his arm.

She slipped her arm through his and drew closer to him as they sneaked their way into the crowd of German tourists now filing out of the bus and making their way up the broad, gravel path which led to the Sphinx. The tourists stopped to look at the column of smoke rising silently from the roofline a few blocks away.

"It's a barbecue," Hawke said as he passed them.

A couple of men were selling hats and water in the shade of a date palm. Hawke stepped over to them and handed them a fifty dollar bill for two hats, which he and Snowcat immediately put on.

"Bastards won't be able to see us now," Hawke said as they made their way into the middle of the crowd.

Hawke turned to see the Apache gain height. It was trying to get a better view of where they were, but also making itself look more like a regular helicopter – just a black shadow against a bright blue sky and no one paying particular attention.

"I just don't understand how the hell they got a sodding Apache on us so fast," Hawke muttered. "But that's a problem for later. For now, we have to give them the slip. We'll pretend to be tourists until that bloody chopper gets bored and then we need to get back to the others as soon as possible… and you have some talking to do."

"Agreed," Snowcat said.

They walked amongst the tourists through the lines of market traders selling thousands of souvenirs – key-rings, paperweights, t-shirts, silk headdresses – and gradually drew closer to the Sphinx where the Germans stopped and took pictures.

"Smaller than I thought it would be,' Hawke said, nodding at the Sphinx. "What about you?"

"Guess so. I've seen it many times."

He nodded and turned to look at the Apache, pretending to point at the Sphinx as he did so. He estimated it was probably around two thousand feet now, and the pilot would be using a helmet-mounted display and zooming in on the crowd to identify them.

He'd known an Apache pilot when he was on tour in Afghanistan and knew how they worked. He knew how they were trained to take in two separate streams of information from each eye – the left one focussed on the cockpit and the right one focussing through the FLIR camera on the outside world. The fact he was being hunted right now by someone with those skills worried him a lot, but not as much as the problem he had with Maxim Vetrov being able to source an asset like an AH-64 and fly it in Cairo airspace at such short notice. Something wasn't right.

Then things got much worse.

The Apache began to lose altitude and fly toward the crowd of tourists.

"They've found us!" Hawke shouted, grabbing Snowcat by the arm. "We have to get out of here – now they've located us we're putting these tourists at risk."

Out of nowhere, Hawke saw the familiar orange flash and puff of white smoke from the pylon beneath the Apache's wing, and then watched in horror as a hellfire missile raced toward them. A second later they heard the screeching sound of the missile in the sky and hundreds of people on the ground looked up and saw the terror rapidly approaching them.

Hawke turned to the crowd and screamed. "Run!"

A wave of panic rippled through the crowd and people screamed and scattered for their lives. A cloud of dust rose up into the air from the stampede of people and camels and blocked Hawke's view of the Apache but he was too busy sprinting for cover to notice.

He and Snowcat hurled themselves toward a low limestone-concrete wall and just cleared it as the hellfire exploded on the road behind them, throwing great piles of rocks and dust into the air amidst an enormous fireball. A thick black cloud of smoke rose into the air and in the distance they heard the familiar wail of sirens.

The wave of terror and confusion all around them gave Hawke and Snowcat a moment to consider their next move.

"I can't believe those nutcases fired on innocent tourists!" Hawke said.

"I can," Snowcat muttered, almost to herself.

"Something's not right here. This can't be about Maxim Vetrov trying to kill us. It just doesn't feel right."

Before Snowcat replied, the smoke and dust began to clear and they saw the Apache turning once again in their direction.

The missile attack had brought chaos to half of Giza, and now the whole area was alive with the noise of sirens and screams and in the distance somewhere a man was shouting orders at the panicking mob in Arabic through a megaphone.

"They're not done with us yet!" Snowcat said.

"Into the pyramid!" Hawke shouted.

The pyramids were a lot bigger than Hawke had thought, and as a consequence it took much longer to get to them than he had judged. With the Apache closing in at their backs, they sprinted closer to the protection of the Great Pyramid, but it just seemed like it never got any closer.

"They're almost on us, Joe!"

Snowcat's warning was backed up by the terrifying chatter of the massive chain gun, rising even above the noise of the four whirling stainless steel rotor blades. Seconds later the ground either side of them was torn apart by the impact of hundreds of thirty mil M788 rounds as they strafed through the dusty gravel and exploded all around them.

Hawke and Snowcat scrambled to their feet and ran along the final stretch of path until they finally reached the entrance to the pyramid. They raced inside and the walls around them exploded into dust as the Apache chain gun unloaded a few more rounds at them.

"They're destroying the bloody pyramid!" Hawke screamed. "Richard would seriously disapprove of this."

"I'm more worried about us, right now…" Snowcat said, looking with despair at the two rounds left in her Makarov.

"And more bad news – just like the wankers in the Escalade, they're bloody Brits as well."

"How do you know?" the Russian asked.

"Engine sound – that thing's running on a Rolls Royce and the Yanks use General Electric. I noticed it back there when they stopped to aim the chain gun. I just can't work out why my own bloody people are trying to kill me."

"Another problem for later, but for now we can presume they will do whatever it takes to kill us."

"Including blowing up one of the world's oldest bloody monuments?"

"The stakes are higher than you can imagine, Hawke."

"Oh *God*," he said, rolling his eyes. "No more bloody secrets, please."

"I don't know what you mean – I have kept no secrets from you. All you need to know now is that your enemies are closer than you think. You can trust me if you like. If you choose not to trust me then it makes no difference to me."

"But no one even knows I'm here in Cairo…"

"No one?"

"Well, only Sir Richard Eden, Scarlet, Lexi Zhang, Ryan and Alex."

Snowcat's words went round in his head – *your enemies are closer than you think* – what could it mean? Between the accents he'd heard and the sound of the

Rolls-Royce engine in the chopper now hovering outside the pyramid, it was obvious that it was the British who were trying to kill him, but the only people who knew he was in Cairo were his friends – or those he presumed were his friends. Had one of them sold him out for some reason? Maybe someone had decided he was getting too close to the truth about his wife – the initial assault on them had happened in the Sheraton before the Russian agent had a chance even to talk to him, after all.

He shook the thought from his mind. He'd known for some time that there was more to Sir Richard Eden than met the eye – but a traitor who would order his assassination in the heart of Cairo? Hawke couldn't imagine the old man making such an order against him, and as for the culprit being Scarlet Sloane or Ryan – or Alex… it was impossible to accept.

That left Lexi Zhang, and he didn't have such a hard time believing that – but she could have killed him at any time – the thought of her somehow engaging Apache attack helicopters to kill him was ridiculous, not to mention the fact she was Chinese and those currently hunting him were all British.

His mind spun with questions but there wasn't an answer in sight. Clearly Agent Snowcat knew more than she was letting on, but as she said, now was not the time to be pursuing the matter.

Because now they were trapped inside the Khufu Pyramid by an Apache chopper which had started to unload its chain gun on them once again.

CHAPTER TWENTY-SIX

With the chopper still blasting huge chunks of limestone out of the Khufu Pyramid, Hawke knew he had to switch his mind to battle mode and do something fast. In a surprise attack situation it was never a good idea to focus on strategy. The smart thing to do was work out what to do about it – think tactically. Revenge came later.

"Give me your weapon!"

"What?" Snowcat looked at him like he was insane.

"Your gun – hand it to me – now!"

"Russian agents do not give their guns to British soldiers."

"*Former* soldier – now I'm just a loveable rogue. Now hand it over." He put his hand out for the weapon and waggled his fingers.

"This is most unorthodox…"

"It's now or never, Snowcat!"

She handed him the compact Makarov and he checked it was loaded and ready to fire. Two rounds.

"What are you going to do?"

Hawke jabbed the gun in the direction of the Apache. "I'm going to shoot that bloody thing down."

"You can't bring down a helicopter with a handgun, Hawke – especially an Apache!"

"I'll be the judge of that."

She sighed. "And just how the hell are you going to do it?"

"We're going to split up. You're going to sprint over there toward that pyramid…"

"The Pyramid of Khafre?"

"If you say so, love."

She looked at him with horror on her face. "You want me to be bait for an Apache helicopter's chain gun?"

Hawke shrugged his shoulders. "Unless you think you stand a better chance of shooting it down?"

Snowcat looked at him and nodded in reluctant agreement. "All right, I'll do it. I am not afraid of anything."

"Good job – you go toward the Pyramid of Coffee or whatever you said it was called, and the bastard will turn to fire at you. When he turns I'll get a clear shot at his rear rotor and bring him down."

"This will work?"

"The slightest obstruction in those rotor blades at the back and that thing's uncontrollable," he said coolly.

"And if you miss?"

"If I miss you get shot with the chain gun and then they'll turn around and put a hundred holes in me as well."

She smiled awkwardly. "In that case, I'd prefer it, Englishman, if you did *not* miss."

"Trust me, I won't."

Hawke watched Snowcat sprint from the entrance of the Pyramid of Khufu past the ancient boat pits and over the road. Just as he thought it would, the Apache responded in an instant, turning to port and moving forward slightly to close in on its new target. The sound of the engine was overwhelming from so close, and its downwash was kicking up a storm of sand and grit.

As Snowcat approached the Pyramid of Khafre, the Apache opened fire. Hawke watched in horror as a trail of bullets flicked up in the sand behind her with the terrible *chak chak chak* sound of the chain gun as it unloaded its lethal thirty mil rounds all over the young Russian woman.

Hawke slowed his breathing and remained calm. The image of Hugo Zaugg trying to kill Lea on the cable car entered his mind. For a second he was standing in the snow of the Alps and taking aim through the sniper's rifle, but then the cold of the snow was washed away with the heat of the Egyptian desert – now it was another woman's life in his hands.

He raised the pistol and cradled it with both hands. He squinted as he took aim, and prepared to take the shot. He knew bringing down a chopper with a single shot from a handgun was going to be hard work – almost impossible, some would say, but he also knew it had been done before.

In terms of its capacity to remain airborne, any chopper, Apaches included, was a very delicate piece of machinery. As a helicopter pilot himself, Hawke knew the function of the tail rotor was to stop the rest the machine spinning around under the force of the main rotors. It applied a counter torque to the force created by the main engine, and kept the whole thing airborne and stable.

Firing at the main rotor blades would achieve nothing. It was common knowledge among those who'd been there that Huey pilots back in the Vietnam War would use their main rotor blades to clear landing areas by pruning tree branches.

He'd done something similar on a mission in the Sierra Leone jungle, hovering his way down into a hole in the trees and having to slice his way back out of it because the downwash had sucked the canopies back over the top of the chopper. It was messy, and noisy, and wrecked the blades, but it was easier to replace a blade than a Special Forces operative so the Top Brass turned a blind eye. The tail rotor, on the other hand, was nowhere near as robust, and yet crucial to the stability of the aircraft.

"Fire!" Snowcat screamed. "They're getting too close to me!"

"No, we have to wait until they slow down or their speed will stabilize the chopper after I hit the rotor."

Having reached their target, the Apache slowed to a hover and turned gently in the hot air to fire the chain gun at the Russian agent for the second time.

"Hawke, this is getting a little too real right now!"

"Another second…"

A slow breath, a gentle squeeze of the trigger.

He fired the penultimate bullet in the Makarov's magazine and hoped for the best.

He wasn't disappointed.

The bullet struck one of the tail rotors and because of the chopper's reduced hovering speed there was no longer enough lift on the vertical surfaces of the machine to help stabilize it.

Hawke watched as the pilot reacted to the loss of the tail rotor, altering the pitch of the main rotors and adjusting his speed, but it wasn't enough. Finally he tried to cut the engine to allow autorotation – the force of the air rushing up as they descended – to force the rotors around, but they didn't have the height.

They had been too greedy in their pursuit of Snowcat and a controlled descent was impossible. It plummeted toward the ground and just before it hit, Hawke directed his final shot into the fuel tank and the crippled helicopter went up in an enormous explosion, leaving nothing but a burned out shell amidst a hot fireball that fell through the sky and crashed into the sand at the southern edge of the Great Pyramid.

As the explosion dissipated and the smoke and dust began to clear, he saw Agent Snowcat was lying in the hot sand, motionless. He ran to her, and checked her vital signs. She was still alive, but her breathing was shallow and she had a flesh would on the side of her head. It looked like she had been knocked unconscious in the shockwave of the chopper when it exploded.

Hawke pulled her over his shoulder in a fireman's lift and pocketed the Makarov before making a call to Eden. Both men of few words, it took just seconds to establish that Ryan had nailed down the Karnak Temple as the location of the other half of the map, and that Eden would send a chopper to pick them up and take them to the airport.

One step backwards, and two steps forwards, Hawke thought. That's how you get where you want.

CHAPTER TWENTY-SEVEN

Joe Hawke watched the runway turn into a blur and then drop away beneath them as the small jet raced up into the Egyptian sky. Far to the west, he saw the massive city of Cairo sprawling either side of the Nile, and rising up behind Giza were the famous pyramids, lit bright yellow in the hot sun. He could still see the columns of smoke from the carnage he had left behind in the shape of a burning Apache, and he guessed by now it would be surrounded by emergency crews, army and police.

As they briefed him on what they had discovered about Osiris, he sensed more tension than was normal among his friends. Ryan was even quieter than usual and seated at the desk on the starboard side of the Gulfstream, buried in a laptop, and Alex was opposite him leafing through Mazzarro's notebooks.

As for him, he watched Snowcat gently breathing on the couch, still unconscious from the shockwave of the explosion back at Giza. Lexi had tended and dressed the wounds on her arm and head and said they weren't serious.

Hawke heard the Russian's words again – what she had said about how his enemies were closer then he thought – and glanced at the faces of his friends for a few seconds. Could it be true that one of these people had ordered the hit on him in Cairo? Now, in their company, it seemed an even more unlikely possibility than it had done in the heat of the fire-fight down in the pyramids.

He watched Scarlet rise from her seat. She wasted no time in hitting the mini-bar, and cracked open a vodka miniature, downing it in one. "Better," was all she said as she pulled a second one from the fridge.

She turned to Hawke. "Tough day at the office, darling?"

"You could say that," he said. "We spent half the morning on a guided tour of Cairo courtesy of some kind of renegade British Special Forces. They even laid on a helicopter."

"A helicopter?" Eden said, eyes narrowing.

"Apache," Hawke replied. "Big black thing with more arms than an octopus. British, as well."

Eden frowned. "I was afraid of this."

"Afraid of what?" Hawke asked.

"I'll explain later – our Russian friend is waking up."

Hawke watched as Snowcat slowly came back to life after the shockwave, and he offered her some water as she sat up and rubbed her head. She mumbled some words in Russian and blinked a few times to regain her focus.

"How long was I out for?" she asked, looking down at her wristwatch.

"Less than half an hour," Hawke said quietly. "We're on a plane going to Luxor."

"Woah – things move fast around you, Mr Hawke."

"They seem to, yes," he said, smiling.

He gave her more water and some time to regain her composure, but his compulsion to know the truth moved him to speak with her about his wife. He had waited long enough.

As he spoke, she unbuckled her seat belt and pulled a hair tie loose, shaking her long, blonde hair free.

"So you want to know what I have to say?"

He nodded. "First, I want your real name. I'm not calling you Snowcat for the rest of the mission."

She smiled and dipped her head in agreement. "My name is Maria Kurikova."

"Thanks, and pleased to meet you, Maria. I'm Joe, so you can leave the 'Mr Hawke' stuff at the door, all right?"

She smiled and nodded her head.

"So why are we going to Luxor?" she asked.

Hawke explained. "Apparently Ryan and Alex worked out that a French Egyptologist called… what was his name again?"

"Champollion," Ryan called over.

"That guy, anyway," Hawke continued, "he discovered a tablet in the desert with similar glyphs to those on our map, and tried to decode it but made very little progress before he died. Decades later some other guy…"

"Pernier."

"Thanks, mate… well, *that* guy discovered something called the Phaistos Disc, an ancient Greek artefact…"

"Minoan," Ryan said. "Do you want me to tell this story?"

"Thanks, but no thanks, mate. Anyway Pernier and Mazzarro used the information on the disc along with Champollion's earlier work and began to create a sort of decoder…"

"A deciphering matrix."

Hawke gave the younger man a look and Ryan shrugged his shoulders and walked off down the aisle to get a drink.

"Anyway, thanks to the deciphering matrix, Ryan and Alex here were able to make sense of the map."

"But we only had half the map, remember," Alex said. "Hi, I'm Alex Reeve, by the way."

"Hello. Maria Kurikova."

They shook hands.

"Like I say, we only had the Poseidon half. We knew from Mazzarro Senior's work on the Phaistos Disc that there had been some kind of ancient war when Poseidon and Osiris fought over possession of the map, and that's why it was torn in half."

"And that's when we realized the other half must be the Tomb of Osiris," Ryan said, returning with a large neat whisky. He took a gulp. "The only problem was where exactly."

"Abydos, surely," Maria said. "The Great Osiris Temple is in Abydos."

"The Great *Temple* is, sure," Ryan said. "And there's another smaller temple dedicated to him at Karnak, but we were looking for a tomb, don't forget. His temple is well-known, and he has a temple because he was a god. But just like with Poseidon, now we know Osiris was really here on earth, we know he must have a tomb, and that's different from a temple."

"I understand…"

"Luckily for us, it looks like Poseidon's trust for Osiris didn't run very far, and he had the location of his rival's tomb written on his half of the map, so now we know where the tomb of Osiris is."

"And it's in Karnak," Alex said. "Just like the smaller temple dedicated to him."

"But not in the same place. The tomb is deep underground, beneath the Temple of Amun, so that's why we're flying to Luxor."

Scarlet got up from her chair and yawned. "Get all that?"

Maria laughed. "I think so…"

"All that matters," Hawke said with quiet determination, "is that we get there before Maxim

Vetrov, stop him getting into the tomb and acquiring the other half of the map, and rescue Lea and Brad."

"Damn right," Scarlet said.

"Then we can translate Osiris's half and finally discover the location of the Tomb of Eternity," Ryan said, finishing his whisky.

Hawke eyed the empty glass with concern, but said nothing. He'd been there.

"Because in that tomb," Eden said quietly, "there exists knowledge that has been hidden from mankind for thousands, or perhaps *millions* of years…"

"And hopefully gold," Scarlet said, causing a subdued ripple of laughter in the cabin.

Hawke waited until the others had returned to their seats and then he lowered his voice. "Now no one's trying to kill us any more, and we've got the Indiana Jones stuff out the way, I have some questions for you."

Maria smiled. "I thought you might, Joe."

"Why were British agents trying to kill us back there?" He glanced at the display on the bulkhead wall to read the flight information. "I can see why they might want to take you out, but not me. At this speed we'll be in Luxor in less than an hour, so you don't have much time to tell me."

Maria inhaled deeply and took her dusty, torn suit jacket off. She draped it over the seat beside her and fixed her eyes on Hawke.

"Joe…those men were ordered to kill us in order to silence me and to stop you."

"Stop me?" he asked, incredulous. "Stop me from doing what? And what does this have to do with my wife?"

"They don't want me to tell you what I am about to tell you, Joe."

Hawke clenched his jaw and rubbed a hand over his tired face. “I’ve had just about enough of secrets. Tell me what you know, and tell me now.”

Without a pause, Maria started to speak, calm and quiet. “Elizabeth Compton was a Russian agent, Joe.”

Hawke narrowed his eyes in shock and disbelief. “What are you talking about? Liz worked for the Ministry of Defence as a translator. She was fluent in German and Spanish.”

“And Russian.”

“No! She didn’t speak a word of Russian.”

Maria offered a sympathetic smile. “I’m sorry, but she *did* speak Russian. I spoke with her myself in the language.”

Hawke was shell-shocked at the revelation and could barely control the thoughts of incredulity and despair that raced into his mind so fast he couldn’t begin to process them all. “You knew my wife?”

The Russian woman nodded respectfully. “Agent Swallowtail and I spoke on several occasions.”

“Agent Swallowtail?”

She nodded and Hawke recoiled in horror. Before she had died, Olivia Hart had used that word to describe the operation to murder Liz, and now the Russian agent was telling him it was his wife’s codename. He felt like the plane was falling apart all around him and he was tumbling to earth without a parachute.

“Your wife was half-Russian, Joe. I know she kept that secret from the Ministry in London, but she never told you either?”

Hawke clenched his jaw as he shook his head in reluctant confirmation of her question. “No, she never told me. In fact, I find it hard to believe. You could be spinning me a web of lies for any number of reasons.”

“I’m not. Please look at this.”

Maria handed Hawke a Russian identity card and passport from inside her suit jacket. The passport was an old one, now many years out of date, but like the card, it contained a picture of a woman who was very clearly his wife.

Subconsciously he shook his head as he stared at the documents. A shaft of sunlight shone through the window and illuminated the tiny images of his wife's face as if to highlight the terrible deceit that was unfolding before him. "I just can't accept this."

Maria pointed at the Cyrillic letters: Елизавета Комптон. "This is her name – Elizaveta Compton."

"Elizaveta?" Hawke asked. "Her name was Elizabeth… and for just one day it was Elizabeth Hawke."

"Her English name was Elizabeth, but her Russian name was Elizaveta. Your wife's mother was Russian, Joe. She was an architect from Kaluga."

"That's not right… Liz told me that before her mother died she'd spent her life in the south of England."

"No. Her mother was part of a Soviet trade delegation that travelled to the West during the détente period. She spent many weeks in England, and that is when she met William Compton. She defected out of love for her boyfriend, later her husband, but her heart was always with the Soviet Union."

Hawke looked into the Russian's eyes but didn't know what to say. He wanted her to say that all of this was an elaborate lie, some kind of terrible deceit designed to manipulate him and slow down the hunt for the map. He knew in his heart it wasn't so.

"Elizaveta grew up and joined MI6, Joe, long after the Soviet Union had collapsed. They thought her background was ideal, but with the influence of her mother she was easily turned by FSB agents and she became a double-agent, working for both sides. All of this was long before she met you."

Hawke's heart began to pound in his chest. He'd tried to keep a lid on things while Maria was speaking, but now it was all getting too much. Here was a woman he had known for less than a few hours telling him more about his wife's true life story than she herself had in all the years he'd known her.

He got out of the seat and walked to the drinks cabinet at the end of the plane. After a few seconds opening doors and drawers he located a bottle of vodka and some ice and made a pretty unhealthy drink. He knocked it back and felt it burn its way south. He didn't flinch. What, after all, was pain like this compared with what he was going through in his mind?

He looked back up the slim jet and watched the Russian for a moment. She was sitting in her seat and staring forward, motionless. Perhaps her eyes were closed. Perhaps she was a liar. Sunlight poured through the tiny porthole and shone on her blonde hair.

He poured two more vodkas and shut his eyes tight. He didn't like to close his eyes anymore. That world was where Liz lived, and now he realized he had never known her it tore him up to see her face in his mind's eye. Right now she was laughing at a joke he had just made while they were rowing on the Serpentine… Now she was standing beside him on a balcony in Madrid as they clinked glasses to toast their decision to move in together.

Was it really all nothing but lies?

He walked the vodkas up the plane and handed Maria one of them. "Some people drink to remember, others drink to forget. What kind are you?"

She smiled and took the drink, but said nothing. Like other Russians and Poles he had known, she made short work of the vodka and set the glass down on the seat beside her. The smell of the spirit mingled with the scent of her perfume, and with the rush of the previous shot coursing through his veins and the shock of everything he suddenly saw her in another way – she was incredibly beautiful, for one thing, but she was smart, together, confident. A lot like Lea, except without the humor, maybe…

"What?" she said, half a smile crossing her red lips.

"Nothing. You just remind me of someone, that's all. Listen, Maria. You told me that you knew about my wife's murder, but all you've told me about is her background – that she was half-Russian, and her codename was Swallowtail."

Another sympathetic nod, another bewitching smile. "I know."

"Now I need you to tell me the rest." He downed the vodka and swallowed hard. "I need to know about Operation Swallowtail."

She looked at him for a long time before replying. He saw sadness in her eyes, and braced himself for what was coming.

"Joe, Operation Swallowtail was a highly covert mission to kill your wife, and I think you've already figured this much out."

He nodded grimly. "Yes. A good friend of mine with senior contacts in the British military told me the kill order came from within the UK. Is this true?"

"Yes. The kill order was given by James Matheson."

The words hit Hawke like a jackhammer and a stunned silence filled the cabin. His mind spun into dizzy chaos in his attempt to process the information he had just been given.

"James Matheson? Do you know what you're saying, Maria?"

She nodded. "Of course."

"James Matheson is the British Foreign Secretary."

"I know this."

A raw, burning rage rose inside him like acid. He had personally met Matheson in a hotel room in Switzerland. He had shaken that son of a bitch's hand and taken orders from him, and the whole time he had been the man who had ordered his wife's execution. Now, thinking back to that day in Geneva, he recalled how Matheson had seemed anxious and on edge during their meeting, particularly when speaking with him personally.

He leaned closer to Maria. "Are you absolutely sure about this?"

"Yes, of course, I have evidence if you need it. Remember, she was a respected and valuable FSB asset. When the British killed her it upset many people in Russia with great influence. Her killers were identified within days."

"Why did they kill her, Maria? And I want the truth."

"Because she was getting too close to the truth, Joe."

"The truth about what?"

"About Matheson and the Athanatoi."

Hawke's head began to spin. He felt almost drunk with confusion, dazed by the sheer amount of information he was supposed to digest and process and react to.

"Matheson knows about all this?"

She nodded. "We think so, yes. In fact…"

"What?"

"We think he might be a part of the Athanatoi."

"This is… *insanity*."

She moved closer to him and placed a hand gently on his arm. "Are you sure you're okay?"

He pulled away from her and scowled. "No, I'm not okay. But I will be, in time."

He walked to the window and watched the desert passing beneath them as they raced south to Luxor. For a moment he wondered if all this might be enough finally to bring him down, but then he remembered what his father had always told him – no matter what, never give in and never give up.

He turned back to Maria. “I was told the killer was a Cuban assassin called Alfredo Lazaro, and that he was killed in a raid in Thailand.”

Maria leaned back a little and narrowed her eyes in confusion. “The hit-man was Lazaro, yes, or the Spider as he calls himself, but he wasn’t killed in any ambush in Thailand. He’s not dead, Joe.”

“Not dead? Are you certain?”

“For sure. Because of what he did to Elizaveta, he’s on a lot of lists in Moscow. The sort of lists you don’t want to be on, you know? I can promise you he is not dead. He was last seen in Mexico about six weeks ago.”

Hawke nodded. He knew well enough that governments kept hit-lists of enemies of the state, but if Moscow thought it was going to get to the Spider before he did then there was going to be a lot of serious disappointment in the Kremlin. As for Matheson… that sort of treachery deserved the ultimate punishment.

He breathed out slowly and took another shot of the vodka. He had to calm himself, but it was tough when the problems kept mounting. Lea was gone, snatched by Vetrov, and now he had just discovered that the two men responsible for his wife’s brutal murder were both alive.

And that was a wrong that had to be righted.

CHAPTER TWENTY-EIGHT

Luxor

Hawke knew Vetrov's plaything was the A380, and noted with dismay that Luxor Airport's runway was, at ten thousand feet, more than long enough to accommodate the giant Airbus both at landing and takeoff. This was confirmed when he looked down from the tiny Gulfstream and saw the A380 parked neatly on the apron to the east of the airport.

Vetrov had beaten them to it, and there was no way to know how far ahead they were. There was also no way to know if Lea Donovan and Bradley Karlsson were still alive. The anger rose in Hawke like a wave of lava as he thought about what he had seen Vetrov doing to Alex back at the dacha, and then imagined the same happening to Lea, somewhere out in the Nile.

Making matters worse was Maria. He was battling hard to put his wife and her slaying out of his mind, but every time he saw the Russian woman's face he lost another part of that battle and had to refocus all over again.

The sleek Gulfstream hit the Luxor tarmac and deployed the reverse thrusters. Moments later it was taxiing to the airport and pulling up not far from the gargantuan A380. Hawke registered with disgust as he read the words VETROV INDUSTRIES written in black on the side of it.

As they walked down the steps of the aircraft, Eden was already on the phone, organizing back-up.

"Peter Henderson again?" Hawke asked him, referring to the British Ambassador.

Eden was hard to read, but there was something strange about the way he looked at Hawke when he replied. "No, an old friend of mine from way back – an Egyptian named Arafa. He's more than half-way up the greasy pole of the Egyptian Army – a Brigadier General. He's going to send a few chaps to help us out, but it might take him a few hours to sort it."

"When we say back-up, we're talking about…"

"Between fifteen and twenty soldiers from the Field HQ of the Southern Military Region in Assiut."

Hawke nodded, always grateful for back-up. It often made all the difference.

"Commander?"

"Man named Koura. He's a *naqib*, or captain, which makes you the ranking officer in command of the mission."

"I was a sergeant, Rich."

Eden gave him a knowing glance. "We both know you were a major before you got demoted. You'll carry that rank today."

"Come off it, no one's going to take orders from a burned-out English Special Forces sergeant out here." He looked up at the Egyptian sun. "Koura can lead his own men."

"Naturally, but he knows literally nothing about what's going on here, Hawke. No idea of the big picture at all. I'm not arguing the point with you. You're the OC today and that's the end of it."

Hawke backed down. Maybe he could lay some other ghosts to rest today as well – like the day those bastards knocked him down to sergeant. But something was bothering him. "Why this Arafa bloke? Why not just call Henderson?"

"We'll talk about that later." Eden put his hands in his pocket.

"Looks like there's going to be a lot of talking later."

Eden's reply was short and clipped, in his usual style. "If we survive the day, yes."

Hawke laughed. "I mean it, Richard. I want answers."

"And you'll get them but for now we're behind Vetrov, so let's get on with it."

They clambered into a couple of hired SUVs and went their separate ways. Sir Richard Eden, Alex, Ryan and Maria went to the Hilton Luxor to set up a base camp while Hawke, Scarlet and Lexi tooled up and headed straight to the Karnak Temple.

It was time to say hello to Osiris.

*

Maxim Vetrov watched eagerly as Kosma placed the explosives on the ancient wall. With Dario Mazzarro's help, it hadn't taken long to work out that the other half of the map was in a secret chamber beneath the Tomb of Osiris in the Karnak Temple. They were now standing at the entrance to this chamber, sealed up countless centuries ago by unknown hands.

Kosma finished his work while Kodiak kept Lea and Karlsson covered with a compact machine pistol. He wanted to kill them, and had told them so, but Vetrov had ordered him to keep them alive. They may turn out to be useful, he had said.

"Do it!" barked Vetrov, sensing his destiny drawing ever closer. "Blow the wall!"

Kosma obeyed and detonated the explosives, blasting the ancient stones to smithereens with the modern technology. When the dust settled, they made their way into the hidden recess behind the wall and descended into the darkness.

The tunnel quickly narrowed and the ceiling grew ever lower until they had to crouch to make their way through to the end. The walls were covered in glyphs and constructed of solid blocks of limestone, perfectly fitted together in a way even modern tools would struggle to replicate. Vetrov slid his hand along them in awe as he studied the workmanship and the hieroglyphs.

He could feel his fate racing toward him like a new dawn. Here, deep beneath the surface of Luxor, far below the Temple of Amun, was the Tomb of Osiris – a real man-god who walked the earth for countless millennia. But like Poseidon, he had been killed and his powerful rule brought to an end, and Vetrov knew who had done it.

The Athanatoi.

They were the ones responsible for Poseidon's death, and they too had killed Osiris, and all the others.

But not him.

He would never let them kill him, because he knew who they were, and the power they wielded. He also knew he was about to seize that power for himself. Dealing with the Athanatoi would be a pleasure he would savor, but it could keep for now. Now, he had more urgent concerns, like securing the final piece of this most ancient of puzzles from Osiris's cadaverous grasp, and sacrificing Donovan and Karlsson to the real gods. Those who had to be appeased.

After that Hawke and his pathetic, indigent army of drop-outs and mavericks could easily be wiped out. Then there would be nothing between him and the greatest destiny any mortal man could ever dream of.

Nothing.

CHAPTER TWENTY-NINE

Hawke scanned the area around the main temple at Karnak. He had never seen anything like it before in his entire life. The site was immense – the ruins he was looking at were all that was left of the ancient city of Thebes, and included the great Temple of Amon. To the west he saw the Nile Quay, which once stretched out into the river when the Nile was higher. Today, the Nile was half a kilometer away through the suburbs of Luxor.

The sandstone and red granite of the ruins was a bright orange in the sunset, and the heat of the day drifted in shimmers into the early twilight. It was late now, and they had arrived at the site as fast as they could, but judging by the dead security guards, it wasn't fast enough and Vetrov was already inside the hidden chamber.

"We have to get in there," he said, still surveying the surrounding area for useful strategic points that might come in handy during the fight. "There's still no sign of Lea and Brad, but while there's a chance they're still alive we can't waste any time. What's the quickest way there?"

"Through there," Scarlet said, pointing at the Precinct of Amun-Ra. "If we go that way there's natural cover, and then we just cut through the east part of the complex and we're in the fight." She lit a cigarette and cocked her pistol.

Lexi turned to Scarlet. "Do you *have* to smoke those damn things all the time?"

"Why don't you…"

“Listen,” Hawke said, cutting Scarlet’s reply dead. “We don’t have time for arguments. We’re going to get Lea and Brad back and take Vetrov out. Everyone clear on that?”

They readied their weapons and moved forward. The usual silence fell on their conversation as they prepared for the fight, each thinking things through in their minds to avoid any mistakes.

They made their way through the dusty ruins, now bereft of the usual horde of tourists because of the late hour. Hawke watched Scarlet and Lexi with pride as they put their differences away and worked together. Lexi’s commitment to the mission since her arrival in Venice was clear, and he had decided to take her word for what happened in Xian. He knew Scarlet was less convinced, but then that was her – always the cynic.

They rounded the east wall of the Temple of Ramasses II and then sprinted between the Sacred Lake and the south wall of the great Festival Hall of Thutmose III as they approached the Temple of Taharka.

“It’s just through there, Scarlet said, jabbing the muzzle of her gun toward an immense wall covered in Egyptian hieroglyphics. “That’s the Cachette Court, and just through there is the part of the complex we’re after – the Ramasses III Temple.”

“And you know this, how?” Lexi asked.

“Because I studied a map of the place on the way here. It’s called pre-mission planning and the SAS are rather good at it. We’re not all just guns and smoke grenades you realize, Lex.”

Hawke suppressed a smile, and not just at the thought of Cairo Sloane studying maps of the Karnak Temple Complex. Despite their superficial differences, he knew they were a lot more like each other than either would ever admit.

As they drew closer to the Amun Temple they heard a loud explosion and felt the ground rock beneath their feet. The shockwave was so great it toppled some of the stones at the top of one of the ruins and they came crashing down into the colonnaded courtyard.

"Bastards are blowing their way into the hidden chamber," Hawke said.

They reached the entrance to the temple, and immediately saw the devastation caused by the explosion. Rubble and dust lay all over the floor of the entrance and in the far wall, and where once had been impressive glyphs of Osiris himself, was an enormous, ragged hole with smoke drifting out of it. Among the rubble, like rubbish, were the corpses of half a dozen security guards, some crushed by the rock that had been blown out of the wall by Vetrov's explosives.

"I see we have another lover of antiquity," Scarlet said as she surveyed the destruction and booted a piece of wall out of her way, totally ignoring the dead bodies. "Those glyphs were thousands of years old."

Hawke nodded but ignored the comment. "Let's go."

They walked into the smoke and found themselves descending inside the tunnel along a shallow slope. Keeping to the walls and guns raised in firing position, Hawke led the way along the ancient tunnel. He paused for a moment to listen.

"I can hear something up ahead somewhere. Maybe we're not that far behind."

"Smashing," Scarlet said. Her words were punctuated by the sound of her moving the cocking handle on her Heckler & Koch submachine gun. "Let's blow some balls off."

Hawke rolled his eyes in the semi-darkness of the tunnel and gave them the hand signal to move on.

They reached the end of the tunnel and Hawke peered around the corner. "Looks like this thing goes deeper than we thought. Whoever I heard is long gone – we have a way to go yet before we catch them up."

*

Maxim Vetrov's eyes widened when he saw the cavern beneath the temple. It was not as grand as he had hoped, but there was no doubt they were in the right place. An enormous statue of Osiris was looming in the darkness on the far wall, and at its base was a small doorway leading into another chamber.

"What was that?" Vetrov said, his voice echoing in the cold, silent cavern.

"What?" Kodiak said.

"I thought I heard water – coming from there." Vetrov pointed his freshly loaded Grach at the doorway in the base of the Osiris statue. "We have no time to waste."

They went through the gateway and found themselves in a rectangular tomb decorated with ornate paintings of the Egyptian gods and goddesses and colourful hieroglyphs all over the walls. The tomb was damp, and musty, and against the far wall was an angular sarcophagus.

"We meet at last, Osiris," Vetrov said as he paced forward and ran his hands over the stonework. Then he turned wide-eyed and saw what was beyond the sarcophagus – a great pool filled with green water. "So the legends are true," he said as he stared at the water. "The true Tomb of Osiris really is protected by the Nile after all – and by the gods who swim in it." As he spoke, Lea saw a movement in the water.

Vetrov moved slowly around the room, no longer hurried by any sense of danger. He caressed the stone edges of the sarcophagus and walked toward the pool of water, his hands trembling with anticipation. He mumbled what sounded like some kind of mantra, and continued talking to himself as he stared into the water of the pool, always keeping a safe distance. This was a man who knew better than most what was lurking beneath the surface.

This was more than a tomb to Vetrov. This was a vindication of everything he had spent his life believing. His rage when he had heard about the discovery of the vault of Poseidon now paled into insignificance when compared to his – the discovery of the tomb of Osiris.

For most, such a discovery would be the crowning achievement of their careers, but to Maxim Vetrov this place was a mere stepping stone to the greatest secret on earth. To most men, Osiris was a god, but to Vetrov he was merely a man who had harnessed the oldest and most powerful energy in the universe, and now he was going to seize that power for himself.

And he was closer than ever before.

Closer than anyone else.

"Kosma – have the men open the sarcophagus. I want the other half of the map and I have waited long enough."

Kosma selected a few men and some equipment and obediently padded over to the sarcophagus. It didn't take them long to lift a gap under the lid with their crowbars and then lash some ropes underneath the heavy slab to raise it up. Kosma had the strength of at least two men, and with the other men also heaving, a few moments later the lid scraped and crunched its way off the top of the sarcophagus and crashed to the ground. Professional excavators would have secured it by tying it off, but Vetrov was only interested in the contents of the tomb, not preserving anything for humanity. Humanity, after all, belonged to him now.

He approached the sarcophagus, his face a study of tentative anxiety mixed with clear madness. He leaned inside and a moment later held up a roll of parchment. “I have it! I have it at last!”

*

Lea sighed inwardly as a wave of despair washed over her. Maxim Vetrov now had the entire map and Dario Mazzarro to translate it. He would reach the source of eternal life first and become an immortal – impervious to attack.

He walked toward her but stopped when he saw some movement in the water. “What’s this?” he said, moving over to the pool. “Ah – the crocodiles are here. This pool is connected to the Nile, you see.” He thought for a few moments, stared at his prisoners, then the parchment and then back to the prisoners.

“I was planning on doing this later, on the river, but now seems like a more fortuitous time. Bring me the woman.”

Kosma moved forward and grabbed Lea roughly by the shoulders. He dragged her across the tomb toward Vetrov and the pool.

“Don’t you touch her, you coward!” Karlsson shouted. “If you need to sacrifice someone to your damned gods then make it me. Just leave her alone.”

Vetrov tipped his head as he considered Karlsson’s plea. Lea watched the Russian billionaire as he thought the proposition over, staring at the American with nothing but hatred in his ice-cold eyes.

“Very well, in that case Kodiak, bring me the American.”

Kodiak waved a pistol in Karlsson's face and made him march closer to Vetrov and the crocodiles in the pool.

"Be careful what you wish for, Navy Seal," Vetrov said.

"Kiss my ass, Vetrov," was all Karlsson said.

Vetrov raised his arm and fired the Grach at Karlsson.

Lea jumped with the shock of the gunshot, which struck the American in the throat and sent him stumbling backwards to the water's edge.

"No!" Lea gasped, and covered her mouth in shock. Bradley Karlsson's eyes swivelled madly as he tried to make sense of things. He was coughing blood and trying to talk, but just managed to stop himself going over the edge. His hands were clutching at the blood which now poured from his wounded throat and he was unable to react when Kodiak turned to him and gave him a gentle nudge with the barrel of his gun.

Lea was unable to move in Kosma's iron grip and watched with horror as Karlsson fell back into the pool, his broad frame hitting the surface of the green water with a tremendous splash and sending a spray of bloody water over the wall opposite them. She was numb with shock as a large crocodile set upon the American, sinking its teeth into the flesh of his neck and shoulder. After a hideous moment when the two of them thrashed about for supremacy, the inevitable happened and the crocodile dragged him under the surface.

"You son of a bitch!" she screamed. She watched the pool desperately in the vain hope Karlsson might suddenly launch himself from the surface but it was silent, and she knew he was dead. The amount of blood in the water told her that, and now not only was Karlsson gone, but she was totally alone in the tomb with these psychopaths.

Vetrov chuckled. He was revelling in the American's death. "Don't get so distraught. He was being a gentleman and he put himself first. Sadly, he only bought you a few seconds of extra life, because now it is your turn to join your friend."

He paused and strutted around the tomb with his hands raised in the air. "This is my first act as a god! Behold it! You must celebrate your death – it is a wonderful and noble thing for a great and powerful immortal like me to use you as an offering to the gods above."

"You're not immortal yet, you arsehole," Lea said, struggling against Kosma's grip.

"It is only a matter of time, Miss Donovan. Time, of course, being a commodity you have just run out of." He waved the Grach in her face. "Go over there, please, and stand beside the crocodile pool."

She kicked against Kosma and began to scream.

"Hush… *hush please*," Vetrov said, raising his index finger to his lips to command her silence. "Please don't debauch this beautiful moment of sacrifice with ungracious behavior. Kosma – please help Miss Donovan to the pool."

CHAPTER THIRTY

Lea struggled against Kosma as he forced her over to the murky, bloody water. She saw with disgust that some of Karlsson's shredded clothes were floating on the surface. The terrifying reality of the situation struck her like a smack in the face. There was no one to help her – Karlsson was dead and she hadn't seen Hawke and the others since the Piazza San Marco in Venice when Eden ordered her to give chase to Kodiak and Mazzarro.

She looked at Vetrov's face – calm, measured, and clearly excited to an unnatural degree by her impending death. It looked like he could hardly wait as the giant Russian had manhandled her across the tomb, her boots kicking out vainly against his might and her screams heard by no one except the ghostly, silent faces on the hieroglyphs.

"This is the greatest moment of your short life, Miss Donovan," Vetrov said, his eyes rapaciously staring at the pool for the first sign of a crocodile. "Soon, you will be gone, but I will be alive forever, and free to impose my will on the human order for the rest of eternity."

"You're absolutely out of your mind, scumbag."

Her mind raced, but all she could do was play for time in the hope someone might intervene and stop this insanity from unfolding.

"I think not. I will shape a world where a tiny elite rules absolutely and forever, served by thousands of generations of slaves. What could be saner than that?"

"A lunatic asylum?"

"And," he replied, ignoring her remark, "there's nothing between me and my destiny except an old map and *them* of course."

Lea saw an opportunity to play for more time. "Who are you talking about?"

Vetrov couldn't resist. "Another curious mind – like your colleague Alex Reeve. She wanted to know the truth as well… but it will do neither of you any good. The real enemy are the *athanatoi*, Miss Donovan. Not me."

Before she could reply, he snapped his fingers at Kosma. "It's time for you to go now."

Then, the sound of gunfire and the blinding white light of muzzle flashes filled the tomb. Deafening shots rang out in the enclosed space and she heard the sound of Joe Hawke as he shouted orders for people to fan out.

She thought she was saved.

Vetrov spun around and aimed his Grach in the direction of the noise. He fired several shots and dived for cover. Kodiak followed suit, firing a couple of short, aggressive bursts from his Bizon and throwing himself behind the sarcophagus for cover. Kosma was slowest to respond, pushing Lea into the pool and moving behind one of the pillars that held up the tomb. The rest of Vetrov's men scattered in all directions as they tried to evade the onslaught of bullets tracing all around them, blasting the tomb walls to pieces in the savage attack.

Hawke led the charge, pushing into the tomb without fear and crouching down on one knee to spray a savage burst of fire from the Heckler & Koch MP5K he was gripping in his hands. His bullets traced over the heads of Vetrov and Kodiak, now cowering behind Osiris's Tomb, but he stopped to re-aim the weapon at one of Vetrov's men who was making a hasty retreat and trying to reach the door. Hawke took him out in a heartbeat, his bullets ripping through the man's chest and propelling him backwards into the water behind him.

And that was when he saw Lea in the pool – desperately trying to swim to the low wall which surrounded the water in order to pull herself out.

Hawke jumped to his feet and sprinted across the middle of the fire-fight to reach her on the other side of the tomb. He didn't see Kosma, who raised his gun and fired at him, narrowly missing his head and obliterating the base of the Osiris statue instead. Hawke's reaction was like lightning, putting his right foot out and throwing himself to the floor. He extended and swung his right arm under body and executed a perfect parkour diamond shoulder roll. Staying inches ahead of the bullets all the way he did a second roll and then he reached the pool.

"Joe, thank *God!* I thought I was dead."

"Not when I'm around you're bloody not. Take my arm!"

Bullets traced all around them as he wrenched her soaking body from the pool and pulled a Sig Sauer P228 from his belt. "Here, take this."

"With pleasure, babe," she said, instinctively checking it was loaded and ready to go.

They took cover behind one of the pillars as Scarlet and Lexi raked the back wall of the tomb with their submachine guns and blasted the decorative glyphs into thousands of irrecoverable pieces. Their efforts worked to keep Vetrov and Kodiak pinned down, but Kosma and the remaining goons were regrouping at the end of the tomb.

A soaking wet Lea scraped her hair back behind her ears and turned a sad face to Hawke. "They killed Brad, Joe."

Hawke made no reply, but clenched his jaw in anger. He knew the time for revenge was always later, and he also knew he could leave it to Scarlet Sloane, who would be crushed about this death, even if she never showed it.

"And Vetrov's got the other half of the map."

"Bollocks – has he?"

"Afraid so. He looked pretty damned smug about it, too."

"We shall just have to take it back off the twat then, won't we?"

Hawke felt the ground shake and peered around the pillar to see what was going on.

"What the hell is that?" Lea asked.

"Giant Russian bastard's got what looks like an old Kord down there."

Hawke watched as Kosma fired bursts from the chunky belt-fed machine gun. The Kord was a heavy machine gun used by the Russian Army, and when needed, by the Russian Police. With a rate of fire of over seven hundred anti-materiel rifle cartridges per minute it was not a weapon to disrespect.

Lea leaned in. "Problem?"

"Maybe. He's got Cairo and Lexi pinned down and it's eating up a fifty-round magazine like a hungry dog with a sausage."

The former Russian KGB man mercilessly fired the Kord at Scarlet and Lexi who had now both dived for cover to escape its lethal fire.

"Where do these guys keep all this kit?" Hawke asked, incredulous. As he spoke he reloaded his H&K and got ready for another assault on Vetrov.

"Tell me about it!" Lea said, also reloading her Sig. "*Every* time I go on holiday I forget to pack my heavy machine gun."

Hawke rolled his eyes and shook his head. "Really, even now you're still trying to be funny…"

"It's my Irish charm, Joe Hawke… it's what attracts you to me and don't deny it."

Hawke laughed. "Between your jokes and those Russians, this sodding elixir had bloody well better be worth it!"

Lea looked back at the pool and saw Karlsson's clothes, now no more than bloody rags floating on the surface of the water. She immediately felt guilty for trying to make Hawke laugh after the American had sacrificed himself to save her life, but it was the only way she knew how to survive.

On the other side of the tomb, Vetrov was attempting to escape using Kodiak for cover as he made his way to the tomb's entrance.

Hawke spun around the pillar and fired at him, the rounds from his H&K exploding in the plaster behind the Russian's head as he sprinted across the tomb's floor, parchment in hand. Hawke tried to take him down, but Kodiak was pouring heavy fire on them with his own weapon and forcing him to keep ducking for cover.

Vetrov was gone, and the order had gone out for his men to retreat. Kodiak, who was lean and fast, took the same route as his leader, but Kosma was slower. The giant Russian padded after them, obscured in the gun-smoke and plaster dust as he moved through the half light of the tomb. He shot at the glow-sticks in an attempt to plunge the place into darkness, but Lexi struck a fresh glow-stick and illuminated everything once again.

No longer pinned down by Kodiak's fire, Hawke spun around from the pillar and fired at Kosma with the MP5K. His bullets tore into the Russian's back and exploded out the other side of his body through his wide, heavy chest as if it were made of paper. He tried to call out but fell to his knees in the dust of the tomb floor where he swayed back and forth for a second before falling forward on his face and landing in the sandy dirt with an enormous crunching sound.

Lea frowned. “Damn it all, Joe Hawke! I wanted to put that bastard in the fish tank!” She waved the barrel of the Sig at the crocodile pool.

“Sorry… I thought you’d be happy.”

“I’ll get over it, I suppose – but Kodiak’s mine!”

“Fine with me – but we have to catch them before we can kill them, and I want to look in that big stone box before we leave.”

Hawke got up and gave the order to give chase to Vetrov and his men while he checked the sarcophagus for any other clues. Inside he saw the coffin of Osiris and beside it was a strange stone object shaped like a small shield and covered in more of the same hieroglyphics. He snapped a picture of it and emailed it to Ryan immediately before snatching it up and joining Lea, Scarlet and Lexi at the mouth of the tunnel and emerging into Luxor once again. Night had now fallen and it was dark and cool. Above them thousands of stars were shining over the Egyptian desert.

“Where are the bastards?” Lexi asked, scanning the temple complex.

“Could be anywhere,” Hawke said.

“Wait a minute,” Scarlet said. “Where’s Brad?”

Hawke and Lea shared a concerned glance.

“Well?” Scarlet repeated.

Hawke stepped toward her. “Cairo, listen…”

“What?” Scarlet said, peering over Hawke’s shoulder and looking back down the tunnel to the tomb. “He’s all right, isn’t he?”

“He’s dead, Scarlet,” Lea said flatly. “I’m sorry.”

“Dead?”

Lea nodded. "He died saving my life. I know how you felt about him, and…"

"You know fuck all about how I feel about anyone," Scarlet snapped. "Shit happens and we need to move on or we get killed."

Hawke knew she was burning up with rage on the inside, but he also knew the last thing Cairo Sloane would ever do was show that she cared about anyone, so he said nothing and moved on. "Everyone keep an eye out – if they're behind any of these pillars or walls we're just sitting ducks."

"They're not behind any pillars or walls," Lea said. "Look!"

A helicopter rose above the ruins, made into a silhouette by the full moon behind it.

"Great…" Scarlet said. "Where are my sodding cigarettes?"

Hawke watched as the chopper flew over them and turned sharply to the left.

"What now?" Lea said. She sounded deflated.

Lexi sighed and collapsed on a block of limestone. "He's won. It's over."

Hawke looked at her, incredulous. "Eh?"

"Vetrov – he's won. He has both halves of the map and Mazzarro. Nothing can stop him now."

"Don't be so defeatist," Hawke said. "It ain't over till it's over."

"You want to say that again?" Lea said, nodding at the line of police cars driving into the vast complex.

Hawke frowned. "Lea, call Eden and tell him we might be indisposed for a while."

"Damn it all!" Scarlet said. "Now we're well and truly f…"

"Never say die, Cairo," Hawke said, cutting her off. "You know that."

Seconds later they were surrounded by police cars, their flashing lights illuminating the great walls of the temples and pylons like multicolored strobes.

"You were saying?" Scarlet said.

*

Their Egyptian police cell was even less comfortable than they had expected, and they had plenty of time to consider it as well, because the authorities took hours before getting them for interview. It seemed the Minister of State for Antiquities Affairs was less than amused with their actions at the Karnak temple complex and particularly enraged about the discovery and then annihilation of the secret chamber of Osiris.

"It takes months for excavation permits to be approved by the Minister," Captain Mustafa Moussa of the Luxor police explained.

"We didn't excavate the tomb," Hawke said patiently. "We already explained this. The tomb was broken into and raided by a Russian named Maxim Vetrov."

"So you say, and yet there is no evidence of this mysterious Russian, but there is evidence that you raided and looted the tomb." Moussa raised the strange shield from a box on the floor and placed it on the desk in front of Hawke and Lea.

"Ah…"

"Ah, indeed," Moussa said. "You were holding this in your hands when we arrived at the complex, Mr Hawke. You still deny being a tomb raider?"

"There is *that* yes…"

Lea rolled her eyes. "This is insane, Captain Moussa! Why are you holding us here when the real culprit has the map and is probably halfway through translating it by now."

"Map?"

Now Hawke rolled his eyes. "Good work, Lea."

"Sorry…"

Moussa leaned forward and joined his hands. "Tell me about this map."

"Listen, we don't have time for this," Hawke said firmly. He had already worked out two ways he could get out of custody without the blessing of Captain Moussa and his men, but knew that would stir up a hornet's nest at the British Embassy in Cairo and wanted to save Eden the blowback.

"Wrong, you have all the time in the world," Moussa said. "You will start talking – and remember, your colleagues are being interrogated and we will be comparing your stories. If you are lying to us then…"

He was interrupted by a knock on the door.

"Come!"

A younger man in a uniform entered the room and they spoke rapidly in hushed Arabic for a few moments. While they conversed, Moussa's eyes narrowed and he stared at Hawke and Lea. He shouted at the junior man and waved him from the room with a string of what sounded like some fairly x-rated words. Then, he sighed deeply.

"You are free to go," the captain said at last. As he spoke, he shrugged his shoulders and shook his head.

Lea glanced at Hawke and then back to Moussa, her face full of hope once again. "I'm sorry?"

"Don't be sorry," Hawke said. "Be gone…" He got up and pushed his chair under the desk.

"But why?" Lea asked, following Hawke's lead and getting up from her chair.

Moussa sighed. "Because when a police captain in Luxor gets a telephone call from the Office of the

President of Egypt telling him to let you go, he lets you go. That is why."

Hawke and Lea shared a quick glance and could barely believe their luck. Hawke reached out for the shield, but Moussa slammed his hand down on it and pulled it away.

"No, my friend. Your liberty you can have, but this stays with Egypt."

CHAPTER THIRTY-ONE

It was after midnight by the time Captain Moussa took the phone call that released them from custody and now their options were limited. Vetrov had both halves of the Map of Immortality and was still holding Mazzarro as a hostage.

On the upside, Ryan and Alex assured everyone it would take Mazzarro at least a day to decipher the map – they knew because they were busy doing the same thing with their fragment of it, so for now, they had done everything they could and it was just a matter of killing time – just one night in Luxor and then onward into whatever hell Vetrov was planning on creating in the Tomb of Eternity.

Eden had not only used his contacts in London and Cairo to have them released from Moussa's custody, but had come through for everyone once again and booked some suites in the Luxor Hilton. The luxurious rooms overlooked the Nile and included balconies, spas and massage tables. Hawke knew Eden had money, but this was getting ridiculous.

Outside their suites, they stood on private patios with cold drinks and watched the sun set over the Nile. The desert air was still warm around them as the moon rose over the east bank of the river, illuminating the date palms and turning them into ghostly silhouettes against a black sky.

"I didn't realize you liked roughing it," Hawke said, turning to Eden with a cold beer in his hand and a cheeky grin on his unshaven face. For the first time since

Lea was snatched in Venice, Hawke was able to stop worrying about her.

Eden, looking as ever the perfect gent in his crisp white suit with silk pocket square, took a look around him. "Oh this? Well, wealth does bring certain advantages, but of course the counterbalance is the tremendous responsibility."

"If you say so, Rich," Hawke said, and swigged the beer.

"I *do* say so," Eden said, smiling. "And now it's time to get back to work." The look Eden gave Hawke left no room for interpretation as he walked inside to check on the progress Ryan and Alex were making in their studies of the image of the shield Hawke had taken back in Osiris's tomb.

The night went on, hot outside but cool in the air-conditioned rooms. Hawke was just dozing off to sleep in the early hours when he was woken by the sound of Ryan shouting. He had done it.

"It's all here – I can't believe it!"

Hawke rubbed his eyes and yawned as he walked to the desk, tripping over one of Lea's boots as he went and nearly knocking himself out on the bed post.

"Sorry, Joe!" she said, picking the boot up and sliding it on.

Hawke gave her a look and turned his attention to Ryan and Alex, around whom everyone else was congregating. All except Lexi who wanted to sleep and had explained that if anyone woke her for anything short of a full-scale assault on the hotel, she would kill them. They believed her.

"So what have you got for us, Mr Bale?" As Eden spoke, he checked his watch and sighed. "Mazzarro must have got to the bottom of it by now, but let's just hope you've beaten him to it."

"This thing – the shield in the tomb… it's a map."

"Another sodding map," Hawke said.

"Doesn't look like a map to me," Scarlet said, confused. "Looks more like a plate or something. Are you sure it's a map?"

"It's a *map*," Ryan repeated.

Lea screamed. "Oh sweet mother of *God*, anything but another bloody map!"

"And you're sure it's a map?" Hawke asked.

"One hundred percent. We're definitely looking at a map of some kind."

Lea was still unsure. "But that tomb was thousands of years old – I didn't even know they had maps back then."

They watched Ryan's face as he pushed his glasses up the bridge of his nose and sighed. There followed the mother of all face-palms. "They used maps in Egypt as far back as the Old Kingdom, which means four and half thousand years ago to you, plus we know the Map of Immortality is from basically *before* time as we know it. Keep up."

"No one likes a smart-arse," Scarlet said.

"No, but everyone needs a smart-arse," Ryan replied, "including you, right now, so shut up and listen. What you discovered in Karnak closely resembles a famous predynastic image known as the Narmer Palette, uncovered in Hierakonpolis and around five thousand years old, which is nearly as old as Cairo Sloane."

"Touché, *boy*," Scarlet replied, raising a cigarette to her mouth.

"And it *does* look like a plate, in fact it almost is a plate."

"So what was this thing used for?"

"Most often for grinding up stuff like copper carbonate for use in the manufacture of cosmetics, but something of this size – like the Narmer job – would have been for use in a temple – it's more decorative. Either way, it's still a map."

"If you say so," Scarlet said.

Ryan sighed again. "All right – it's not a map in the way we would understand it but it *is* a two dimensional representation of a geographic space, and for its time it was pretty groovy. At the bottom of the smiting side of the Narmer Palette you can see what basically looks like just another hieroglyphic, but in fact it's a bird's eye view of what is probably a walled garden, so that is pretty much a map. Well, we can see that on your *palette*, if you want to use the word, we have a similar style of glyph, so…ergo, this is a map. More than that, along with the famous scorpion macehead also discovered in Hierakonpolis in the temple of Horus, it gives us a very early image of an Egyptian king."

"King who?" Lea said.

"Narmer of course," replied Ryan.

"Oh, sorry… I thought Narmer was the name of the dude who found it or something."

"Narmer, was the successor to the Scorpion King during the Early Dynastic Period. Seriously, Lea, what did they teach you in school?"

"Well… not *that*, that's for frigging sure, but I did learn what happens if you spray shaving foam in the exhaust pipe of the geography teacher's Fiat or what happens if you go behind the bike sheds with Ronan Murphy..."

"All right," Hawke said, "I think we're drifting from the point a little. Ryan, just how does all of this help us?"

"I was waiting for someone to ask that," he said, clearly beginning to enjoy himself again. "None of you can see it?"

"See what?" Eden asked, leaning in to the computer.

"No?" Ryan repeated, zooming in on the image of the shield.

"Ryan," Scarlet said in a whisper. "My boot is hurtling toward your nuts. You have half a second to tell us what's going on before it's Deep Impact time between your legs."

"I've already told you. This is the map."

"Yes," Eden said. "I think we just established that."

"No, not *a* map, but *the* map."

"I don't understand…"

"This is a copy of the original Map of Immortality – the one torn in half by Poseidon and Osiris."

"Eh?" Hawke looked confused.

Ryan explained. "You can see here that it's clearly a representation of the map we took from Poseidon's tomb, but with the other half in addition – the hieroglyphic similarity is undeniable – it's not exact like a rubbing or something, but a copy in the sense Osiris must have ordered to be made from the original at some point."

Hawke looked at Ryan, impressed once again with his determination to get to the truth. "So basically, Osiris must have double-crossed Poseidon and made a copy of the map before they tore it in half?"

"Pretty much, only we could never have found it without Poseidon's half of the map because only on that was there a reference to Osiris. Poseidon probably had no idea he'd been duped by Osiris."

"Wow," Lexi said, walking over to them and yawning.

"Quite, and when you consider just how *old* this thing is – so old it had Osiris and Poseidon arguing over it and tearing their map in half – I think it really deserves a double wow."

"Double wow,' Snowcat said, her words drifting into the stunned silence.

"But there's one thing that bothers me," Ryan continued. "I was poring over Lexi's picture of the Poseidon half of the map when I noticed there was a slight discrepancy with the Osiris copy on the palette."

Eden looked concerned. "What sort of discrepancy?"

"It's not much – just a few simple glyphs, but they seem to be referring to something that doesn't make much sense to me."

"Great," Scarlet said. "If it doesn't make much sense to you then the rest of us are properly fucked."

"So what doesn't make sense?" Lexi asked.

"It just seems incongruous in the context of the other details, which are basically a treasure map. It reads… let me see if I've got this right… *the golden mean is your measure*."

"Any idea what it means?" Snowcat asked, moving closer to Ryan.

He shook his head. "Not really, and the thing is I'm struggling to see the relevance of it to be honest. It's not got anything to do with the location of the source, whatever it is, and was clearly added much later after Osiris had made his copy."

Eden cleared his throat and straightened his shirt. "If you're happy that it has no relevance, then it's time to ask the big question."

Everyone stared at Ryan. They knew what Eden was about to ask him, and they knew Ryan already had the answer.

Eden raised his chin and spoke without emotion. "Mr, Bale, where is the elixir of eternal life?"

"Beyond Upper Egypt, without a doubt."

Lea cursed. "Damn it, we just came from there, right?"

"Eh?" Ryan said, perplexed. "What are you talking about?"

"Cairo – we just came from the Upper Nile."

"Upper Egypt means the *south*," Ryan said patiently, trying to suppress a second face-palm.

"But north is more *up* on a map," Lea said. "That's just obvious, right?"

"To you, maybe, but upper and lower are references to the Nile, not which way up Lea Donovan is holding an iPhone."

"I miss this kind of pillow talk, Ry."

"Yes, thank you both for that," Eden said. "But 'beyond Upper Egypt' is not precise enough, Mr Bale. Where, exactly?"

Ryan flicked on Google Earth and zoomed in on an area he'd already marked with a pin. He spun around in the chair and grinned at his audience before speaking.

"The source of eternal life, Sir Richard, is *there*."

He pointed the tip of his pen at the laptop screen.

The Ethiopian Highlands.

*

After the revelation they had been waiting to hear for so long, they decided the best thing to do was get some sleep before loading the choppers and heading south. It was dawn now, and they were exhausted. The journey from the British Museum to here had been long, demanding and dangerous. Their three dead colleagues were a testament to that, not to mention the narrow escape Lea had endured back in the Moscow fire.

They went back to their rooms, Hawke leading Lea by the hand. It was a strange and unusual moment of quiet the two of them rarely enjoyed together, and neither really knew what to say.

She went to draw the curtains but he stopped her. She watched him as he drew closer, the way the sun struck the thick stubble on his chin and wide jaw line. She felt like she fell in love with this man all over again with every new day, and now it was happening once more. Times like this, she thought, are when we get to forget about the killing and carnage. Times like this, she thought, are when I can really lose myself, just for a moment in time.

He stood in front of her, his broad shoulders blocking the Egyptian sunlight which shone low over the city behind him. He lifted his hands to her face and brushed her cheek. She had seen those big hands in a fight, and sometimes struggled to believe he could be so gentle with them.

"Don't stop," she whispered, and moved closer to him.

He made no reply, but simply lifted her off her feet and carried her back to the bed, lit soft amber by a flickering candle in the dawn's low light. She felt his heavy, scarred body press down on her. He lowered his head and kissed her neck and her eyes widened with pleasure. Now, he ran his fingers trough her tangled hair and she closed her eyes.

*

Hawke opened his eyes and woke to feel Lea beside him, still asleep. She was resting her head on his chest and using it as a sort of pillow, the way she did sometimes. The morning sun was higher now and streamed through the thin voiles. Everything looked different in the daylight.

He smiled as he recalled the day they met in London, and when they had shared the ski chalet in Switzerland that night. Just one solitary night with each other beside the fire. When all this was over, he promised himself, the two of them really had to get away from it all.

Beside him, Lea awoke.

"Hot or cold?" he said quietly.

She turned to face him, her hair bunching up on the pillow. "What?" She smiled.

"When all this is over," he said, turning onto his side so they were face to face. "We should get away somewhere. Where do you fancy – somewhere hot or cold?"

"After Egypt, I'm going to say somewhere cold. Maybe we could get back to our little ski chalet in Zermatt?"

"Why are you grinning?"

She shrugged. "No reason. It's just that was the place you seduced me…"

"You seduced me, more like!"

Hawke smiled and turned on his back. The ceiling fan whirred slowly above them. He didn't care which way around it was. He hadn't been this content for years, not since the second before his wife's murder. Yes, it was true he had unfinished business – James Matheson would pay the ultimate price for his crimes, but it wouldn't be easy – Eden was right. Matheson was the British Foreign Secretary and had some of the chunkiest and best trained security in the West. No, Hawke knew he would have to bide his time on that one… but in the meantime, he had Lea, and that was enough for him.

He turned to her but she had fallen back to sleep.

Rangers he thought, with a smile.

He climbed out of bed and started to get dressed. Today was the day he ended this war. Today was the day he found the elixir of life.

CHAPTER THIRTY-TWO

Ethiopian Highlands

When they got to the airport they saw Vetrov's A380 parked on the apron, glistening white in the hot sun, but with the addition of several dozen armed soldiers crawling all over it. Arafa had delivered on his promise to Eden. In addition to the men guarding Vetrov's plane, there were around twenty soldiers waiting for them, headed up by Captain Koura, a short, lean man with a serious moustache.

The sight of Vetrov's aircraft in quarantine had sent up a cheer among the group, but it was short-lived. Koura explained that witnesses had already told him how Vetrov, Kodiak, Mazzarro and a team of his best men had left the airport hours earlier in three heavily armed Kazan Ansat choppers which he had transported to the desert himself in his Airbus. Koura explained that the witness had claimed Vetrov had gone south with what he described as a small army. Hawke was unfazed.

They wasted no time in their pursuit of him, powering away from the airport and heading south in half a dozen ageing Mil Mi-8s which had once belonged to the Egyptian Air Force but were now mothballed in a hangar at Luxor International Airport. Just a few minutes after taking off there was no longer any sign of civilization below them at all as they headed out into the desert – just endless sand dunes to every horizon.

In the lead chopper, banter was light but good-natured as they raced low across the south of Egypt and then gained altitude as they crossed the Ethiopian border and slowly flew up into the mountains. Hawke's mind was clear and he was ready to fight, as were the others. Scarlet looked like she could skin a live grizzly bear – she was obviously thinking about Karlsson, but refused to talk about it.

"I'll let this do the talking," she said when asked, and pointed to the Heckler & Koch MP5 she was holding between her thighs.

They arrived at the site – a vast plateau of elevated ground deep in the Highlands. It was a scrubby landscape at lower altitudes, but up here the mountainsides were covered in a thick, lush rainforest and a dense, steamy mist hung in the air.

Hawke looked out across the terrain from the chopper and was filled with something approaching despair. Endless forest stretched everywhere he looked, obscured here and there by the low cloud and he half expected to see a dinosaur plodding through the jungle. The place was as isolated as anywhere he had seen on earth, and there was an ominous feeling of despondency inside the chopper.

Hawke thought about Vetrov and how his insane hunt for the elixir had led them all to this forgotten corner of Africa. He thought about how Vetrov had gotten so much further than the others – so far in fact it looked like he could beat them to it and seize the ultimate power for himself. Inwardly he was shocked by all the things that had happened to him over the last few weeks and could hardly believe what he'd learned about the world in that short space of time, but there was no time for speculation now. Now was the time for focus and fighting.

Beside him, Ryan studied the landscape carefully on a couple of Apps as the chopper moved deeper into the mountains, looking out for a lake he had seen in the

Osiris Palette. When he found it, it was just a matter of correlating its location with several of the closest peaks until the rough location was found.

Then he saw it – the Semien Mountains came into view – an ancient World Heritage Site often called the Roof of Africa.

There at last was a fifteen thousand foot-high peak rising high above the misty clouds and stretching into the blue African sky.

"We're almost there!" Ryan said, the excitement rising in his voice. "That's Ras Dashen, the highest mountain in Ethiopia and the tenth highest in the whole of Africa… plus this place still has Egyptian wolves, leopards and the Masai Lion."

Scarlet scoffed. "Thank you for that totally fucking useless piece of information, boy."

"I take every opportunity I can when it comes to enlightening you, Cairo. I'm even hoping to get your IQ into double digits one day."

She scowled at him. "No one calls me Cairo!"

Hawke smiled as they began to descend into the jungle. He pulled a compass from his pocket and set it on the map.

"What's that?" Ryan said.

"It's a compass, mate. Never seen one?"

"Of course, but we've got this." He held up his iPhone.

"Sure we have. But when the battery fails in this humidity or you drop it in a steaming pile of Masai lion dung , we'll still have this." Hawke waved the compass in his face and smiled. He checked his weapons and secured his pack and then gave the order to the pilot to tell the other choppers to get ready for disembarking. This was it.

As they descended closer to the edge of the plateau they had chosen as the most appropriate landing zone, Hawke noticed there was still no sight of Vetrov's choppers or any of his men – or Mazzarro.

"Are you sure this is right?" Hawke asked Ryan.

"Joe, it's me. I don't make mistakes."

"Modest," Lexi said, strolling past them with an assault rifle over her shoulder and an ammo belt slung around her waist. "I like that in a nerd." She strapped herself in and prepared for the landing as the chopper swung violently to the left and executed a sharp descent to make the landing site. As it touched down, Hawke unbuckled his seat belt and swung open the door. He ordered the others to get out and as they assembled at the edge of the clearing the other choppers in their contingent touched down all around them.

The gradient of the slope meant they had to land the chopper half a kilometer from the entrance to the tomb. They hiked through the rainforest, sniping at one another with the occasional barbed comment, but it was all just to relieve the tension. There was a heavy feeling of anticipation in the humid air as they drew closer to the long-awaited site.

"I can't believe we're finally here," Lea said.

"Sure," said Scarlet. "Just one problem – where the hell is that Russian psycho?"

She was right. They knew that Vetrov had left Luxor before them, but he was nowhere to be seen.

"Maybe Mazzarro led him to another location to protect the source?" Lea said.

"Or maybe your ex-hubbie led us to the wrong location," Scarlet said, looking over at Ryan.

"Maybe their chopper got a flat tire and or they had to stop for sandwiches," Hawke said. "Or maybe we should just shut the hell up and get going?"

They made their way through the jungle at the speed of the slowest man, who, as usual was Ryan Bale. Hawke was in the lead, followed closely by Scarlet and Lea, with Lexi bringing up the rear. Snowcat stayed back with Ryan, ostensibly on the grounds of protecting him, but Hawke thought maybe there was another reason as they chatted to each other up the hill. Captain Koura and his men were marching behind them in the distance, fanning out with guns raised ready for firing. They were professional, active soldiers but they knew the local terrain no better than Hawke's crew.

Then they saw it.

It reminded Hawke immediately of some kind of ruined Aztec temple, only the architecture was somehow different. They were looking at two stone columns that had obviously once supported a beam of some kind and formed what once would have been a grand entrance to the tomb. Now, they were broken down into rubble and covered in wild coffee plants and fallen gum leaves.

"Oh my *God*," Ryan said, approaching the ruins slack-jawed. "It's like the Lagunita temple… this is *amazing*."

"The *what* now?" Lea said.

"Lagunita – it's a massive set of ruins in the Yucatán Peninsula in Mexico. We're talking about an entire palace that was lost in the Campeche jungle for two thousand years."

Scarlet laughed. "How can these nerds not have found an entire palace after hundreds of years of explorations? Idiotic."

"Not really – in jungle that thick you could be as little as a few hundred feet from an entire lost city and never even know you'd walked past it."

Scarlet raised an eyebrow. "You mean there could be more of these places?"

"More?" Ryan offered a low, condescending laugh. He liked it when people relied on him for information, especially Scarlet Sloane. "I guarantee there are literally countless palaces and temples lost in those jungles, just waiting to be discovered."

"Just waiting to be looted, you mean," Scarlet said with a smirk.

"If you're of that mindset," Ryan said haughtily. "Others would see it as an opportunity to fill museums and extend knowledge."

"Yeah, right," she replied. "If you ask me, they just sound like giant cash machines, sitting around waiting to be emptied."

"Well, Cairo," Hawke said. 'No one did ask you, and now we know why."

"Bloody SBS."

"Hey, James Bond was a Navy man, just remember that." He turned to Ryan and they both looked up at the ruins. "Crazy, but you're right – it really does look like some kind of Aztec temple."

"Not crazy at all," Ryan replied, taking his jacket off and fanning his face. "There are certain legends which claim it was the same people who built all these temples thousands of years ago – that one ancient antediluvian mega-civilization spanned the entire globe."

Hawke shook his head. "Leave it to you to give me nightmares."

They moved closer to the ruins and finally saw what they were looking for – the entrance, but it was nothing more than a fissure in the rainforest floor. At first it looked like a simple mess of tree roots and a shallow ditch, but Ryan assured them it was the location. His explanation about how it lined up with the circumpolar stars and the peaks of three specific mountaintops was barely heard by the others as they lowered their ropes into the ground and cracked open the glow-sticks.

Hawke felt the excitement grow, but he was determined to keep a lid on it. They weren't there yet, plus they still had no idea where Vetrov and his men were. It had been a long slog from London via Zaugg's insane vanity and the tortured mind of Sheng Fang, but now they were here and they had to end this the right way. "Ryan – call Eden and Alex back at Luxor and tell them we've arrived and that we're going in."

Ryan pulled out his phone. "Sure thing."

Then, after a short briefing with Koura who divided his men into several sub-units, including five to guard the choppers, Hawke led the first team into the mountain, forcing their way through the narrow slit in the rock and lowering themselves into the hole one by one.

They reached the bottom of the hole and began to shine their torches around.

"I don't like the look of *that*," Lea said, shining her flashlight along the crumbling shaft ahead of them. It seemed to twist downwards, and the stark halogen light of the torch picked out every detail in the face of the rock, carved out thousands of years ago by long-dead men, probably the slaves of whoever had given Poseidon and Osiris the map.

"Neither do I," Scarlet said. "But I hardly think the ancients were going to leave the source of all their power just lying around for any old nob, dick or fanny to pick up. This is the challenge, so let's get on with it."

Hawke smiled and they made their way along the winding tunnel until coming to an artificial man-made arch which opened onto a large cave.

He stared at the enormous cavern in front of them. It was a natural space, formed by the rainfall of millennia as its cumulative power dissolved the limestone which towered all around them. All over the bottom of the cavern was a spectacular man-made labyrinth, receding into a silent darkness too overwhelming for their tiny glow-sticks and flashlights to penetrate.

Lea stood next to him and gasped. "Would you look at that, Joe Hawke! It's incredible…" Her voice trailed away into the eerie silence of the cavern.

He turned to look at her as she spoke and saw she was totally captivated by the immense sight before them. "Yes, it is," he said quietly.

Scarlet walked over to them and pushed some chewing gum inside her mouth, tossing the foil to the tunnel floor. "Looks like the same crap we saw back in Osiris's tomb," she said dismissively. "But is there any gold in here, that's what I want to know?"

Hawke rolled his eyes and sighed. "Still worried about your retirement, Cairo?"

She nodded, missing the note of sarcasm in his voice. "I'm still way off retirement levels, Joe. I wonder what price I could sell the water of life for?"

"I don't know but it looks like you're in luck," Lea said.

Hawke looked at her. "Eh?"

"What's that over there?" she asked, pointing to where something sparkled in the darkness. "Gold, right?"

Hawke looked at where she was pointing and saw something sparkling vaguely in the distance. "Could be gold," he muttered. "Diamonds, maybe."

"Diamonds?" Scarlet said, raising her eyebrows and spitting out the gum. "Even better."

"Let's get over there to those pylons," Hawke said.

"I don't see any pylons," Lea said.

"Right in front of you!"

"Oh sorry… I was looking for those things with wires that make your TV work."

Hawke rolled his eyes. "I mean those two enormous stone towers over there at the entrance to the tomb."

"And how the hell did *you* know they're called pylons, ya big fool?" said Lea, slapping his shoulder.

"How'd you think?" he said, and laughed, jabbing his thumb back at Ryan. "Someone told me…"

They walked down the broad stone steps carved in the side of the cavern, careful not to slip on the smoothness worn into them by thousands of years of use. As they went, it grew colder and damper, and the eerie silence seemed to wrap around them like a cloak the deeper they went.

At the ground level they walked through a miniature version of the giant pylon at the entrance to the Karnak Temple back in Luxor, but this one was covered in the same hieroglyphics as the map.

"Looks like we did it," Lea said.

Hawke smiled. "At bloody last."

"And we beat that bastard Vetrov to it as well," Lexi said, her voice quiet as she brought up the rear. "He *has* to be lost in the jungle somewhere."

Maria clicked her tongue in disapproval. "Don't divide the pelt of a bear until he's dead…old Russian proverb."

"Eh?" Hawke said.

"Don't count your chickens till they've hatched, darling," Scarlet said.

"Oh…"

They followed what looked like some kind of main boulevard through the labyrinth, stopping occasionally to shine a torch down a silent side-street, not seen for thousands of years, or longer.

But then they stopped in their tracks.

"Bloody hell!" Lea said.

Hawke shared the sentiment as he raised his flashlight from their level on the ground slowly up the wall in front of them and illuminated another pylon. This one was carved into the far side of the cavern and covered in similar glyphs. Thanks to Ryan, Hawke recognized the one at the top – it meant *eternity*.

"This obviously marks the end of the labyrinth," Scarlet said.

"And the start of something else," Hawke said, shining his torch through a small archway at the base of the pylon.

"And I think we all know what," Lexi said, the excitement in her voice obvious to everyone.

Like the others, Hawke's mind was racing with a mix of elation and anxiety. He had already uncovered the truth about his wife – not only that the hit in Vietnam was intended for her and not him, but that she was in fact a Russian double agent codenamed Swallowtail. Worse, he had discovered that she was killed by none other than the British Foreign Secretary who officially had ordered the murder on grounds of national security, although in reality he knew it was something to do with this group calling itself the Athanatoi.

Now, the journey which had started out in the British Museum was also coming to an end – or so he thought. He was finally about to come face to face with the source of eternal life – the elixir of eternity that Hugo Zaugg, Sheng Fang and now Maxim Vetrov had all sought at any cost to human life – and all failed to find. Their failure had been eclipsed by the success of him and his team. Part of him couldn't wait to walk through into the tomb, but another big part of him wanted to blow up the entrance and bury it forever.

Without saying another word, they moved slowly forward and stepped through the ornately carved arch.

They were met with a small fountain built into a natural recess in the cold rock-face. It was covered in the same ancient hieroglyphs that had led them to this place. It was so beautiful it looked like something from another world, but at the same time there was something simple about it.

"The glyphs are so intricate," Lea said, her voice almost a whisper.

"But it looks sort of *pre-historic*," Ryan said, leaning forward and pushing his glasses back up the bridge of his nose.

"Whatever it looks like…" Lea said, "…we bloody well found it!"

The others directed the beams of their torches toward the fountain and illuminated it. In the vast space it looked almost insignificant.

Hawke was stunned. Water trickled from the top of the fountain which was shaped into the face of what looked like some kind of god, and shimmered in the torchlight, mesmerising him. So this is what it was all about.

"What *is* that stuff?" Lea said. Her words drifted into the half-light and once again the only sound was that of the water falling from the lower tier of the fountain and splashing on the circular marble reservoir that formed the base.

"It looks like it's flecked with something – gold maybe, but it seems brighter somehow."

Hawke studied the water and saw it had gold and silver sparkles within in it. At first it looked like it was simple regular water reflecting their flashlights but closer inspection showed that the sparkling was coming from within the water.

Ryan leaned in to touch it, but Hawke reached for his arm and stopped him.

"Wait! We don't know what it really is or what it does yet, mate. Best off leaving it alone."

"Agreed," Ryan said. "But we should get a sample."

Hawke frowned. "All right, go ahead – but be careful."

He watched as Ryan leaned forward with a small vial and gently collected a sample of the water.

"We need to report this to Eden," Lea said. "He's going to want to know about this – *believe* me. He's spent his life searching for this, and he deserves to know."

"But only I am deserving of it!"

The voice was shrill and loud and came from the entrance to the chamber.

They spun around to see Maxim Vetrov and Kodiak standing a few yards from them, flanked on either side by several men, all aiming suppressed submachine guns at them.

CHAPTER THIRTY-THREE

The Athanatoi gathered in solemn silence and waited for the Oracle to speak. Athanatoi, as the great Oracle told all new initiates, was the Greek word for *immortals*, and was originally used to describe the elite military unit of the Byzantine Empire over a thousand years old. Today, they were a much smaller but far more dangerous elite – a secret society of men and women who had learned to harness the power of eternal life.

The Oracle knew the import of his decision today and chose to contemplate the matter for another few minutes as he stared out of the room's vast window. Outside, the snows of late winter were still blowing, far away from the steamy tropics of Africa where the fight for their precious secret was currently being played out.

He turned to the man beside him and spoke. His words were ice-cold and echoed in the silent space of the ancient chamber.

"And you're *absolutely* certain they're in the tomb right now?"

The man spoke nervously. "Yes, sir."

"Then bring me the sphere."

A ripple of discontent crossed the room, followed by a long silence as the Oracle considered the implications of what he was ordering. It would mean the destruction of the Tomb of Eternity. This was not the first time they had come under attack, neither was it the first time their secret had almost been discovered – extreme curiosity could drive the most determined of men almost anywhere – but it was the first time anyone had ever got this close to the truth.

And it had to be stopped.

"Perhaps there is another way?" a woman asked.

His expression was grim. "No. We have no choice. We must activate the sphere."

Another collective gasp of horror went around the assembled elite as the implications of the Oracle's words sunk in. A moment later a man in robes brought a strange chest to the Oracle and opened it. Inside was a kind of dome covered in a black velvet cloth.

"But this will destroy the tomb, sir," said one man.

"We will be weakened," said another.

"This is unprecedented," said a third. "In all of our ancient history nothing like this has ever been ordered."

The Oracle glared the man. "In all of our history we have never faced a threat like this."

The man looked away in fear. It was never wise to argue with the Oracle, or question his decisions.

"Besides," continued their leader, "the other two sources are safe."

"But for how long?" the woman said coolly. "We all have a lot to lose."

"We have *everything* to lose," said another man. He looked like he was going to be sick and another murmur of anxiety rippled over the room.

Yes, for how long, indeed, the Oracle considered. The Athanatoi had protected the sources since the beginning of almost everything, and now one of them had finally been uncovered. He would have to work hard to prove he could safeguard the remaining two sources.

"I have made my decision. May the Gods have mercy on me."

Another gasp.

"Activate the sphere."

The man beside him opened the dome to reveal a smooth, glass sphere. A faint blue glow emanated from beneath it.

The Oracle ordered the man to lift it. "Proceed with the activation," he said calmly.

The man turned the upper half of the sphere and the neon blue grew brighter, eerily under-lighting the faces of those present.

"It is done," the man said.

The Oracle's face was frozen in a rictus of fear. He nodded his head slowly and spoke, raising his voice for all to hear. "It is done, and cannot be undone. Return this to the other spheres."

The man walked away with the chest, now re-cloaked in the strange velvet cover.

Half a world away in Ethiopia, a mountain was about to fall apart.

*

Hawke kept his eyes fixed firmly on Maxim Vetrov as he moved gradually closer to the fountain. His eyes were wide, staring saucers as he drew closer to the sparkling water, protected in his oblivious state by Kodiak and the men at his rear who were covering everyone with their submachine guns.

"And you can forget about Koura and his cavalry. They are all dead, as is Dr Mazzarro." Vetrov gestured toward the silenced submachine guns in their hands. "It wasn't even a challenge."

The Russian billionaire stepped over the low wall and walked slowly across the tiled courtyard. Clearly apprehensive now, he slowed as he drew ever closer to the ornate fountain where the magical water tumbled in a stream from the mouth of the carved god none of them could name.

As the Russian began to get closer, he began muttering to himself about how finally he had met his destiny. He plunged his hands into the stream of cool, silvery water and scooped it up to his face, drinking greedily. It dribbled out of his mouth and ran down his chin on to his shirt.

"It tastes like nothing on earth!" he gasped, obviously exhilarated by the moment. He plunged his hands in a second time and guzzled more of the gold-silver water. "Nothing has ever tasted like this before…*nothing!*"

"He's obviously never had Vimto," Lea whispered to Hawke.

Hawke rolled his eyes and gave her a look.

"What?" she said. "Not the right time for jokes?"

"Vimto? What the hell made you think of that?"

Kodiak took a step toward them and aimed the Vityaz at them. "Silence, you scum, or I rake you with this!"

"Not an unreasonable request under the circumstances," Hawke said.

"I mean it, you English vermin!" Kodiak came closer and pushed the cold steel muzzle of the submachine gun in his stomach. "Say one more thing, and I fire."

Hawke knew the others were all looking at him, pleading with him to keep his mouth shut and right now it was the right play. There was nothing he could do but comply with his orders and shut his mouth, inwardly vowing revenge on the Russian hit-man.

Across the chamber, beside the fountain, Vetrov finished guzzling the water and turned to face them. His chest heaved up and down as the excitement of the moment coursed through his veins like fire. His arms and legs began to shake almost immediately.

Hawke took a step back and gave the others a look to do the same thing. He was starting to have grave concerns about the future of Maxim Vetrov, and it wasn't that the Russian billionaire was about to turn into a living god and live forever.

"Ha!" Vetrov screamed, the veins bulging in his neck. "Ha! I am electric!"

"If you say so, matey-lad," Hawke said.

Kodiak's eyes widened and he too began to move away from Vetrov and the fountain. On seeing the former Spetsnaz sniper shying away from their boss, the rest of Vetrov's goons followed suit and shuffled back toward the rear wall of the chamber.

"Behold as I become a *god..!*" Vetrov began to hyperventilate and Hawke saw his eyes were turning red. "Where countless others failed, I have succeeded. I have turned myself into a god!"

"A god-forsaken mess, I *think* is what you mean," Hawke said.

Vetrov laughed maniacally and turned to stare at Hawke and the others. "When you are nothing but ashes I will rule the entire world. I am your god! I will live for…"

He stopped talking, a look of strained terror spreading across his face.

Hawke watched as he dropped to his knees and clutched at his throat.

"I…I…*am your god...*"

Vetrov's eyes were now dark red with blood, and the veins in his neck and temples were bulging hideously and throbbing with the beat of his racing heart. He began screaming and tearing at his throat, his fingernails clawing into his own flesh and making it bleed.

"Help me! Kamchatka, *help me..!*"

Kodiak took another step back.

"Maybe a Panadol might help, mate?" Hawke said.

They watched in horror as Vetrov's skin began to turn a pallid color like clay and drop from his face in dry peels. His hoarse, terrified screams filled the chamber as the realization of his true destiny dawned on him.

"Bloody hell," Ryan said. "His eye just exploded!"

Vetrov fell to the floor now and began rolling around in the dirt, screaming and clawing at the ground, his agonized death throes convulsing his broken, decaying body.

"Looks like someone put a set of jumper cables on him," Hawke said. "Which is funny because…"

His sentence was cut off by a deep, low rumble echoing inside the tomb. Seconds later it reached the inner chamber and sent chunks of rock from the ceiling crashing to the floor. A stalactite broke lose and skewered one of Vetrov's men, and two more ran from the chamber in terror.

"Time to go, I think," Kodiak said, watching his boss as he squirmed on the ground in agony. "But not for you, English vermin."

He raised the Vityaz and fired at Hawke.

"No!" Lea screamed as she pushed Hawke aside, but she was too slow.

One of the bullets tore through her chest and she dropped to the floor of the chamber just a few yards from the convulsing Vetrov, who was now more a skeleton than a man, and yet still writhing in the dirt.

"Lea!" Hawke screamed. He dropped to his knees to help her while Scarlet took advantage of the confusion of the earthquake and gave Kodiak the benefit of a well-aimed and lightning fast Krav Maga slap kick. Her heel struck him like a sledgehammer and tore into his flesh.

He staggered back, dazed and bleeding, randomly firing off the Vityaz at the ceiling as he went, but before he could get his balance back, she planted a second slap kick on him, and Lexi did the same to the remaining goon, who hit the floor before scrambling away like a frightened crab.

Scarlet gripped Kodiak between her thighs in a scissor hold, and slowly his face began to turn purple.

"Shoot my friends and I have a tendency to lose my temper," she said. "And you won't like my temper very much, you little worm."

She squeezed her thighs and further constricted his windpipe.

All around them the tomb was shaking.

"What the hell is going on?" Snowcat asked Ryan.

Ryan, who had joined Hawke at Lea's side turned to face her in the confusion.

"Some kind of earthquake, I guess," he said. "But a bloody big one. We have to get out of here, Joe!"

Hawke nodded and hoisted an unconscious Lea over his shoulder.

In the corner, Scarlet was literally squeezing the last breath of life out of Kodiak when Hawke screamed at her to move out. She stepped over his limp body, snatching up his Vityaz as she went. "Been waiting to do that since Berlin."

"What about him?" Lexi said, pointing at Vetrov, who was now croaking on the floor and heaving hoarse breaths into his crumbling lungs.

"What about *it*, you mean," Scarlet said, and fired a burst of rounds into Vetrov's head, blasting pieces of the desiccated skull all over the fountain. "That's you sorted then, you tit."

A foot-wide split appeared in the roof of the chamber and cracked its way down the wall behind the fountain and started to snake along the floor.

"The whole place is breaking in two!" Ryan shouted, peering into the newly formed gap. He shook his head in awe. "It just goes on *forever.*"

"Right, everyone out…*now!*" Scarlet shouted.

They sprinted out the chamber and along the tunnel which led to the entrance, seeing daylight after what felt like the longest race of their lives. As they ran they saw the corpses of Koura and his men lining the tunnel, lying dead where Vetrov's men had killed them. Finally they saw Mazzarro's dead body with a single bullet hole in his forehead.

As they sprinted toward the light, the tunnel behind them began to collapse and they only just got to the entrance before the whole thing began to crush in on itself and spew a great plume of dust and ash out into the jungle – the last dying breath of the ancient tomb.

"When that thing collapses no one's ever getting back in there, that's for damned sure," Scarlet said.

While the shockwave slowly dissipated, Hawke laid Lea down on the soft leaves of the rainforest floor. A few seconds later the final part of the tunnel shaft crumbled into itself as the weight of the mountainside pushed down onto it and sealed it forever.

Hawke looked down at Lea, dying in his arms. The race to escape the collapse of the tomb had knocked her from unconsciousness for a few short moments.

"You're going to make it, right?" he said, tearing off her t-shirt to see the wound. There was a small bloody hole an inch above her heart.

She tried to smile at him as he studied the wound. "You better not fuck this up, Joe Hawke…" her words were faint now, and drifting into the steamy air of the jungle. All around them the cacophony of cicadas echoed off the trunks of the myrrh trees and from somewhere in the thick canopy above their heads they heard the calming call of a lone greenshank as it returned to the trees after the mysterious earthquake.

"So what is it then?" Lea asked, barely able to ask the question as the blood filled her lungs.

Hawke choked back the tears. "What's what?"

"Your name. You told me back in Switzerland that I'd never find out, but I'd like to know."

Hawke clenched his jaw and held her tighter. It was all coming back again, the unassailable terror of his wife's brutal murder – the way he'd held her that terrible day in Vietnam in the heat and humidity, the way she'd looked up at him with her dying eyes while the pedestrians scattered in fear of more bullets. Now, he was being forced to relive the same dreadful moment all over again, only this time they had slain Lea, and right in front of him, just like before.

"My name?"

"Sure, ya *eejit*." More coughing. The light in her eyes started to fade.

This can't be happening again, he thought. *She doesn't deserve this…* He held her tighter and looked into her eyes.

"Josiah."

She tried to smile, but the pain was too much. "Josiah Hawke. I like that." This time she managed a smile, and reached out to stroke his face.

And then she was gone.

CHAPTER THIRTY-FOUR

Hawke stared at Lea, now lifeless in his arms, and for a moment nothing else existed. Was any of this really happening? He thought about the pain Ryan had gone through dealing with Sophie's death – how she had died selflessly taking a bullet for him, and now Lea had done the same for him. The idea of her sacrificing her own life for his made him feel sick with guilt even though he knew he would do the same thing for her over and over.

He looked up at the others and saw nothing but desperate faces as his friends waited for him to make the next move.

"Is she dead?" Ryan asked.

"I'm not sure," Hawke said. "I think there's a very faint heartbeat but it's fading fast. Get over here and bring that bloody vial of water!"

A look of expectant surprise crossed the faces of the others as they realized what Hawke was proposing.

Ryan stumbled over to him, tripping on his way and landing in a pile of rotten leaves and weaver ants. He staggered to his feet and handed Hawke the vial he had taken from the fountain before the tomb had collapsed.

"Here!"

"Are you crazy?" Scarlet said. "Didn't you see what just happened to Vetrov?"

"He took too much," Hawke said.

"My God, he's right!" Ryan said. "Remember the ancient Delphic riddle on Poseidon's half of the map – the golden mean is your measure?"

Scarlet screamed. “Now is not the time for one your lectures, Ryan!”

“Let him speak,” Hawke said, cradling Lea’s head in his arms.

“The golden mean is an ancient Greek concept advocating moderation. Poseidon was giving an oblique warning to anyone who found the map that the elixir must be taken in moderation… great moderation if what happened in *there* is anything to go by.”

Hawke wasted no time and took the vial in his shaking hands. He unscrewed the tiny metal lid and lowered the vial to Lea’s lips.

“I hope you’re right about this,” Lexi said, watching the life slip away from Lea.

“We have no choice whether he’s right or wrong,” Hawke said, looking at her dying body in his arms. “She was shot very close to her heart. She’s losing a lot of blood and she’s about to die. I thought I’d lost her in Russia in the fire and that was enough for me, thanks. We have to do whatever it takes.”

“But Joe, what if the same thing that happened to the Crocodile King in there happens again, to Lea?” Scarlet said again.

“Like I said… no choice.”

He finished pouring the water and watched as the strange white-gold liquid ran over her dry, cracked lips, wetting them slightly. For a few seconds nothing happened, but then the water sparkled slightly and seeped inside her mouth. It looked almost like it was being *controlled* to flow inside her.

She coughed and opened her eyes with a terrific gasp as she struggled to reinflate her lungs.

Then he watched the bullet hole slowly grow pale and heal right before his eyes. The blood dried and flaked away and the color of the wound changed from scarlet to crimson and then to paler skin tones. Finally, the skin puckered and a faint glow appeared before the wound was gone and the skin was smooth again.

Lea coughed more violently and blinked several times as she tried to focus on her surroundings.

"*Where…*"

More coughing.

Hawke put his hand to her lips.

"Shhh, it's okay. You're going be all right now."

"Yeah, so get up you lazy cow," Scarlet said. She looked at the shocked faces of those around her. "It was just a *joke*… bloody hell."

"SAS humor," Hawke said. "Best ignore it."

Lea tried to smile, but was too weak to hold it for long. "Did you save my life twice on this mission?"

"Who's counting?" Hawke said.

"I am, *Josiah*…" she said with a smirk.

Then a single gunshot slammed into the tree trunk an inch above Hawke's head. He looked up, stunned, and saw Kodiak standing on the ridge. Vetrov's Grach was in his hands.

"It's that bloody Russian!" Scarlet said, automatically returning fire. "Oh… sorry Snowcat."

"Forget about it," Maria replied, also returning fire at the assassin. "We can be very bloody."

Lexi cursed. "He must have been right behind us in the tunnel and got out just before it collapsed."

With Scarlet, Lexi and Maria returning a savage wave of fire at the Russian hit-man, Hawke and Ryan moved Lea down the hill toward the chopper.

Kodiak maintained the attack, using his sniper skills to pin them down, but he was outgunned three to one, and gradually they were able to turn the tables on him, moving back to the clearing.

When they returned, one of the choppers was already fired up, and the rotors were whirring fast ready for take off.

They climbed inside and Hawke raised the collective, lifting the helicopter off the ground and above the trees.

"How do you fancy some target practice, Cairo?" Hawke said through the headset.

"You know me so well, Josiah," Scarlet said.

Hawke rolled his eyes, already regretting letting his full name out of the bag. "You know what to do."

Cairo swung open the side door and loaded the rapid-fire heavy-machine gun bolted to the chopper floor.

"I know she's good," Ryan said. "But surely not even Cairo Sloane can find that psycho down in all that jungle?"

"Correct," she said. "But I'm not aiming for the psycho."

Hawke made a low pass and she opened fire on the remaining choppers, exploding them all one by one, including the three Vetrov's team had arrived in. Great plumes of burning oil smoke and fire twisted into the sky as the wrecked flying machines now burned themselves out in the rainforest.

"Let's see the little bastard get out of this place without one of those," Scarlet said through the headset. "And no one calls me Cairo anymore, boy."

CHAPTER THIRTY-FIVE

Scarlet Sloane tried for the third and final time to get Sir Richard Eden drunk, and then gave up and turned up the stereo, cigarette hanging from her lower lip. She'd been on the bottle since she'd got back to base, but denied it had anything to do with Karlsson's death. Eden's toast to Bradley Karlsson had caused a few tears, but not in Scarlet's eyes.

A day had passed since they'd dispatched Maxim Vetrov and watched a mysterious earthquake come out of nowhere and bury the Tomb of Eternity under thousands of tons of Ethiopian mountain.

Lea had made a full and startling recovery. What surprised everyone was how fast it had been – within a few short hours of getting shot and almost dying she was up and running in full health without a sign of the bullet wound. That raised a lot of questions in everyone's minds, most of all Hawke's. When he asked her if she remembered anything after being shot, she shook her head and smiled.

Hawke himself still had battles to fight, even with Vetrov dead and buried and the source located – even if it was lost to humanity forever. For one thing, he had to arrange a meeting with James Matheson, the British Foreign Secretary. The two of them had a few things to discuss, and Matheson wasn't going to like the subject of conversation.

He escaped the throbbing bass of the music coming from inside the suite and moved to the balcony for some peace and quiet. Looking up at the sun as it started to sink in the western horizon, he knew he was also owed an explanation from his new friends about why they had been lying to him, and it was to come sooner than he thought.

His mind turned to his family back in England. He hadn't talked to them for a very long time, and some would say with good reason, but maybe now it was time to lay some ghosts to rest and talk again. Maybe he should introduce them all to Lea – or then again, maybe not…

Before he could consider the matter any further, Sir Richard Eden appeared on the balcony and stood beside him.

"Good work, Hawke," he said in his usual business tone. "HMG is pleased Vetrov was taken out, even if it did mean destroying the tomb."

Hawke sighed and shook his head.

"What's the problem?" Eden asked.

"First, I don't care what HMG thinks because I don't work for them and I didn't do it for them, and second, as I told you before, we didn't destroy the tomb. I don't know how it happened – maybe we triggered some self-destruct device like Indiana Bloody Jones or something – I don't know, but we did *not* destroy that tomb." He paused for a second. "And don't think I've forgotten about what you said on the flight out of Cairo when you found out about my attackers being British."

"That's easy. It pains me to say it but I think we have a leak at the British Embassy. When we got to Cairo, as you know, I went straight to my old friend Pete Henderson, the ambassador. I apprised him of our situation and asked him to make things as easy as he could for us during our stay in the country. He said he'd help out. He was the only person I spoke to, Hawke."

"You trust him?"

"I did, but not any more. I strongly suspect he leaked your presence in Cairo to Matheson – they were old friends in the Foreign Office for many years. After what you told me about Matheson being behind your wife's murder, it all seems to fit together. Certainly that would explain the Apache and how the men in the Escalades were able to track you all over the city – working for Matheson they would have had access to real-time sat surveillance data. I also suspect he was the reason Maria was locked out of the Russian Embassy. He must have spoken to a contact inside the Russian Government and pulled some strings."

Hawke listened carefully to the words as the old man spoke. It all made sense, he decided, and it all led back to Matheson. Inwardly he was ashamed he had doubted some of his closest friends, and he was grateful he hadn't accused them of anything to their faces. Only Maria knew of his doubt, however fleeting it had been.

"All right, I accept that," Hawke said. "It just makes me more determined to make Matheson pay for his crimes." With lightning reactions he swatted a mosquito on his neck and its mangled body fell silently to the decking.

Eden sighed. "He's the Foreign Secretary, Hawke. He has some of the toughest security on the planet. You're not going to get anywhere near him."

Hawke frowned. "We'll see about that. Besides, he won't be the Foreign Secretary forever, Richard, will he now? I know how to play the long game… but there's more you've been keeping from me, am I right?"

Eden nodded but said nothing for a long time. Like Hawke, he was momentarily mesmerised by the sunset over the Sahara desert. Hawke, for his part, fought hard to control his curiosity and not look too keen in front of the other man. He had waited a long time to hear the truth, but he knew that the truth usually hurt more than lies.

"I'll come straight out with it, Hawke, so listen up."

Hawke leaned over the balcony and watched a boat moving up the Nile. As it passed north it broke the reflection of the setting sun in the water into a thousand ripples. *Here it comes*, he thought.

"You're right about Scarlet never having been in MI5, and the same goes for poor Sophie Durand who we lost in Tokyo. She was never in the French DGSE either. Both of them worked for me."

"I don't understand," Hawke said, turning to face Eden. "I was there in Geneva when Sophie burst in on us. It was obvious no one knew her."

"An act I'm afraid. Sophie worked for me for many years. I was the one who told her to join you in Geneva as back-up when it looked like things were getting out of control in the Zaugg case."

Hawke frowned, and felt the anger rising inside him. An act? They had deceived him right in front of his face and now Eden dismissed it as a simple act. "And Lea? She works for you – that much is true, right?"

"Yes and no. She works for me, but not, as you believe, as my personal security."

"Excuse my French, Rich, but just what the fuck is going on here?"

"You have to remember we didn't know anything about you back then and we couldn't take any risks." He sighed and sounded like he meant it. "Lea, Scarlet and formerly Sophie all worked for something called ECHO. There have been others but…"

Hawke shook his head. He couldn't believe the level of deceit they had subjected him to. "And what the bloody hell is ECHO?"

"Eden Counter-Hostile Organization. I established it some time ago as a semi-autonomous unit to deal with threats like the ones you have been handling over the past few weeks. It is, as you will appreciate, *extremely* covert, and not even the British Government knows about it."

"And not one of you trusted me enough just to tell me?"

Eden sighed. "It wasn't like that, Hawke. People do not simply *join* something like ECHO. They are proposed by members and then tested. This is what happened when you gave chase to Zaugg's men on that day at the British Museum."

"I don't believe this…"

"And don't think about taking this out on Lea Donovan. She wanted to tell you from the start, but she was under my instructions not to say anything."

"If you say so."

"I do say so, Hawke. It's nothing personal, but after the loss of Sophie Durand I felt the last thing the team needed was a new member to adjust to, and that is why I told Lea to keep it to herself. As it happens, everyone in the team, myself included, is highly impressed with you and we want you on the team."

"*Do* you now?" He shook his head in disbelief.

"Yes, we do. Our headquarters are based on a private island in the Caribbean – it's called Elysium, but we are a very fluid, and very rich, organization with safe-houses all over the world. You will be given these locations if you become one of us. If you do, you can expect to be up against the likes of Vetrov all the time. It won't be easy, but I know you're up to it."

Hawke knew Eden was still talking but could no longer hear the words. Instead, his mind was full of anger and betrayal over the way they had kept him in the dark – all of them knowing they were a team and not telling him… and not an apology in sight.

"I will of course give you time to think it over."

"That's very kind, Rich, but I don't need any time. You can stick your job up your arse and fuck off round the corner while you're doing it."

Eden looked shocked, but before he had a chance to reply, Hawke put his drink down, stormed inside and picked up his kit bag.

Lea saw the look on his face and knew what had happened.

"Please, Joe – don't be like this."

"I can understand *her* not saying anything," he jabbed his thumb at Scarlet who was currently fighting Lexi for the last shot of vodka, "but *you*?"

"I just couldn't say anything, Joe!"

"So you put me on fucking probation like an office gopher?"

"That's not fair!"

"What's going on?" Ryan said, confused. Hawke looked at him and saw he was now squashed under Maria and had her lipstick all over his face.

Lea saw the glance. "And before you say anything don't you dare say anything to Ryan – he never knew anything about it, either, and another thing – wait… where are you going?"

Hawke flicked her hand from his arm and walked over to Alex Reeve.

"Just calm down there, cowboy," she said, pushing her wheel chair back a foot or two from the red-faced Englishman. "Whatever you're pissed at don't make it me because I don't know what the hell is going on here."

"I know you don't," he said calmly. He fished around in his bag and pulled a tiny vial of sparkling water from it.

"What the hell?" she said.

"Here," he said. "This is the only remaining water from the source. I didn't use it all on Lea. I want you to try and use it to repair your legs. It brought Lea back to life, so maybe it can help you to walk again. Obviously, just a drop of the stuff because we saw what too much did to Vetrov. It's all that's left of the elixir, Alex, so make it count."

"I'll give it a go, Joe. Thanks." She held his hands firmly as Eden walked back into the room.

"Please, Hawke – why don't you reconsider joining the Echo Team on Elysium? We could really use a man like you. No one can say you haven't proved yourself a thousand times to all of us, and the island really has to be seen to be believed. We have all kinds of natural and manmade training facilities and everything you could wish for."

Hawke saw they were all staring at him, waiting for his response. He knew what they wanted him to say, but he felt betrayed. He felt like a fool who'd been taken for a ride and dumped in the middle of nowhere. Part of him wanted to forgive them and say yes, but another part, the angry part, wanted never to see them again. Especially Lea – her betrayal had been the worst. He had told her his most private thoughts about his wife and her murder, but she had kept this to herself. Maybe he was being unfair, maybe it was just the shock of almost losing Lea not once but twice on the same mission – he didn't know and at the moment he just didn't care, not anymore.

"No," he said firmly. "I don't think so, not now. I need time to think. Time to myself."

He slung the canvas sack over his shoulder and walked back out to the patio, leaping the balcony railing with a simple side vault and landing on the soft irrigated grass outside the suite. The air was still hot, and a little sweat trickled down into his eyes. He glanced up at the first stars of the new night for a few moments and then stepped out toward the desert, leaving the others behind him and walking toward nothing but the sunset.

THE END

AUTHOR'S NOTE

The Tomb of Eternity is the final part of the arc concerning the hunt for immortality which started with *The Vault of Poseidon* and followed on with *Thunder God*. These books were a lot of fun to write and I hope you enjoyed reading them just as much. I have left a few points unresolved, so who knows what Hawke might have to face in the future…

I'd like to take this moment to thank everyone who has read the series so far, and also to say to those who have enjoyed the stories that more Rob Jones books are planned for 2016, including, among others, a brand new rip-roaringly fast and furious standalone adventure for the increasingly beleaguered Joe Hawke. I will post new information relating to Hawke and the ECHO series on my website www.robjonesnovels.com and also on my Twitter and Facebook pages.

So, Mystery Reader, my sincere thanks to *you* once again, and as I'm writing this note in early January, here's wishing you a Happy New Year for 2016!

Rob.

The Joe Hawke Series

The Vault of Poseidon (Joe Hawke #1)
Thunder God (Joe Hawke #2)
The Tomb of Eternity (Joe Hawke #3)
The Curse of Medusa (Joe Hawke #4)
Valhalla Gold (Joe Hawke #5)
The Aztec Prophecy (Joe Hawke #6)
The Secret of Atlantis (Joe Hawke #7)
The Lost City (Joe Hawke #8)

The Sword of Fire (Joe Hawke #9) is scheduled for release in the spring of 2017

For free stories, regular news and updates, please join my Facebook page

https://www.facebook.com/RobJonesNovels/

Or Twitter

@AuthorRobJones

62675830R00178

Made in the USA
Lexington, KY
14 April 2017